I0671963

ENTICED & SEDUCED

SHELLEY MUNRO

MUNRO PRESS

Enticed & Seduced

Print ISBN: 978-1-99-106381-6
E-book ISBN: 978-0-473-44608-6

Editor: Evil Eye Editing
Cover: Kim Killion, The Killion Group, Inc.

Munro Press, New Zealand.

First Munro Press electronic publication July 2018
First Munro Press print publication March 2025

DEDICATION

For Paul, my husband, partner in crime, and fellow adventurer.
Every day is a good day.

INTRODUCTION

Some days, getting out of bed is a mistake...

Kaya Ignatius loves her job, working as part of the *Indefatigable* crew. But this isn't a normal morning. Gryffnn Drake, a hunky dragon shifter, has a problem with another clan and wants her to act as his betrothed. It's a chance to smash a dry spell and help the man who has become a good friend. After all, what's not to like about steamy sexual encounters?

But everything after that is downhill.

She's slimed by a stinky plant, her brother arrives with bad news and dumps a huge, scary responsibility in her lap. Suddenly, her life is full of drama and nasty surprises.

Gryffnn has always lusted after Kaya, but she only saw his older brother. Now things have changed, and he has a plan to capture the sassy Kaya and woo her to his way of thinking. A move by an opposition clan forces him to escalate his romantic plan. Things proceed well until the past struts in to say hello and creates havoc with his love life and his dragon clan.

Never mind bed, Gryffnn and Kaya are too busy putting out dangerous fires and trying to stay alive to worry about the future...

CHAPTER 1

THE PROPOSITION

The *Indefatigable* landed at the Narenda spaceport, the pilot powered down, and silence fell, broken only by the squawks of a flock of scarlet birds, unsettled by the noisy arrival. Dragon shifter Gryffnn Drake's chest rose and fell on a harsh exhalation. Tension slid through him, finding an outlet in clenched fists.

The doors slid open, and the Indy crew appeared—leopard shifter Ryman Coppersmith, his mate Camryn O'Sullivan, the pilot Nanu, their medic Mogens, and the luscious and unpredictable Kaya Ignatius.

A whisper-soft sigh released from Gryffnn once he confirmed Kaya was with the crew to fulfill their quarterly contract. Something about this woman called to him, to his dragon, yet she only had eyes for his older brother Ransom.

A sad fact, but this time, he had a strategy.

A plan.

The crew spotted him, waved, and strode down the ramp in his direction. Gryffnn averted his gaze from the woman who'd claimed his attention from their first meeting and nodded in greeting.

"Gryffnn." Ry Coppersmith held one of his twins. "How is Ransom?"

"Is he showing signs of coming out of his coma?" Camryn held their other wriggling twin.

"He's about the same." A wave of anxiety and sadness struck Gryffnn. His older brother's unexplained coma concerned him. While Gryffnn didn't mind temporarily stepping into the chieftain's shoes, he'd prefer it if Ransom regained consciousness, especially with this new complication. "He's reached a plateau, neither improving nor declining further."

"Will Sable be all right minding the twins?" Camryn asked. "They're a handful now that they're mobile."

"Niran's youngest daughter intends to help my sister," Gryffnn said. "They're both responsible and will take good care of your offspring."

"We're more worried about Sable and Niran's daughter," Camryn said drily. "These two are hell-on-wheels."

Gryffnn grinned, getting the general idea even though he didn't understand the words. Camryn came from a distant planet, and sometimes, her colorful language perplexed him. The *Indy* crew often borrowed words from her, meaning he had to concentrate. Ransom had also confessed to confusion at their word choices, which made Gryffnn less agitated with himself.

"Have you seen activity around the mine?" Nanu asked, the tendrils of his hair stirring and hissing.

Whoa! That was new. "We've tried to watch from afar," Gryffnn said, eyeing Nanu's hair. "But we're wary of getting too close."

"We'll check out the area when we collect more precious stones for you," Ry said. "What about those plants?"

Someone—probably pirates—had introduced a carnivorous plant to the planet. They'd thrived in Narenda's tropical climate, creating a new hazard for those who collected the raw materials he and the other dragons used to make their renowned jewelry.

"We've kept away from the mountain range," Gryffnn said. "But rumor says the plant numbers aren't increasing as they were. The salt spray you used to deter them has worked well."

"We've come prepared with more," Kaya said.

Without warning, a solution to his problem zipped into his mind. Gryffnn stilled, stunned by the audacious scheme, which was even better than his original idea. It might work...

The child Ry was holding shrieked, throwing up his arms.

The flight of dragons in the distance—all youngsters in training—wheeling through the sky indicated the source of the child's interest.

"Something wrong, Gryffnn?" Camryn set down her squirming daughter, who scampered away to explore the colorful red flowers to their left.

"A complication," Gryffnn said. "Let me collect your daughter, and we'll walk to the compound."

A short time later, the *Indy* crew sat with Gryffnn in Ransom's office. Even though he spent many marks each cycle here, he still thought of it as his brother's domain. Books lined two of the three walls, while the large windows in a third wall overlooked the training field where the young dragon shifters practiced their flying and other battle skills. At present, two bright green dragons were practicing their flame-throwing. One opened its maw, and flame flared outward, almost striking their instructor. Gryffnn stifled his burst of humor. They required better aim to progress in the ranks.

"As I mentioned, we have a complication," Gryffnn said and glanced at Kaya. She cocked her head, interest flitting across her face. He caught a quick peek of one pointed blue ear before her straight blue hair settled back into place. Those pointed ears of hers intrigued him.

"Oh?" Ry said, his big body straightening.

Nanu wrinkled his nose, and his hair hissed.

His attention diverted, Gryffnn stared in fascination at the copper-colored dreads. "Why is your hair hissing at me?"

Nanu flashed a broad grin. "I have a mate. You remember Jazen?"

"Yes, the nurse. Your mating changed your hair?" Gryffnn asked.

"Yes," Nanu said. "I'll tell you the story later once we hear about this problem of yours."

Gryffnn heaved out a harsh sigh. "Fifteen rotations ago, I took one of the Gwilym dragon clan as my mate. The clan is based on Dalcon. It was a way to stop the war between our clans and introduce peace. Our pairing was not without problems. I left the Gwilym to return here and brought our son with me. We've kept a tenuous peace ever since, with little contact between our two clans. Aideen Gwilym, the leader of the Dalcon clan, contacted me yes-cycle requesting a meeting."

"Why is that a problem?" Camryn asked.

"We've tried to keep Ransom's illness quiet, but I believe word is out, and she is visiting to discern the truth herself."

"What happened to your mate?" Kaya asked. "Is she part of the visitor contingent?"

"That is the other problem." Gryffnn's voice hardened. "There was mention of an apology and a resumption of the relationship between our clans. I refuse to spend time with that she-devil."

"What about your son?" Mogens asked. Streaks of black writhed across the medic's cheeks as he studied Gryffnn.

"Another thorny problem," Gryffnn said. "I don't wish them to have contact with my son. My opinion—they're testing us. Our strengths and weaknesses. They believe we are vulnerable. I fear we are on the brink of war, and if our clan loses, Aideen and her tribe will force us to leave Narenda. This means Niran and his people are in danger, too. With Ransom out of commission, Aideen considers us ripe for pillaging."

Ry tapped his fingers on the wooden float-desk top. "Your men are well-trained. You're doing an excellent job. Ransom couldn't do any better. Perhaps they'll visit and leave."

"Aideen is not one for polite chitchat. We've had no communication, and that thrilled me. The downside is we have no knowledge of their current situation. I heard a rumor about the limited supply of precious stones on Dalcon, but I have no idea if this is truth or fallacy."

"You think they're after your resources?" Ry asked.

Gryffnn yanked at his tunic collar and unfastened a toggle. "That is my suspicion. I've nothing to base it on, but my gut is jumping and bouncing like a dragon unused to flying."

"Wait, what about this ex-mate of yours?" Camryn asked. "What happened after your split?"

"She mated with another dragon. I heard he died, but I haven't determined the nature of his death." Gryffnn scowled. "This is the first formal contact between our clans since I left Dalcon."

"They can't force you to mate with her," Ry said.

Gryffnn eyed Kaya, trying to read the warrior woman. "No, but their desire for talks means they might prolong their stay for many cycles. I don't want them here. Their visit won't thrill Ransom either."

"When are they coming?" Ry asked.

"I haven't replied to the correspondence yet. I wanted to discuss the matter with you first."

"Lad, you don't require our input," Mogens said, his violet gaze drilling into Gryffnn. "You are a capable leader. You have proved yourself already. Ransom is proud of you. I am certain of this."

"I have an idea I wanted to run past you before I reply to Aideen." Gryffnn hesitated before turning to Kaya. *No, this was a good idea.* A sound one, and if it meant he got to spend time with the beautiful Kaya, it couldn't be wrong. This was his opportunity to woo and win the courageous woman. "Actually, Kaya, my plan involves you. I wondered if you would be amenable to acting as my betrothed, my intended mate."

Kaya's blue, blue eyes widened. A spurt of amusement filled him on seeing her unattractive gape.

"Me?" Her brow wrinkled and she pressed her palm to her chest.

Gryffnn tried not to stare at her plump breasts, diverting his gaze to her eyes. "If I already have a mate, Aideen can't use betrothal talks as an excuse to prolong their visit."

"I guess I could pretend to be your mate," Kaya said.

"No." Gryffnn watched her closely. "Forgive me, but I need to be blunt. We'll need to have sex so you take on my scent."

"Friends with benefits?" Camryn asked.

"This term is new, but yes. That sums up my needs."

"We'd have sex?" Kaya demanded.

"Yes." Gryffnn was having difficulty reading the woman. Was that intrigue he saw in her expression? He wasn't certain.

Kaya stared for a fraction longer while the other members of the *Indy* crew remained silent. Finally, she nodded. "It wouldn't be a hardship having sex with you. At least I'd break my dry spell."

"Kaya!" Nanu said.

"Oh, Kaya." Mogens tsked.

Camryn and Ry both chuckled.

"Excellent." Gryffnn struggled for impassive when he wanted to leap to his feet and cheer. Once Kaya got to know him, without Ransom hovering in the background, she might decide she wanted to keep him. It was up to him to become the mate of her dreams.

"You said you were mates. I thought dragons developed bonds in the same way as feline shifters," Ry said, his green gaze piercing and intelligent.

"We do." Gryffnn's mind leaped to the past and his naivety with Caley. Slightly older, she'd never wanted him. Their pairing had been political. Expedient. Not that his father had forced him into the arrangement. Gryffnn had seen his pairing as a way of helping his clan. He shook himself away from the painful betrayal. "Dragons pair. After a rotation together, they take stock of the relationship, and if they wish to stay together, they exchange dragon fire. It is this that cements the bond. Caley refused to take this last step."

An abbreviated history of his failure.

Caley had ripped out his heart and stomped on it, laughing the entire time. Worse, she'd rejected their son, and he'd never forgive her cruelty.

"So there is no danger of a mating bond springing a trap on my unwary head if we have sex?" Kaya asked.

Gryffnn fought a grin. "I repeat. Our bond will differ from Ry's and Camryn's."

"Or me and Jazen," Nanu said.

"All right," Kaya said. "I'll do it, but I'll need details to pull off this con."

"We'll talk later," Gryffnn promised. "Our soldiers have been watching the comings and goings on the planet. Entry through the spaceport is easy since we require everyone to request the right to land, but it isn't easy to monitor the mountain range. None of my people wish to go close to the mountains after Ransom fell into a coma. I don't blame them. A short flight left me vibrating for half a cycle afterward."

"We'll do a flyover and check out the mined area, see if things have changed since our last visit," Ry said. "Once you know when your guests will arrive, we can watch your back."

"What if the tender malfunctions again? We've never pinned down the cause of our crash," Nanu stated. "Jazen is expecting me back home after this visit with all my bones intact."

"We'll collect the load of precious stones first," Ry said. "Make sure you have enough in stock before we investigate the mine. Have you considered hiring a third party to guard your property on the other side of the mountain range? Someone is sneaking onto Narenda, and that is the obvious point of entry."

"Our spaceport isn't picking up anything on radar," Gryffnn said. "This is frustrating as hell. The mine worried Ransom. That's why he was so insistent on flying over the region. We dragons are a possessive lot when it comes to our wealth."

"As long as you don't think you own me," Kaya said, her chin rising with attitude. "No man possesses me."

"No man would put up with you," Nanu muttered.

Kaya glared at Nanu, and Gryffnn fought to keep his amusement contained. He enjoyed her sharp tongue and sass, her take-no-prisoners arrogance, and the way her nose lifted in defiance. And she bore integrity, which was necessary after his dealings with Caley.

"When do you think the dragon contingent from Dalcon might arrive?" Camryn asked.

"I received a formal comm two cycles ago," Gryffnn confessed. "I've been trying to think of a reason to deny their visit. Tradition and protocol mean I must welcome the contingent even though I don't trust them."

"Why can't you tell them it's not a convenient time to visit?" Kaya asked.

"Because I can't risk them taking offense and starting a war. My father worked hard to bring peace to our clans. I'm only the caretaker of the chieftain role. Once Ransom recovers, he'll take over again. I don't want to thrust him into a conflict."

"You suspect these dragons will try something with Ransom out of commission?" Ry said.

"They don't consider me a leader, not after what Caley put me through. To them, I'm weak and ineffectual." A tic fired to life at his jaw. He was *not* a soft touch and intended to prove it to all those doubters. He'd do it for Ransom, and he'd do it for himself and their clan.

Ry pulled a leather tie from his tunic and confined his long black hair into a tail. "You are a leader, Gryffnn. We're here to aid and offer moral support. Tell us what you need."

"I hate to put any of you in danger, especially your children," Gryffnn said, although the offer pleased him. "The Dalcon dragons have no awareness of our strong ties with the Incorporeal people since the Incorporeal are recent arrivals to our planet. Once Aideen learns of their existence, it will make us even more attractive."

"What does Niran say?" Kaya asked.

Gryffnn tapped his fingers on the float-desk top. "He's worried, but he's refusing to leave."

Ry nodded. "I understand their desire to remain in their homes, but their young will be vulnerable. Perhaps I can convince Niran to send them to Viros. Leeam and Sheera would care for them. King Lynx will do everything he can to help."

"Niran wanted to greet you, but his oldest daughter is having her first child," Gryffnn said. "I'll speak with him again about their safety."

"I'll comm Lynx and Jannike," Ry said. "We had intended to relax this end of the cycle and collect precious stones tom-cycle—"

A strident buzz came from Kaya's comm, interrupting Ry.

"Sorry." Kaya plucked her comm from her internal jacket pocket.

Gryffnn watched her scan the screen and the tinge of healthy color seeped from her cheeks, leaving her features a delicate blue. She jumped to her feet.

"I'm sorry. This is urgent. I have to take this call." She darted away before Ry continued.

"Will she be all right?" Gryffnn asked.

"I bet it's one of her many boyfriends." Nanu smirked. "Maybe one of them is pregnant."

"Nanu," Mogens chided.

Gryffnn's body heated as his dragon sent a shower of disapproval cascading over his skin. The tattoo on his left biceps glowed as he fought for control. The jealousy lashing his mind refused to leave without a struggle. "I'd consider it a favor if you'd observe our battalion of dragons at training," he gritted out. Speech helped to release his tension, so he continued. "Niran wanted to discuss security with you. He decided basic training for all Incorporeal adults made sense, and my trainers have aided them. He thought you might have helpful advice since he's heard how well Leeam and Sheera are doing."

"They're good kids," Ry said. "We're happy to help, but we'll get those stones for you first. You'll want to keep up production."

"Yes, I want everything to proceed as normal. I'm lucky Ransom included me in his plans. He is more hands-on than our father, which has made Ransom's illness easier to handle. I owe my brother a great deal."

"Which you are repaying with your careful guardianship," Mogens said.

A burst of pleasure suffused Gryffnn. "I'm doing my best, but I worry about Aideen. The dragon woman is cunning and unpredictable."

A faint tinkle filled the air, along with a chilly burst. "Welcome, Niran," Gryffnn called.

An instant later, Niran and three Incorporeal men shimmered in to view.

"Good welcome." Niran, the leader of the Incorporeal people, pressed his hands together and bowed his head. "Excellent. You're here, Ryman. I have three volunteers to aid you when you travel to collect stones."

"No," Gryffnn said. "It's dangerous for them on the other side of the mountains. What if they spring a pirate's trap? I can't let you do it."

"Our scientists have been working on a method to make the invisible traps visible," Niran said. "An excellent opportunity to test our invention."

Gryffnn exchanged a glance with Ry and caught his imperceptible nod.

"We intend to leave at once instead of tom-cycle," Ry said. "What preparations do you require? Are you ready to leave?"

Kaya pressed the return call button on her comm, her hand trembling as she waited for her brother Tayte to answer. Her gut hollowed, and she paced the corridor to rid herself of the nervous energy residing in her middle.

"Kaya?"

"Yes. What is it? What's wrong?"

"Mother is dead."

Kaya swallowed, her hand tightening on her comm. "What happened?"

"A coup."

"Oh, goddess," Kaya whispered. "I wish I'd taken the risk and called her. She's been on my mind. I picked up my comm half a dozen times..."

"She understood," Tayte said. "It was too dangerous."

"How did you learn of the coup?"

"That's the other thing," Tayte said. "I need to speak with you in person. I'm on my way to Viros and will arrive in three cycles."

"We're currently on Narenda, completing a contract for the dragon shifters."

"No problem. That's closer."

"It's a closed planet," Kaya said, her mind racing in dozens of directions at once. Her mother dead. Tayte on the way to visit her.

A relationship with Gryffnn.

"Kaya," Tayte said, his tone sharp. "It's imperative I see you, and I don't have much time. Fix it for me. I'll see you soon."

"Yes, of course," Kaya said, his arrogant, bossy big-brother abruptness dialing back her panic.

"I will arrive tom-cycle. See you then." A shrill cry sounded on his end, and the comm disconnected.

Kaya frowned. She didn't see her brother often. The last time had been a brief stop-off after their Christmas visit to Earth and Camryn's people.

The door to the office opened as she slid her comm back into her pocket. Her mother was dead. She blinked, refusing to let tears fall. When she'd fled Sitnam, she hadn't cried. Weeping now changed nothing.

Her mother was dead.

If the leaders of the coup learned of her existence, she'd die.

No, crying wouldn't solve a thing.

"Kaya, we're leaving to collect stones now," Ry said. "You ready?"

She nodded. "Yes. I need a quick word with Gryffnn before we go. Two, three mins tops." Without waiting for an answer, she hustled into the office to find Gryffnn still seated behind the big desk, his dark head bowed and an air of defeat clear in his mien. "Gryffnn, am I interrupting? I need to ask you something before we leave for the collection fields."

Gryffnn straightened, his hazel gaze piercing her. "Problem? Have you changed your mind?"

No, if anything, seeing Gryffnn's rare vulnerability when he usually swaggered and oozed confidence firmed her decision to help him. Sharing her body with the dragon shifter wouldn't present a hardship. Like his older brother, Gryffnn drew the eye with his shaggy black hair and robust build. She'd only seen his dragon twice but still recalled his vibrant red as he'd zapped through the sky while teaching his son to control his fire.

"No, I'm fine with that. I've made a promise and won't go back on my word. It's something else." She hesitated.

"Speak freely, Kaya. You have nothing to fear from me." He rose and rounded the desk, clasping both her hands in his. He squeezed them, his gaze serious. "We're friends, aren't we?"

She nodded, taking in his height and powerful physique. His broad shoulders and a peek of his tribal tattoo. Having seen him shirtless, she knew his tattoo extended across his chest and back. His skin was much darker than hers, a deep tan, while his eyes bore a faint slant. At times of high emotion, as with any of the dragons, his scales became more visible. Red, in his case, to match his dragon.

"Tayte, my brother has something urgent to discuss with me. He wishes to speak with me in person and was flying to Viros. I told him I was here. Can he have clearance to land? He should arrive later this cycle or early tom-cycle."

"Has Ry met him?"

"Yes. We stopped at his home base for two cycles before we arrived at Viros." Kaya didn't mention specifics or the considerable distance between Slyvia and Viros. Habit kept her silent to protect her brother.

"All right," Gryffnn said. "He is welcome. Ry expects to return later this eve. If you're delayed, I will greet him myself."

"Thank you." Kaya started to retreat.

"I believe we should seal our bargain with a kiss," Gryffnn said.

Kaya froze. Her tongue slid along her bottom lip, moistening it. "Ry is impatient to leave."

Gryffnn strode toward her, intent in his gleaming hazel eyes. "He can wait."

"I...um..."

Gryffnn halted her dithering by drawing her close and sealing his mouth over hers. His lips were hot yet soft, his tongue bold as he wrapped strong arms around her and kissed her as no man had ever kissed her. She clung, her knees no longer holding her upright, and enjoyed the hell out of the embrace.

When he parted their mouths and released her, she had difficulty processing her reaction. One thought bashed inside her head like those pinball games Camryn had introduced them to on Earth. Gryffnn bore hidden depths, and now curiosity filled her. She'd thought she'd enjoy pretending to be his mate, but now, after his decadent kiss, she looked forward to completing the favor.

"I'd better go. I'll see you later."

Gryffnn smiled, and it held enough smug male satisfaction to fan her temper. He'd better not consider bossing her around or expecting her to run around after him and emulate a slave.

"I look forward to our evening," he said in a rumbly, sexy purr. Then, he straightened, resolve settling on his features. "I'd better explain this to Hallam before Aideen and her clan contact us about their expected arrival."

Kaya's irritation seeped away at the mention of his son. "Will Hallam be all right?"

"We've discussed his mother and why we no longer live together. Don't worry. He's a good kid. He won't make life difficult for you. I want him to understand what's happening so Aiden and Caley won't take him unawares."

Kaya nodded and bolted, aware of her friends waiting. She'd be a stand-in mother for Hallam. Perhaps, with her lack of experience, this charade wasn't the best idea.

"Kaya!" Ry shouted.

She put on a burst of speed and ran down the passage and the stairs leading to the ground floor.

"Sorry, I had to ask Gryffnn a favor. It was important."

Ry's nostrils flared, and his eyes narrowed. "We're on a timeline. Save your friends with benefits for later."

"We didn't make out," Kaya said indignantly.

"Then why do your clothes reek of Gryffnn?" Camryn inserted herself into the conversation.

Kaya scowled and lifted her charcoal gray tunic to her nose. She sniffed and shot a glance at Ry and Camryn. Her friends were grinning, their amusement digging into their features.

Kaya huffed. "I don't want to talk about it." She stomped to where Nanu had landed the tender, trying to outrun her friends' laughter and the anxiety that had seized her mind when her brother said he needed to speak with her in person.

Both concerns followed her as if attached by invisible strings. She swallowed as she stormed up the ramp and dropped onto a tender seat. Her past had caught up with her. If she hadn't sensed that already, the prickling of her pointy ears was the next big clue.

CHAPTER 2

THE BAD, BAD, MOST HORRIBLE CYCLE

Kaya stared out a porthole, taking in the stone wall and buildings that made up the dragons' main compound. One large stone mansion where Gryffnn's family lived and at least twenty smaller homes. Colorful plants in red and green, blue and yellow, contrasted with the gray stone of the buildings. Outside the wall surrounding the grounds was the road leading to the township where many other dragons lived alongside the Incorporeal people. To the left was an immense flat green area where the dragons trained and the youngsters played and learned to control their dragon powers.

Narenda was a tropical planet with a profusion of plants and a pleasing heat that Kaya enjoyed, yet it had a mountainous region, the spine of the mountain range running the length of the largest land mass. This was the source of the stones the dragons used to make the jewelry they sold for enormous sums. But something contained within the mountains caused a dragon sickness known as resonation. A double-edged sword since the dragons relied on the precious stones for their livelihoods.

Ransom Drake lay in a coma, suffering from the resonation because he'd risked going too close to learn more about the mystery mine high in the mountains.

Lucky for her and the rest of the *Indy* crew, the dragon's problem became a lucrative contract.

Nanu guided the tender toward the mountains, skirting the range until they reached the lower peaks at the far end. A river began here from a myriad small streams that ran down the slopes and converged into one silver rush of water.

She glimpsed a turquoise blue lake, which tossed her back to her childhood. Even though she'd ruled their people, her mother had stolen time from her duties and responsibilities to take her and Tayte to the wilderness area. Happier times before custom and tradition interfered with her childhood, thrusting her into adulthood too soon.

Phrull it. What did Tayte want to discuss? He'd informed her of their mother's death. What else could be so hush-hush he'd refused to tell her over the comm system?

"Kaya. Kaya, child? Is something wrong?" Mogens's gentle voice ripped her back to the present.

"I don't think you've listened to a word of our plan," Ry said. "If your mind is in the gutter and thinking about sex with Gryffnn, stop. This is business. We're committed to our contract with the dragons, and I refuse to fail."

"She's daydreaming about flying through the skies on a dragon's back," Nanu said with a sly wink.

"No, I wasn't. Grata, you keep telling me dragon flying is reserved for mates. Gryffnn and I will be pretend mates, so it's against the dragon rules." Kaya swiped her hand over her face and sucked in a deep breath. "Gryffnn wasn't on my mind. I have thought little about my promise, to be honest."

"You've been weird since you took the comm call," Nanu commented. "Is something wrong?"

"No. Yes. I don't know," Kaya said, frustrated with her brother and the insistent prickling of her ears.

Camryn wrinkled her nose. "Well, which is it?"

"No idea," Kaya said, trying to decide if this unsettled sensation in her gut held merit. "Tayte has something to discuss with me, something he wouldn't or couldn't tell me on the comm. He's visiting and should arrive either this eve or early tom-cycle."

"Tayte's coming?" Ry asked. "I'll enjoy meeting him again."

"Me too," Camryn said. "You should've said earlier. We could've done this trip without you." She smiled at the three silent Incorporeal men who sat beside her. "We have extra help."

"No, it's best if I keep busy." Despite trusting her friends with her life, habit made her refrain from mentioning her mother. Maintaining her cover and her safety meant keeping quiet about her connection with the Sitnam tribe. It could place her friends in danger. With luck, the distance between this galaxy and the solar system encompassing Sitnam meant they remained safe.

Aware she'd drive herself crazy if she continued in this vein, she forced her mind to the upcoming task. "What's the plan for our collection this cycle?"

Ry rolled his eyes. Obviously, he was repeating himself, which was why he was giving her attitude. "For safety, we're splitting into teams. You and Seedric. Nanu and Wen. Mogens and Roden. Camryn is with me. Once Nanu lands, we'll split into these pairs and collect as much as possible in four marks. I want to leave enough whitelight for us to check the area where we discovered the mine.

"We're not certain about traps in this area. We won't sense them, but Seedric, Wen, and Roden will test their invention. If you discover a trap, send out an alert, and we'll work out a way to spring it without the Incorporeal people getting injured. Clear?"

"Yes," Nanu said. "Do the dragons require a particular colored stone this trip?"

"Gryffnn informed me he wanted a mixture, and if we come across the purple-blackish stones—the Narendanite—we should grab that. Questions?" Ry asked.

"No," Kaya said.

"Your plan is logical," Seedric said. "Can we patch our comms into your system? With other Incorporeal people, it's not necessary. We can shimmer to whoever we wish to speak, but your people don't enjoy our unannounced presence."

"Sure." Ry held up his comm to the one Seedric produced. He repeated the procedure with the other Incorporeals. "One last thing. Watch out for those plants. Make sure you pick up the salt water pistols before leaving the tender."

"Slimy suckers," Kaya muttered. "I intend to stay far away." She scanned the open, stony grounds below. "I can't see any in the dry creek bed down there. I still suffer nightmares about them trying to eat us. And the smell." She wrinkled her nose.

Camryn shuddered. "I had nightmares about them for cycles afterward."

Nanu landed the tender on a flattish area and powered down. The purr of the propulsion unit ceased, and along with the others, Kaya disembarked.

"Four marks, then meet back here," Ry said.

"Aye, captain." Kaya gave him a cheeky salute that had Camryn grinning. "Are you ready, Seedric?" Kaya scooped up a collecting bag, handed it to Seedric, and picked up a second for herself. She draped it over her shoulder, shoved a water pistol into her pocket, and straightened. "We'll go east," she said to Seedric.

The gravel and dirt crunched beneath her boots as she strode toward the valley she'd noticed as they landed. Both she and Seedric scanned the ground for the stones favored by the dragons.

"Perhaps we'll have more luck in the next valley," Kaya said. "We've collected here several times and picked the area clean."

A man of few words, Seedric nodded and continued walking at her side.

Once they crossed the dry creek bed and rounded a cliff, the chatter from her friends faded. Kaya scrutinized the ground and let her mind wander back to Tayte and whatever he wanted to discuss with her.

"Ah." Seedric pounced on several small pebbles and picked them up. "You were right. There are better pickings in this valley."

Kaya nodded. "Keep an eye on me, and don't wander too far away. I will not be the one who has to tell Niran I lost you."

"I am an adult."

"You are," Kaya agreed. "But other species and races consider you a prize. Relaxing your guard or overconfidence might end in capture."

Seedric searched her face, his white eyelashes fluttering. "The voice of experience?"

As a young girl, she'd thought herself impervious to their planet's enemies. Her mother's private guards were the best, and they watched her. Once she grew older, she trained with her mother and increased her proficiency in fighting and self-defense. A botched abduction attempt had shown her confidence had been misplaced when unknown assailants had injured her and almost spirited her away. Now, she trained hard and kept her wits about her. Her mother had lost her life, and she'd been strong and well-trained.

She shook herself. Mind on the task. Ah. A reddish glitter caught her attention. She picked up a stone the size of her palm and scrubbed away the dirt clinging to it. Two smaller stones grabbed her attention, and she scooped them up. Soon, the added weight dragged her collection bag on the back of her neck. Now and then, she scanned their surroundings to check for plants and ensure Seedric remained safe.

Oh! A purple stone. It glinted under the whitelight, drawing her closer. With another glance at Seedric, she darted toward the violet sparkle. From her position, she could see into the next valley. A shiny flash of silver caught her attention. She straightened, trying to make out the moving object. A person. It was an upright figure in a suit, and they were collecting stones.

Kaya retreated until she no longer had a view into the neighboring valley. She turned to Seedric and gestured for him to come to her. Secs later, he shimmered into position at her side. Even though she'd expected him to appear, she still jumped.

"What's the problem?" Seedric asked.

"Someone else is harvesting stones in the next valley," Kaya said, once her heart rate evened out to normal.

"I can get closer without them seeing me."

"No," Kaya barked. "There might be traps, then we'll be in a worse mess than we are already."

"I can summon Ry."

"It's best if we stick together. We'll comm Ry and head back to the tender."

"All right. Are you sure they didn't see you?"

Kaya readjusted the collection bag on her shoulder. "I'm sure. I only saw one, but my gut says he wasn't alone." She called Ry, and his return communication took secs.

"Intruders?" Ry demanded.

"I saw one, but they're harvesting the dragons' stones."

"Wait where you are, and we'll come to meet you. I want to see the intruders myself. Camryn is contacting the others now. Sit tight."

Kaya disconnected and turned to Seedric. "We're to wait here until Ry and the others arrive. We might as well gather more stones while we wait. Stay close. Please, I repeat. I don't want to face

Niran and tell him I lost you."

Seedric grinned. "Are you frightened of our illustrious leader?"

"Let's say I'm aware of his powers, and I'd hate to get on his bad side."

Kaya spied a green glint on the ground in front of her and pried the stone from the dirt surrounding it.

"Look at those stones," Seedric said, gesturing at the numerous stones of various colors strewn on the ground to their right. He trotted forward, and Kaya followed.

A horrid stench hit her. Eye-watering and putrid, it stopped Kaya in her tracks.

She slapped her hand over her mouth, searching for the carnivorous plants, yet not one appeared on the rocky landscape around them. Kaya took a step forward and felt the ground vanish beneath her.

Then she was falling, a cloud of dust obscuring her vision.

"Kaya!" Seedric shouted.

Kaya hit the rocky floor of the pit with a thump that squeezed the air from her lungs. She gasped for breath and the putrid scent of rottenness seared her lungs and pushed tears to her eyes. A squawk. A hoarse cry alerted her to the fact she wasn't alone.

The stench intensified, and without warning, a hand—no, a leafy tendril grabbed her arm. A burning sensation on her skin made her yelp and pull away, but not before another tendril attached to her face. The associated hissing pushed her to action. She yanked free and retreated until her back hit the side of the pit. Stars, her skin burned something fierce, the slime expelled by the plant dripped down her tunic and soaked through her trews.

"Kaya!" Seedric's face appeared from above her.

"Careful," she shouted. "Don't fall in with me." She eyed the three hissing plants and kicked at their reaching tendrils. With a trembling hand, she fumbled for her blaster. Her belt was empty. Goddess. Gryffnn and her brother had rattled her mind. Her blaster was sitting in her chamber. She plucked out her water pistol and fired salt water at them. For a sec, their pained hisses pushed guilt through her.

"What should I do?" Seedric called.

"Chuck me your water pistol and wait where Ry can see you. Warn him about the pit and tell him there might be others."

Kaya plucked the water pistol from the air and fired at the hideous plants again. Goddess, the stink. She gagged, her belly revolting at the rancid stench.

She eyed the edges of the pit while closely watching the three hungry plants. The sides appeared slick and without purchase. She wouldn't be leaving this hellhole without help.

"Are you all right?" Seedric asked.

"No, I'm in a hole with three alien flesh-eating plants."

"Oh." Seedric peered down at her. "Is that Viros humor?"

Kaya muttered a curse and yanked at her strained patience. "Can you see Ry yet?" One plant edged toward her, and she sprayed it with her water pistol. It hissed and jerked back. The other two plants chattered.

Ugh. Plain creepy.

"Should I collect more stones while I wait for Ry?"

"Fine, but do not wander far and watch for danger. If you get injured or captured, I will hunt you down and skewer your pretty face with my sword."

"Huh. You must catch me first," Seedric said.

"Is that Incorporeal humor?"

"I see Ry and the others," Seedric informed her, offering her a delighted smile.

Thank the goddess. "Have they seen you?" She glanced up to see Seedric and his two Incorporeal friends staring down at her.

"You reek," one said.

"You've ruined your clothes," the other declared.

Seedric grinned.

"Thank you for telling me the obvious." A burning stab on her leg loosed a shriek of protest from her. "Shoot them with your water pistols."

The pair gaped at her.

"Give me your pistols," Seedric ordered.

They handed them over, and Seedric shot at the plants, one pistol in each hand and a gleeful grin curling across his white face.

"I'm glad I'm entertaining you," Kaya bit out.

"That is Viros humor," Seedric informed his friends.

"Kaya," Ry said. "You okay?"

"Ugh!" Nanu wrinkled his nose. "I'm not sitting by you on the way back to the dragons' compound."

"Is that Viros humor too?" Roden wanted to know.

"Shut up or I'll smother you with my tunic," Kaya snapped, wiping at her streaming eyes.

"No, but that is," Seedric said.

"The Incorporeal trap-finder didn't work." Camryn bit her lip, but Kaya saw the humor sparkling in her eyes, and Mogens's mouth twitched.

"Nanu and I will free Kaya. This area has a surplus of stones. Camryn, you and Mogens watch the boys while you collect stones. Stay close and be careful. There might be more pits. We'll check out the next valley together." Ry issued the orders while wrinkling his nose at the stink.

Kaya didn't blame him. She didn't enjoy smelling herself either.

"What about the plants?" Camryn asked.

"We'll make sure they're dead before we leave. As much as I dislike the things, making them suffer is not right. Seedric, before you go—can we ask you to make us a coil of rope?" Ry asked. "We'll need it to pull Kaya out of the pit."

As he spoke, Nanu shot at the plants, blasting them with his weapon. The hisses ceased, and the plants grew limp.

"Why didn't you shoot them?" Ry asked.

Heat collected in her cheeks. "Stupidly, I left my blaster in my chamber at the compound. This cycle..." She shook her head. Not a great excuse. If she wasn't more careful, she'd land in even bigger trouble than she was right now.

"Why didn't you ask Seedric to produce a ladder for you?" Nanu asked.

The heat in her cheeks intensified, and she suspected her face shone a bright blue. "I'm having a bad cycle."

Ry tossed the rope down to her, and she tied it around her waist.

"I didn't think of a ladder either," Ry said. "Are you ready?"

"Yes. Don't drop me when the worst of the pong hits you. I suspect I have bruises on my back now. I don't want them on my butt too."

"Are you daydreaming of Gryffnn in your gel-bed?" Nanu taunted.

"No. I didn't tease you about Jazen. Much," she added. She braced herself and walked up the slick sides of the pit as Ry and Nanu pulled. "Gryffnn and I are friends."

The truth. They'd become friends during their last visit to Narenda, and she enjoyed his company. Before Ransom had become sick, she'd only seen the leader, but Gryffnn was just as strong and decisive as his older brother, and the clan hadn't suffered during Ransom's absence. Gryffnn had stepped into the gap, and she admired him. He differed from the men she favored, not afraid to disagree with her when their opinions varied, and he challenged her.

With a final heave, Kaya cleared the lip of the pit.

"Grata, I didn't think the stench could get worse," Ry muttered, wrinkling his nose in a catlike manner.

"Bite me," Kaya snapped.

"Thanks for the offer, but no," Nanu said as he backed away from her.

"Ry!" Camryn shouted, pointing past them.

All three of them gazed in the direction she indicated. A sleek black ship headed in their direction.

Weapon fire peppered the ground,

"Take cover," Ry roared.

Kaya tried to rip the rope from her middle, her hands clumsy in her haste. Shots sprayed up dust at her heels as she ran. She increased her speed and promptly tripped over the trailing rope. *Phrull it!* She pushed to her hands and knees. The rope dropped away, and another pass of the black ship prompted her to roll. Just in time. More shot. *Splat. Splat. Splat.*

She dived behind a rock, her heart drumming against her ribs.

Her eyes narrowed on the ship. Not a single marking marred the matte black surface. She'd never seen the ship before. It made another pass of the slopes, where they hunkered down before departing.

"Everyone okay?" Ry demanded.

"Yes." Kaya rose from hiding, as did the others.

"I'd intended to walk to the next valley, but let's return to the tender and fly over. If the thieves were on that ship, they're gone now, and we'll check the area for stones where Kaya first sighted them."

Back at the tender, they unloaded their collection bags.

"Anyone notice the lack of loose stones in this valley?" Camryn asked.

Kaya waited her turn to empty her collection bag. "I was certain there were more stones during our last visit. Someone else has picked the area."

"That's my guess." Ry stalked closer and recoiled. "Grata, Kaya. You can't get on the tender wearing that stink."

"Well, what am I meant to do? Trail after you like a balloon?"

"Perhaps I can help. Remove your clothes, and I'll conjure you more," Seedric suggested.

Kaya stomped away from the tender and sat on a stone to remove her boots. Standing, she tore off her tunic and stripped off her black trews—her usual casual daily attire.

Seedric, who had trailed her, blinked at her hot pink underwear—a matching bra and panties she'd purchased on Earth. "Is that all?" he asked.

"I am not discarding my underwear." She planted her hands on her hips and glared at him.

"I could conjure you more."

"These are my favorites." She'd purchase more lingerie, but a visit to Earth to obtain more of what she was wearing was out of the question. "I appreciate the suggestion, but your clothes emit a chill."

"You're right," he agreed. "I'll dress you to save time."

Secs later, a pair of tight trews—black with red, orange, and green splotches—covered her legs, and a more feminine blouse in bright red draped across her breasts.

"I resemble a signal light," Kaya muttered.

"Incorporeal humor," Seedric said, his features impassive. She caught the masculine smirk in his eyes in the instant before he shimmered.

She stomped to the ship, grateful for the clothes since she smelled marginally better. It would still take several hot showers and Mogens's cleansing salve to get rid of the plant odor.

Camryn's mouth twitched as Kaya approached. Ry grinned while unwisely, Nanu sniggered. Kaya pointed her finger at him. "Don't. Just don't. I will ask Gryffnn to place you in his dungeon. I'm sure the dragons have one."

"Let's move." Ry cut in on the argument. "Kaya, sit at the back. Sorry, but you still reek."

About to park her butt on her normal seat, Kaya retraced her steps, storming to the rear seats.

Nanu lifted off and flew them to the next valley. Dead plants littered the banks of a shallow stream running down from the mountains. As Nanu flew a circle over the valley, Kaya saw the extent of the mining.

"Ransom was right to worry. Someone has set up a lucrative operation," Ry said.

"But Gryffnn said they'd spotted no intruders on their security system." Camryn's brow crinkled as she studied the scar on the mountainside.

"Looks as if they've left the area for now," Nanu said. "They've kept the mine small enough to conceal their presence."

"What will we do?" Seedric asked.

Ry scowled at the vista. "Land near their mine, Nanu. I doubt they've laid any traps there. We'll try to collect enough stones to fill our bin before we return to the compound. All the plants seem dead but take care. They might have laid other traps."

Nanu landed. "We interrupted them. Look at the blocks of Narendanite stone ready for transport."

"We'll take them," Ry decided. "Ransom said this stone is rare. That's how we'll track them. If they're brazen enough to steal, they might be stupid enough to flood the market."

"At least we can figure out a plan to stop them now," Camryn said.

Mogens exited the tender and ambled over to the stacked stones. "I thought the dragons preferred fist-size stones."

"They do. I'll comm Gryffnn now and get him to organize a safe storage area," Ry said.

"I can contact Niran," Seedric offered. "The dragons built a secure facility—to store larger stones and surplus ones."

"I haven't noticed it," Camryn said.

"No, we make it invisible for the dragons."

"Thanks, Seedric." Ry patted the man on the shoulder. "That will leave me free to help the others."

Blacklight was chasing away the white by the time they finished loading the tender.

"We should've caged Kaya at the rear of the tender behind the stones," Seedric said, holding his nose.

Exhausted from hauling stones, Kaya sank onto the tender floor. "We'll make you unload this by yourself," she said without heat. The physical labor had taken her mind off her problems for a short time, but now, with the compound in sight, her worries stalked her like hungry beasts.

She'd never see her mother again.

Her brother held troubling secrets.

She'd agreed to help Gryffnn and his clan.

Plants had accosted her, and someone had shot at her.

And most troubling at the present, she stunk with the ferocity of a putrid Niffum swamp.

The law of averages meant the next cycle would be better. Right?

CHAPTER 3

KAYA'S CYCLE GETS EVEN WORSE

Kaya helped to unload the stones at the facility on the other side of the village. Her friends kept a healthy distance and made rude and cheeky remarks about her delicate scent. Clearly, they were using sarcasm and making the most of the payback for when Kaya had teased them on other occasions.

Gryffnn greeted them when they finally returned to the spaceport. He blinked at Kaya's colorful appearance and took half a step toward her before he halted, his eyes widening in shock. "What is that stench?"

"Me." Kaya sent him a guarded look. "It's been a hell of a cycle."

"Use the showers at the training field," Camryn suggested. "I'll get you a clean set of clothes and some of Mogens's wash."

Kaya brushed a lock of hair from her face, fatigue forcing a yawn from her. "Yeah. Okay."

Gryffnn remained where he stood, and she didn't blame him. "Your brother has arrived. I've put him in my private parlor."

"Thanks. I'll be as quick as I can." Kaya forced her legs to a jog and headed to the training field while her mind sprinted back to the worry she'd carried the entire cycle.

In the ablution block, she tore off the bright red tunic with its inappropriate frills and stripped off her skinny trews. Her nose wrinkled at the offensive reek coming off the clothes Seedric had gifted her. The plant slime stuck to the garments and her skin.

Kaya sighed. "Shower on."

Hot water poured from the control above her head. Her skin—chilled from wearing the fabric conjured by an Incorporeal—protested the blast of heat. She edged away from the stream of water, ducking her head under a bit at a time. She closed her eyes as her hair plastered to her head, and the heat seeped into her aching muscles.

"Kaya. Kaya!"

She jumped at the sound of her name since her mind had drifted back to her brother. She poked her head around the shower screen. "Camryn, I didn't hear you over the blast of the water. You gave me a fright."

"Are you worried about helping Gryffnn?" Camryn raised her voice so Kaya could hear.

"No." She wished she felt able to confide her fears to Camryn. The habit of keeping her life private kept her quiet. "My mother is dead," she blurted.

"Oh, Kaya. Why didn't you say earlier?"

"I can't do anything to fix it." Kaya reached for the wash Camryn had set in the wall recess.

"You could've taken the cycle off."

"And miss giving you all a good laugh?" Kaya picked up a brush the dragons used to scrub their scales. As long as she didn't press too hard, it should work. "It was better that I worked and kept busy."

"Can Ry and I help?"

"No. Thanks. No, wait. Can you tell Tayte I'll be there soon?"

"Of course. I've left your clothes on the pegs."

Kaya rinsed, applied more of Mogens's wash and scrubbed her skin until it tingled. Aware of the ticking secs, she switched off the water, dried, and dressed. Her pulse raced as she stalked from the ablution block.

She found Gryffnn waiting for her.

"Your brother asked to wait in private. Should I tell him about our arrangement, or do we keep it between us and the *Indy* crew?"

"I'll tell him," Kaya said. "You can trust my brother."

"I haven't met him," Gryffnn pointed out.

"Let me speak with him first. I'll introduce you later." Kaya placed her hand on his forearm. He wasn't as calm as he pretended, although he did a first-rate job of hiding his unease. She got it. He'd had to step into Ransom's shoes, and soon, he'd face an even bigger test. Now, a stranger had arrived. Yes, she understood. "Will that do?"

"Yes."

They strode through the entrance hall and down a long passage to one of the rooms she hadn't entered before.

"How did things go with Hallam?"

Gryffnn smiled, the strain in his expression fading. "That was the easy part. Hallam thinks you're cool, and he can't believe his old dad has captured your attention." He halted in front of a closed door. "Call if you need me."

"Thanks." Kaya sucked in a quick breath and knocked on the wooden door.

"Come," a deep voice said.

A high-pitched shriek filled the parlor as she stepped inside and closed the door.

Kaya stared at the pale blue infant in her brother's arms. Her brows rose. "Something you forgot to tell me?"

"This is Lys, our sister." Her brother had grown his black hair long. The wavy locks hit his shoulders. He wore a sleeveless leather vest in deference to the heat on Narenda, and this revealed his peak physical condition, plus several tattoos. Taller than her, he glared down at her in the big-brother stare that always jerked her chain.

Except for this instance.

Kaya's gaze darted from him to the infant and back. "Sister? You're kidding me. Really, who does the kid belong to?"

"Your brother isn't lying to you." A man stepped from the shadowed corner of the parlor. "Lys is your sister. Gleneese's third child."

"Father?" Kaya glanced at Tayte, a rush of goose bumps breaking out on her limbs. "But-but you're dead." Except the man stood in front of her with his pale blue hair as straight as hers. He was taller than Tayte and didn't have as much muscle, but she recalled the strength in his arms and the speed with which he could run.

"Kaya, have a seat," Tayte ordered. "We have much to tell you."

With another glance at the wailing infant, she walked—or rather wobbled—to the nearest gel-chair and fell onto the seat.

"What is that stench?" her father asked.

"It's me. I washed and rinsed three times, but it takes a while for the scent to fade. I got slimed by one of the carnivorous plants on the other side of the mountains. Tell me about Mother. What happened?"

The baby ceased wailing when her father took her from Tayte and tickled her tummy. "Are you hungry, sweet Lys?" her father crooned.

He produced a bottle from a bag Kaya hadn't noticed and soon the child—her sister—drank with gusto.

"A faction developed who believed our race would be better off without Mother's rule," Tayte said.

"Phrull, don't tell me you expect me to return to Sitnam. I don't want to rule. I-I... I'd make a terrible leader."

"Listen, Kaya, and we'll explain everything before we leave," her father said.

Kaya pressed her lips together. She understood none of this. Her father was alive, and she had another sibling?

Her father stared at her. "You're so beautiful. You have the appearance of Gleneese."

But her mother was dead. Another thing she didn't fathom. Her mother was a strong woman, an experienced and canny leader. It sounded as if her attackers had taken her unaware.

"Kaya, you, Lys, and I are full siblings, not half, as is the tradition among Mother's people," Tayte said. He held up his hand when she opened her mouth. "Father is from Morph. He and Mother met when they were young, and they fell in love. They didn't care that their people were enemies. Mother and Father made a plan to mate and stay together for as long as they both lived."

Her mother, a romantic?

"As a Morph, Father can change his appearance at will. Show her."

Kaya blinked as the man they assured her was her father—he resembled him—transformed in front of her to the younger male she'd seen in depictions her mother had shown her when she was young. Then, as she watched, his appearance shifted again to a handsome man who in no way resembled her mother's first two husbands.

Kaya blinked. "Father?"

The man transformed back to the father she'd known as a child before tradition demanded that her mother get rid of him. *Let the celebrations begin.*

"I can also shift my appearance in the manner of our father," Tayte informed her. "Our special talents mean we can help certain races with delicate matters."

"You're spies?"

"Not quite, but all of our work is undercover," her father said.

"But why didn't anyone tell me?"

"We're telling you now," Tayte said with clear impatience. "Kaya, time is scarce. We're in the middle of an important mission, so we must leave Lys with you. Keep her safe."

"Wait...what...? No! I have no experience with children. If they screech, I hand them back to their mothers. Wait—is this payback for us dumping Olivia Polo with you?"

"No," Tayte said. "Although I owe you. That Earth girl is a menace to my sanity."

The trace of confusion in her brother cheered her. She'd known the Earth woman would intrigue him. "Olivia is an intelligent being. Oh, wait. Has she caught on to your spy games?"

Her father chuckled, and for an instant, Kaya felt normal. She had a family.

Tayte straightened, his scowl menacing. "Father and I are in the middle of something dangerous. I don't want you or Lys caught in the trouble. You are Lys's sister and will act as her guardian."

"Please, Kaya. There is no one else we trust, and you should spend time with your sister. It's not normal for the children of your race to have close ties, but you and Tayte get on well," her father said.

"You said she's in danger?" Kaya asked, her gaze flitting across to the now quiet baby. *Phrull*, she knew nothing of raising a child. Although Camryn and Jannike had children. Perhaps they would help her. Offer her aid.

Grata! She could imagine Jannike's evil chuckles now.

"You're both in danger from the new ruler," Tayte said.

"All the more reason to separate us," Kaya blurted.

"No," her father said. "We're stronger together. I am proud of my son and older daughter. You are warriors and capable of great things."

"You're not giving me a choice, are you?" Kaya asked, staring from her brother to her very-alive father.

"I'm sorry, sweetheart," her father said. "You and Lys will have to rub along together."

Kaya gulped. She'd rather face a herd of hell-horses than this one child. She understood more about hell-horses than offspring. Her shoulders slumped, then straightened. "All right. Who should I watch for? One thing first. I am—" She broke off her intended lie. "I agreed to do a favor for Gryffnn, the leader of the dragons. Another dragon clan from a nearby planet has declared their intention to visit. Gryffnn has a history with the other clan. He believes they have heard of his older brother's illness. He's in a coma," she added. "It's just as dangerous for Lys on Narenda. I need to tell Gryffnn the truth. My friends, too."

"Secrets shared have a life of their own," her father said.

"These people are my friends. I hold their secrets, and they will do the same for me," Kaya snapped.

"Could you pass off Lys as your child? Would this Gryffnn agree to this and protect her as his own?" Tayte asked.

Kaya lifted her head and met her brother's and father's doubts. "He has a child from his first mating. I would protect his son with everything I have, and Gryffnn will offer the same protection for me. He is a good man. A decent one. Ry and Camryn, Nanu, Jannike, and Mogens would protect Lys with their lives too."

Grata, she couldn't believe she'd agreed to this plan.

"Gryffnn. He is the dragon who showed us to this parlor?" her father asked.

"Yes."

Her father nodded. "He spoke highly of you."

"He's an honorable man and trustworthy," Kaya replied as the baby—Lys—gave a tiny hiccup.

"All right. I agree," her father said. "But remember this well, Kaya Ignatius. Every person you tell places not only you and Lys in danger but Tayte and myself too. Gleneese has died protecting her family. You must take care."

"How will the danger present?" Kaya asked, tension sliding down her backbone. Her ears tingled, and she fought to stay her hands at her sides. She wanted to itch that pesky tingle away.

"Watch for a single assassin," Tayte said. "From Sitnam, I'd say. At least they'll stand out with their blue skin."

"The assassins are more likely to chase Tayte or me," her father said. "Narenda and your home base of Viros are far enough away from Sitnam, which is why we brought Lys to you."

"Are you returning to Sitnam?"

"Morph," Tayte said.

"But isn't that dangerous? Won't they see your true faces once you land there?"

"Neither Tayte nor I registered as Morphs," her father said.

"Every bit of information you offer gives me more questions," Kaya commented. "You can tell me the story once your mission ends. You will survive. Won't you?" she added in a hard voice.

"We'll do our best." Tayte picked up a package she hadn't noticed earlier. "This is Mother's sword. She always intended to pass it on to you. I had a faithful servant retrieve it once I heard of Gleneese's death."

Kaya took the wrapped sword, feeling the magic of it radiating through the wrapping. Tradition said the sword chose its master, not the other way around. Until she felt the prickle clear to the tips of her ears, she'd never believed the stories, dismissing the information as fantasy and gossip. "I will treasure this sword."

"Practice the routines you learned as a youngster," her father instructed. "Gleneese always boasted of your talent. If an assassin comes after you, you'll require fast feet and a strong arm."

"All right. I train each cycle. Adding in swordplay is easy enough."

"Lys's clothes and supplies are in the two bags." Tayte pulled out a third bag and removed a woman's dress as he spoke. The flowing type that older matrons wore.

Her father handed Lys over, and Kaya accepted her sister awkwardly since she still held her sword. Although she'd been around Camryn's and Jannike's babies, she'd escaped close contact. Tayte yanked off his vest, tossed it aside, and pulled the dress over his head. Secs later, her brother morphed into a middle-aged female with stark black hair and an ample bosom. By the time she turned to scan her father, he also had transformed to an older woman.

Her father embraced Kaya, taking care not to squash his youngest daughter. He stooped to kiss Lys's forehead. He stepped back, his blue eyes bright with emotion. "Take care, my daughter," he said in an old-lady rasp to match his appearance.

"You too," Kaya murmured, blinking at the difference in her father and brother even though she'd witnessed the change from male to female.

"Kaya." Tayte approached and hugged her.

"Stay alive," she murmured as he kissed Lys.

"Please thank your Gryffnn for his hospitality and consideration," her father said. "We will meet another time."

Kaya nodded and watched as her father and brother minced from the parlor and disappeared.

With a sigh, she frowned down at her sister. The infant had an angelic appearance with her blue curls and blue-tinged skin. Her little pointy ears. Then, she opened her mouth and screeched.

"Oh no. Oh no. Please don't cry. Please don't cry!" Kaya jiggled her as she'd seen Camryn and Jannike do with their children. Lys promptly vomited all over Kaya's front. "*Grata!* Camryn! Camryn!" Kaya strode from the parlor, heading toward the family room where Gryffnn's family hung out. She figured—prayed—Camryn and Ry were present.

Her father and brother had left her holding the baby. A screaming, angry, sick one at that.

CHAPTER 4

THE SCARY RESPONSIBILITY

"Kaya?" Gryffnn had hovered close enough to give Kaya aid should she require it but far enough away so he didn't eavesdrop with his superior hearing. Oh, he'd wanted to listen, but decency forbade him to intrude in this manner. Two men had entered his parlor, and two elderly women departed, yet he'd remained in position, trusting Kaya despite the odd situation.

Kaya appeared in the doorway, holding a squawking baby. The stench of vomit wafted in the air. Kaya's eyes were wide and round, and her muscles clenched tight. "She won't stop crying! She cries and cries. I don't know what to do."

Gryffnn took in the vomit on Kaya's tunic, the fear on her face, and his heart melted at her panic, the chink in her tough warrior armor.

"Here, let me." He scooped up the wailing infant, held her

against his chest, and rubbed her back. The child burped and quieted, her frantic sobs reducing to sniffles. Gryffnn continued to stroke the child's back, enchanted by her similarity to Kaya. "Has your brother left?"

"Yes. I need to talk to you, tell you something in private."

She stared at him weirdly, her mouth opening and closing until she resembled an inexperienced dragon youngling who'd burnt his lips on his beginner fire.

"Whoa," she muttered and shook her head.

"Why don't we discuss whatever you need to tell me in my chamber? You'll want to change your tunic. Hallam moved your possessions for me. Well, he started to until he got to your underwear drawer. I had a maid finish the rest of the packing while Hallam did the toting back and forward." Gryffnn waggled his eyebrows and grinned. "He has questions for you."

An un-Kaya-like moan slipped from her. "Maybe I could redo this entire cycle. I'm a warrior, not a nursemaid. Two children in one cycle. It's way too scary for me."

Gryffnn wanted to smile at her flustered air. Her ruffled manner made her more interesting, as did learning of her family. She had a brother, which meant he'd have another brother if he got his way. A dragon could never have too many siblings guarding his back.

"This is my chamber," Gryffnn said, stopping before a carved wooden door. He placed his palm on the recognition plate, and the door swung open. "I'll code the door for your palm later this eve."

Kaya shut the door behind them and turned to him. "This is my sister, Lys. My mother died, and my father and brother believed if those responsible caught up with either me or Lys, they'd try to kill us. They suggested I pretend Lys is my daughter. Children are a mystery to me. What if I break her?" Kaya almost wailed.

"That's a lot of information for my poor male brainbox to compute. Start again and tell me everything," he said.

Although he'd received the gist of what she said, the lift of her nose and the straightening of her shoulders told him Kaya was regaining control. She set the wrapped package she carried in the corner of his chamber.

"What is that?"

"My mother's sword. Tayte said she wanted me to have it."

"Are you talented with a sword?"

"I used to train with one. It won't take me long to regain my muscle memory and strength."

The baby in his arms cooed and grabbed a strand of his hair. She yanked it hard. "Ow. The little one is a warrior like her sister." He freed himself, and the baby laughed at him. His heart melted with a fierce wave of emotion. If he and Kaya had a child, they might resemble this baby or turn into a big hulking dragon. Either way, he'd celebrate.

Normally, dragons didn't mate outside their species, but he and Ransom had discussed the matter when his older brother had noted his fascination with Kaya. Ransom had informed him anything was possible. He'd confided to Gryffnn that if he discovered a woman who called to him, he'd follow his heart—no matter the lectures the remaining elders gave him.

Good enough for him.

Aware his thoughts had wandered onto a different path, he glanced at Kaya. She'd sunk onto the corner of his gel-bed. The next step would be getting her naked.

"Your eyes are glowing."

Gryffnn blinked. The baby was staring at him too. Best he get his randy thoughts under control. Lys cooed and flung up her little arm, smacking him on the jaw.

"Lys." Kaya cast her gurgling sister a scowl, and Gryffnn controlled his amusement with difficulty.

"What happened to your mother?"

"She was the ruler of Sitnam. From what my brother said, there was a faction on the planet who wanted to overthrow her, and they succeeded. The ruler of Sitnam is always a female. My race never values males, which was why my brother left at the age of twelve rotations. My mother sent him away, but now everything I thought I knew is upside down."

"Why? Can you tell me?" This slice of her life fascinated him.

"In my mother's world, a male serves one purpose. To provide seed to produce the next generation. Once a female is breeding, the female kills the male. My father didn't die until I was around four rotations, which is unusual on our world."

Gryffnn blinked yet again. "Kills them?"

"Yes. I thought my mother had followed tradition, since my father differed from Tayte's. But now I find she fell in love with a man from an enemy planet. A man from Morph. Tayte, Lys, and I all have the same father, who is still alive. I-I think he raised Tayte and ensured his safety. Tayte kept the secret and never told me." She sounded confused and disgruntled.

"That was your father with your brother?"

"Yes."

And the Morph connection explained why two women had left. He'd let them go without questioning their changed appearance since he'd been more worried about Kaya.

"Your father and brother think you and Lys are in danger?"

"The faction who overthrew my mother may search for us. We're a danger—well, me—since I have the bloodlines to stir the people to rebellion."

"Are you royalty?"

"Not royalty, but I possess the bloodlines to lead—if I want."

His breath caught, his mind racing. He couldn't leave Narenda. Not again. This was home, and he was needed until Ransom recovered. "Do you want to lead?"

"I left the only home I'd ever known after my maid tried to poison me. My mother asked me if I wished to lead, and I said I preferred to explore life outside Sitnam. In our history, mothers have done away with ambitious daughters."

"You think she tried to kill you?"

"No. My mother loved me, and if I wanted proof, I have it now. She kept my brother, father, and me safe, and now Lys, too."

"How long has it been since you saw your mother?"

Kaya's forehead puckered. "Ah, about five rotations."

"How did you meet with Ry?"

"I'd never left Sitnam, and it didn't take long for thieves to part me from my currency. Ry stopped two creepy aliens from abducting me. He offered me passage away from the planet I'd landed up on and later gave me a job on his ship. Ry collected all the *Indy* crew that way."

"He's an honorable man."

"Yes. Meeting Ry was a lucky cycle for me."

"All right. This is what we'll do. We'll tell everyone Lys is our child. A baby won't interest Aideen. It's you who will draw her attention. I'll make certain I hold Lys for her to take on my scent."

"So we need not have sex?"

Gryffnn wished he could read Kaya, but she'd settled and regained her balance. "You'll be under scrutiny. If I'm reading Aideen right, she expects me to hook up with her sister again. That will not happen. Have you changed your mind?"

Please say no. Please say you want me.

Tension slid through him as he waited for her answer. Perhaps he should take a leaf from his grandsire's teachings and abduct her. He'd keep her contained until she agreed to a mating between them.

"I gave my word I'd help you. I stand by that. But what about Hallam? I'd hate him to get hurt by our pretense."

"I've explained everything to him." He'd told his son the truth about the Dalcon dragon clan and what he hoped to achieve with Kaya. His son would keep Gryffnn's confidence.

Kaya nodded. "Okay, as long as you're certain Hallam will be all right."

Unable to force his relief into casual speech, he dipped his head. He glanced down at Lys and smiled as she sucked her delicate blue thumb, her eyelids almost closed. "Lys is exhausted. Why don't we take her down to meet your friends, my son and sister, and then to the nursery with Camryn's offspring?"

"Just as well you know what you're doing. I'm clueless."

"You'll learn. I'll teach you." Lys's presence might prove helpful and cement them into a family.

Kaya gulped, and Gryffnn wanted to take her into his arms and kiss her until they both trembled. *Too soon. Play the long game.*

He stroked Lys's head, her blue hair silky beneath his fingertips. "Are you ready?"

"Yes." She stood and straightened her shoulders. "Wait. I'd better change my tunic. Where are my clothes?"

"In the closet over there." Gryffnn gestured with his free hand and watched as she whipped off her dirty garment and donned a clean one. He caught a flash of tempting curves and pale blue skin before he forced himself to study Lys instead.

Kaya's chin rose as she turned to him. "Let's do this."

"Do you want to carry her?"

"No." Kaya backed away, alarm bleeding the healthy color from her cheeks.

"Perhaps it's best if I keep holding her so she absorbs my scent."

"Excellent idea." She marched to the door and flung it open, allowing Gryffnn a chance to free his grin. No doubt about it, Kaya presented an enticing challenge, and he intended to enjoy every moment.

Gryffnn followed Kaya into the communal room. The animated chatter fell silent as they entered. "I'd like you to meet our daughter, Lys," he said. The mite had fallen asleep, and a surge of protectiveness filled him.

"I have a sister." Hallam bounded over to them, all long legs and gangly youth.

"You do. Do you want to hold her?"

Hallam nodded, accepting his word without asking any questions. The adults wouldn't believe the story so easily. His son was a good kid, responsible and mature despite his tender years. Almost twelve rotations old, he'd flown earlier than his peers, making both Gryffnn and Ransom proud.

Hallam stroked her cheek with a fingertip. "She is so tiny."

"Support her head," Gryffnn murmured. "Sable, will you go with Hallam to the nursery and put Lys down for the evening?"

"My pleasure." His sister's swift glance promised myriad questions in his future.

Hallam exited the room with his aunt.

"I suppose you have questions," Kaya said.

Gryffnn moved to stand by her and reached for her hand. He squeezed it in silent support. She started before relaxing.

"Is this secret squirrel stuff?" Camryn asked.

"Yes." Kaya leaned into him.

Gryffnn forced himself not to react, but every part of him registered her scent—still tinged with plant stink—and the weight of her body against his hip. "What is a secret squirrel?"

"Private stuff," Nanu said, acting as an interpreter.

"I-I can tell you, but it's better not to share the truth with you. All you need to know is that Lys is m-my d-daughter."

"And mine." Gryffnn rearranged Kaya against his chest. He felt the tension in her but refused to let her wriggle free. He bent his head to nip her earlobe, and she froze. A tiny moan squeezed past her pastel blue lips. "We have more important things to discuss. Tell me again about these intruders. You have no idea of their identity?"

"None," Ry said. "With the arrival of the Dalcon dragons, do you have enough soldiers to guard that perimeter? Kaya, she isn't your daughter."

The abrupt subject change had Kaya stiffening in his arms.

"My sister," Kaya said with a sigh. "But to everyone else, Lys is my daughter. Understand?"

"Interesting." Nanu's hair stirred with a whispery sigh. "You never discuss your family. I'd decided you and Tayte arrived via giant bird."

Gryffnn's concerns lightened on hearing Nanu's good-natured insults. "Continue," he said to Ry. "We have enough soldiers, but the mountain resonance worries me."

"Ellard wanted to offer his soldiers more training. Would you be willing to have them do the job with Ellard overseeing them?" Ry asked.

"Not a bad idea. I'll comm Lynx and Shiloh as soon as we finish dinner." Gryffnn said as he absorbed the offer. "I'd prefer to keep my men on hand here to watch Aideen and her flight. Meanwhile, can I get you to set up surveillance equipment where the thefts are occurring? We didn't pick up any arrivals or strange ships in our flight space on our system here."

"Their ship appeared sleek and modern. It's possible their technology is new and undetectable."

"It's superior if they can steal our resources from under our noses," Gryffnn said drily.

"Has your brother left?" Camryn asked.

"Yes, he has urgent business," Kaya said.

"I'm sorry we missed him. Did he mention Olivia? Has she returned to Earth?"

A quick grin flashed across Kaya's face. "Olivia is driving him nuts, jolting him from his routine. He hasn't sent her packing yet, which I find interesting."

A servant tapped for entry. He approached Gryffnn. "The dragons from Dalcon have arrived," he said instead of announcing dinner.

Damn and blast. This was typical Aideen, always doing the unexpected.

"I'll meet them at the spaceport. Kaya and I will leave now."

"Their ships have landed on the training field," the servant said.

"What do you need us to do?" Ry asked.

"I need two guards on Ransom's chamber. The visitors must not see him. I also need Hallam kept away from them. I don't trust Aideen."

"Mogens and I will take care of Hallam," Camryn said. "Does he understand why he must avoid the Gwilym dragons?"

"Yes," Gryffnn said tersely. "He understands, but can you reinforce that Lys is his sister and he mustn't mention her either—to keep them both safe."

"Nanu and I will watch over Ransom and free up your guard," Ry said. "Anything else? Where are you housing them?"

"Decorum states I must have them here at the compound. I'll decide on the exact arrangements once I see who has arrived. Kaya, with me."

Gryffnn stalked from the communal room, his mind racing in a dozen directions at once. Kaya strode at his side and her silent solidarity shored up his fears. He refused to let Aideen and her clan get the better of him, and he'd protect his brother and their clan to his dying breath. His only regret—he and Kaya hadn't cemented their bond yet.

"Aideen will scent we're not mates," he said.

Kaya winked. "Maybe not. She'll take one whiff and avoid me."

"I get a lungful now and then." A burst of humor shot through him. "With luck, the stench has transferred to me, and Aideen will keep her distance."

Goddess, he wasn't looking forward to this meeting.

"You've got this, Gryffnn," Kaya said as they stalked outdoors and headed to the training field.

Gryffnn's chest swelled, and he tugged Kaya to a halt.

"What?"

He hauled her into his arms and kissed her with all the desperation he'd felt when he'd thought Ransom wanted Kaya. He caught her gasp with his mouth and teased her lips with his tongue before he took the kiss deeper. Sweetness burst over him at Kaya's acceptance of his rough and unrestrained ardor.

"Well," a strident feminine voice declared. "A fine meeting to be sure. You'd rather dally with your doxy than greet us. With Ransom out of commission, I expected disarray, and I wasn't wrong."

CHAPTER 5

UNWELCOME GUESTS

G ryffnn stiffened at Aideen's mocking voice. She still thought
the solar system revolved around her.

Kaya brushed a kiss against his ear. "You got this," she
whispered. Then, she pulled away to face Aideen, her lips curling
in a sneer. "Who the devil are you calling a doxy? I'm no common
trollop."

Proud and buoyed by Kaya's attitude, Gryffnn reminded
himself he was no longer the same young, inexperienced male
who'd gone to Dalcon to join Aideen and her clan. He angled until
Aideen entered his peripheral vision.

"Aideen," he said, not giving her the usual incline of head—a
show of respect to those of higher rank. "If you'd troubled to tell
me of your arrival time, we would've greeted you. Instead, you
arrive unexpectedly and have the discourtesy to land in the middle

of our training fields instead of at the spaceport. I expect your pilots to clear our fields and park your ships at the spaceport. *Now*. And you will apologize to my betrothed."

The dragon leader hadn't aged since he'd last seen her almost eleven—or was it twelve?—rotations ago. No, it must be eleven since Hallam had been a newborn. Her copper-bright hair lay in loose curls around her shoulders while her green eyes held surprise at his order. The leader of the Dalcon dragons stood tall for a female since she was only half a head shorter than him. Sculpted muscles packed her upper body and arms, and if one looked closely, her copper-colored scales were visible beneath her skin.

"I wouldn't want to inconvenience you." Aideen signaled to a member of her silent entourage. "Unload our luggage and have the pilots move the ships to the spaceport. I presume there will be room for our six ships?"

Six ships? Why had she brought such large numbers of her people? Gryffnn hid his concern in polite acquiescence. "There is room. If you have six ships, your people can deal with your luggage. I have arranged for you to stay in the guest cottages. The overflow can stay in the guards' quarters. I will have my staff ready the cottages for you."

"Oh, what about the main house? We are family."

"Not true," Gryffnn stated in a hard voice. He recalled his ex-wife and Aideen telling him he would receive no help from them, and he couldn't expect a return of his bride price. They'd invested the currency and the marriage contract had stated it was non-returnable. During all these years, they'd displayed not a scrap of interest in his son. "I haven't heard you apologize to Kaya."

"I hadn't heard of your betrothal." Aideen avoided the apology and sent a glower at her people when one or two dared to titter. "And we have ties in common. Your son."

"Why would you have learned of our happiness?" Kaya snapped. "I understood your clan has little contact with Gryffnn's."

54

A brief silence fell as Gryffnn measured Aideen. He found her lacking, her arrogance as devious as ever. There was no way he intended to let Aideen or her traitorous sister get their dragon claws into Hallam. The boy—his son—was the one good thing that had come from his short relationship with Caley Gwilym.

"You wish to discuss private matters in front of your people?" he demanded.

"No, you're right. Discussions can come later. What you say about our clans is true. It's time to change this," Aideen stated. "Hence the overture and this friendly visit." She turned to Kaya. "We seem to have started our meeting badly. Please accept my words of sorrow. I did not wish to offend."

Kaya glared at Aideen, not cowed by the fact the dragon woman stood several inches taller than her. Pride surged in Gryffnn as his breath eased out. Kaya's confidence made him think he could do anything.

Kaya sniffed, not hiding her dislike of Aideen. "We will show you to your accommodation."

Gryffnn smothered his amusement at Kaya's reaction as she gestured Aideen along the path toward the cottages. He didn't trust Aideen. Once burned by her and her sister, he'd never offer his back to this witch. Given the chance, she'd likely shove a knife between his shoulder blades.

"This way," Gryffnn said. "This path leads to the first cottage. Decide who you wish to stay with you, and I will contact housekeeping to determine if the other cottages are ready for habitation." He gestured the entourage down the path, his gaze locking with a member of the party he hadn't noticed to date. "Caley, I didn't realize you were part of Aideen's group. I understood you'd left the clan."

"You thought wrong," Caley said with a sniff and a toss of her head.

Like Aideen, Caley Gwilym was beautiful with her red hair,

creamy skin, and flashing green eyes that, at this moment, held malice. The beautiful exterior concealed a rotten heart. He'd learned this soon enough—material wealth interested the dragon woman, that and her own pleasure. She'd never wanted a mate. Not him, at any rate. He'd been too young. Too green. Too unsophisticated for a dragon woman of her needs. She remained unchanged and still wished to bend him to her will. But she'd learn he'd matured, and she and her sister could no longer shift him around like a game piece on a board.

When he remained silent, she rushed into speech.

"It is time for me to meet our son."

Gryffnn bit his tongue with difficulty. Hallam might have emerged from Caley's body, but that didn't make her a decent parent. No, she'd fled with her lover, spurning both Gryffnn and their son. She didn't get a second chance.

"Before I left Dalcon, you signed away your rights regarding my son. You will see him over my dead body."

Caley sniffed again and brushed past him, her long skirts rustling with displeasure. She muttered as she stalked away.

That could be arranged.

He was certain he'd heard her mumbled words correctly.

Gryffnn continued to count the number of *guests* in Aideen's party. The count ended at forty-three, and he wondered why Aideen had brought so many of her people with her and if she'd left any at their Dalcon enclave. *Grata*, he hadn't numbers for the crew on the ships yet.

Once the last person trailed past, Gryffnn followed in the rear. Hurried footsteps behind him had him slipping off the path.

Aideen's second-in-command jogged past, a tall, muscular dragon with a scarred face and long black hair braided into a tail that hung down his back. Assured this male was the last, Gryffnn followed Dilan. Rumor had said Dilan was Aideen's lover, but Gryffnn didn't know for sure.

Dilan slowed his steps and Gryffnn closed the gap between them, walking at his side once the path widened.

"I ordered the ships to the spaceport. They will leave as soon as the luggage is unloaded," Dilan said.

"Thank you. My training captain will be relieved to have his field cleared," Gryffnn said. "You have a large party."

"Yes." Dilan glanced ahead and slowed once again. "Be careful, Gryffnn."

"Of what?"

"Aideen has a plan."

"Aideen always has a plan," Gryffnn said. "I learned this to my cost. Why are you telling me? You're her second-in-command and have her ear."

"No longer," Dilan said. "Times change. Alliances."

"Speak plainly, man." Gryffnn didn't trust Dilan either, yet the dragon shifter appeared sincere in his warning.

"I can't say more. Aideen will know I spoke with you. Watch your back. That's all I'm saying."

Gryffnn eyed him, attempting to discern truth and lie. Dilan appeared genuine, but he'd ask Kaya her opinion later. "I need to speak with my staff and organize a meal for your clan. Go. I shall rejoin you shortly."

"Thank you, Gryffnn." Dilan gave a quick bow, inclining his head at the same time before hurrying around the corner in the path.

If Aideen and her clan were trying to set him off-balance, they were succeeding. Seeing Aideen again, then Caley. Gryffnn snorted, remembering the innocent youngster he'd been and his determination to be a good mate and make his father proud. Aideen had wanted ties between their clans, and he'd ended up the sacrifice since his father didn't wish to lose his heir. He wondered what his sire would feel now that Gryffnn was leading the Drake tribe.

Leading? *Bah!* He was bumbling through a series of crises, faking his confidence while he prayed Ransom would fully recover.

Kaya stomped toward the compound after arranging the *guests* in accommodation. Gryffnn was right to worry. The leader and Gryffnn's ex-wife had a goal in mind that went far beyond extending the hand of friendship.

A flash of color caught her attention. *Phrull it.* She upped her pace to a jog to intercept one of Aideen's people.

"You! Where are you going?"

The young male with dark hair and slanted amber eyes paused to grin at her. Twin dimples dug into his lower cheeks. His was a face to make young maidens sigh and coo. Too pretty for his own good.

"Merely stretching my legs after the flight from Dalcon."

"It's not that far from Narenda to Dalcon," Kaya said. "This part of the gardens is private. Stretch your legs on the training fields."

He shot a surreptitious gaze at the line of windows to his right before shrugging. "Can I entice you to take a stroll with me?"

"No," Kaya snapped. "Don't come here again."

The male tried to grasp her hand, and instinct had Kaya plowing her fist into his belly.

"*Oomph*," he said, watching her warily now and taking a rapid step back to increase the distance between them.

Frag it, her hand ached. This male might appear young but his body comprised tight muscle. One of Aideen's soldiers, she presumed. A spy.

"Tell your people the gardens are out of bounds. You are guests here and must abide by our rules."

"Some might assume you're hiding secrets."

"They can think what they want," Kaya said, maintaining his gaze. "If I catch you trespassing, I'll shoot first and ask questions later. I'm an excellent shot."

"You need a strong male to keep you in line."

Gryffnn stepped into the light and curled his arm around her waist. "She has a strong male, and I enjoy her sass and attitude just fine."

The young male stared at them for a fraction longer before giving a minuscule dip of his head, the show of respect almost an insult. He whirled and strode away until he blended with the blacklight.

"Are you all right?"

Gryffnn didn't release her, and his scent filled her lungs. A hint of amber. A dash of cinnamon, fragrant spices, and the smoky, salty tang she was coming to associate with dragons.

Her pulse beat a little faster at his proximity. "I'm fine. That *is* Ransom's window over there?"

"Yes."

"I caught Aideen's dragon creeping along here. He intended to peer inside."

"We need to move Ransom to an interior room," Gryffnn said.

"That might be best—if you wish to keep them from learning more about your brother's condition."

"I'll arrange a new chamber for Ransom tom-cycle. Aideen...I didn't expect her to bring so many of her people," Gryffnn said. "Her contacting me was suspicious before, and more so now since most of her entourage are young dragons." He thumbed his comm and spoke to his guard captain to arrange security around the family quarters. Once he ended the call, he said, "That will be sufficient for this blacklight. We have plenty of security. Aideen will learn that soon enough."

"Her people are battle-fit." Kaya tugged Gryffnn toward the

family quarters. "She hasn't come here for a friendly visit. She has other plans."

Gryffnn sighed. "My initial thoughts were that since she's heard Ransom is ill, she is testing our strength."

"Will she attack?"

"My gut says yes. She has always envied our precious stone deposits. Her hunger to better herself starts with taking us over."

They entered the dwelling and walked down the cool passage toward the family room. Their boots thudded on the stone floor tiles.

"I wonder if it might be a good idea to remove Ransom and take him to Viros. That way, you wouldn't have to worry about your brother, and you could use those men elsewhere. Discuss it with Ry and ask his opinion. Bring Jannike and her men in on the conversation. You intended to speak with them about extra security for your mineral deposits, anyway."

Gryffnn exhaled heavily. "The burden of leadership is a heavy weight."

Kaya halted him and gripped both his biceps in her hands. She stared up at his strong tan face and into his hazel eyes. They held kindness and determination, and warmth bloomed inside her. "You're doing a good job in Ransom's stead. You picked up the reins and have barely stumbled. That snooty Aideen and her friends don't stand a chance. I have confidence in you." And she stood on tiptoe and pressed her lips to his.

He groaned, wrapped his beefy arms around her shoulders, and took over the kiss. *Well, she'd managed the confidence boost she'd intended.* Kaya looped her hands behind his neck and clung, enjoying the hell out of his dominating kiss. The press of lips. The tangle of tongues. The brush of bodies.

She'd imagined sex with Ransom often but had never set her sights on Gryffnn. A mistake. This dragon shifter had hidden depths, and better still, she'd come to like and admire him when most males needed to work hard to impress her.

Gryffnn pulled back, separating their mouths.

Huh! That was interesting. His eyes had shifted, the pupils transforming to mere slits. Sexy.

Kaya concentrated on regulating her racing pulse and breathing. She expected he'd set her on her feet, but he surprised her again. He pressed his forehead to hers and closed his eyes, breathing in her scent.

"I love your perfume."

"Even though I still wear odor of plants?"

"I'm not noticing that so much now. It's the crispness underneath I can smell. It reminds me of when I'm flying high on a cool day, and the tropical winds are blowing in my face and buffeting my body."

Heat collected in Kaya's face. No doubt her cheeks wore slashes of cobalt blue, but this dragon shifter didn't offer pretense. Oh, their relationship was fake, but the dig of his cock into her body told her he wanted her. If she were honest, she craved him with the same intensity. She hadn't wanted a man like this since Ry's brother...

No, she refused to waste thoughts on that worm and his magical spells that had turned her into his sex slave. His evilness. Good riddance to him. Best she concentrate on Gryffnn and the present rather than a dead man.

"Are the pair of you coming in for dinner?" Camryn asked. "We've been waiting while you canoodle in the passage, but I'm starving." Her stomach let out an audible rumble.

Gryffnn let Kaya slip down his body to regain her own feet. "What is canoodling? I have not heard this term."

"It comes from Camryn's place of birth," Kaya said, a fresh wave of warmth suffusing her face on witnessing the male heat in his dragon eyes. "It means we were doing kissing stuff."

"I suppose I'd better feed you before we canoodle some more."

And with that, Gryffnn ushered her toward the dining room door.

When they entered, everyone was waiting, and the scent of a rich, meaty stew drifted to Kaya.

"Start eating," Gryffnn said. "Kaya, can you serve my dinner for me? I want to check in with my security team to make sure they're in place, and Aideen's people aren't running amok. I won't be long."

He strode from the room, and Kaya watched him until he disappeared. When she returned her gaze to her dining companions, she found each of them grinning at her. Even Hallam.

"You like my father," Hallam said, and he sounded pleased.

Her crewmates didn't speak, sparing her any teasing in Gryffnn's son's presence. Their expressions, however, said volumes.

"My new sister wouldn't stop crying," Hallam said. "She sure cries a lot."

Shame that she hadn't spared a thought for Lys engulfed her. Kaya half stood, intending to go to her before Camryn halted her.

"When I stopped by, my twins had crawled from their beds and were chattering to her. My two refused to stay in bed, so I ended up making one big bed for the three. The close contact seemed to quieten them, and when I peeked in later, the kids were all asleep," Camryn said.

"Thank you," Kaya said, and it was heartfelt. Lys's crying scared her. *Phrull*, what was her brother thinking? He knew she had little experience with children. She accepted the bowl of stew from Nanu and served a generous ladle onto Gryffnn's plate before adding a smaller one to her own.

Gryffnn strode back into the dining room and took his seat beside her. "My soldiers are in position, and they've already forced away two different dragon shifters."

"Aideen is here to cause trouble then?" Ry asked.

"She's testing us, learning our weaknesses," Gryffnn replied.

"What are you going to do?" Nanu queried.

"I can't challenge her outright without reason. All I have at present are suspicions. My gut tells me to get Ransom away from here. Hallam too. Your children and Lys should leave as well," Gryffnn said. "Could I send them to Viros?"

"Let's finish dinner before we contact Jannike," Ry said.

"Nanu and I could fly Ransom and the children back to Viros," Mogens said, flashes of black dissecting his cheeks and turning his skin darker as he spoke. "We could leave after dinner before your visitors understand what is happening. Gweneth will take charge of the children. We could send Hallam to Jarlath and Keira. They'll keep him busy at the farm with their other charges. This is a sensible choice. I disliked the cloud's appearance before whitelight turned to black."

"That is an excellent idea," Ry said. "Camryn can go too."

"I'm happy to help with our twins and Lys on the journey back, but I will return with Nanu," Camryn said in a don't-mess-with-me voice. "I am capable."

"Of course, you are, sweetheart. But like Gryffnn, my gut is signaling trouble."

"Which is why I'm returning," Camryn declared. "I love our children, but I wish to set a good example. What kind of friend would I be if I didn't stand up for my pals?"

Ry picked up a goblet of cacjuice and lifted it in a silent toast. "I can't argue with that, but I will growl and roar if you get injured."

"Right back at you," Camryn said.

"Now that your domestic argument has ended," Kaya said. "This is a good plan. I'm sure Jannike and her men will agree with our suggestions. Bring back the soldiers with you. Gryffnn, maybe you can offer Ellard's men a bounty for each one of those creepy plants they kill?"

"Not only that, I'll pay them for guarding our lands," Gryffnn said.

"You must distract your visitors while we get Ransom and the kids to the *Indy*," Camryn said.

"If you don't mind taking charge, Kaya and I can see Aideen and make sure she has everything she requires," Gryffnn suggested.

"Are the Incorporeal people still here, or did they leave?" Nanu asked.

"Niran is still here along with his two oldest sons. The rest of their people removed to Tiraq, a planet near Dalcon."

"Will Niran help move Ransom and Hallam?" Ry set down his cutlery. "Camryn, Nanu, and I can take the babies, and it will appear as if we're going back to Viros. If anyone asks, you can tell them your friends are leaving. No need to mention that I'm staying or the others are returning with reinforcements."

Kaya witnessed the struggle in Gryffnn. He didn't want to send his brother or son to Viros even though he knew it was for their safety. She pushed her dinner plate away and reached for Gryffnn's hand. She curled her fingers around his bigger, callused ones, her heart tripping at the contact.

"This is only temporary. You never know. A change of domicile might jerk Ransom from his coma. Mogens will stay with him, and every castle resident will protect him," Kaya said.

"I know you're right," Gryffnn said.

"Yay!" Hallam's jubilant arm flinging sent a plate flying. It struck the floor and broke into three pieces.

"Hallam," Kaya said, trying not to laugh.

"Sorry, Ma," Hallam said. "What should I pack?"

A choking sound came from Nanu, and Camryn turned to face Ry.

"Don't call me Ma," Kaya snapped.

"Don't you like me?" Hallam took on a wounded expression, his young face creased in frown lines, and...were those tears?

Oh, *frag it*. She was messing this up. *Phrull*, she was right to worry about breaking Lys. "Um, sorry," she mumbled. "You're a good kid, okay?" What should she do now?

"Why don't you call her Kaya, the same as you always have?" Mogens suggested. "She is still your mother, and you must mind her as you would your father." A wave of white dissected his right cheek. "I suspect Kaya is still getting used to having two children."

Two children. She swiped a hand over her face. *Holy Hannah*. Things were moving way too fast for her. Two children and a husband in one cycle were too much for her beleaguered mind to cope with, even if it was a pretense. She sucked in a quick breath.

"I'll come and help you pack, Hallam. We must do it quickly so I can aid your father with his visitors." Kaya stood. "I'll be back soon. You'll need to confirm with Viros before we go to see Aideen, anyway."

Hallam brightened and gamboled at her side, reminding Kaya of one of those puppy-pets that Amme and Marcus had purchased for their daughter. Did parents get their children these things? She should've paid more attention to Camryn and how she dealt with her twins.

Holy phrull! She had two kids. *Two*. Now each of the *Indy* female crew had a pair of children. Even though her children were temporary, the responsibility hit her hard.

"Will I be able to practice my flying on Viros?" Hallam wanted to know.

"Jarlath's mate is a crow shifter," Kaya said. "She might help you."

"I've never been away from Father before," Hallam said.

Okay. That was clear. He was nervous now. "You'll have fun with Jarlath and Keira. They have a farm and will teach you about animals. Their cook makes delicious meals."

"But I'm a jeweler," Hallam said. "Father is teaching me."

"You'll still be a jeweler," Kaya said. "But a wise person learns everything they can. New skills are never wasted. Jarlath and the boys he fosters practice their sword skills and wrestling. They learn about farming and selling things in the market. These are skills you can use as a jeweler."

Hallam nodded even as she prayed she was telling him the right thing. Actually, she was repeating the lecture her mother had given her when she hadn't wanted to train one day. She'd told her mother she preferred to dress in pretty clothes. Funny how things changed. She'd never imagined this life in a trillion rotations, yet at the end of each cycle, she fell asleep, happy with her achievements. She wished she could tell her mother that.

But it wasn't too late to tell her father.

He had given her variations of the same lecture.

Kaya turned to Hallam. "Throw in a few tunics and trews. Leave your comm here because it's possible to trace them."

"Can I take my jewelry-making tools?"

"Yes," Kaya said. "As long as it will fit into the bag with your clothes. Will you watch out for Lys for me? You won't be staying at the same place but on the journey to Viros?"

Hallam nodded, and to her surprise, he wrapped his arms around her waist and hugged her. "I'm glad you're mating with my father. He has been lonely. You make him happy."

Kaya opened her mouth to dispute this, then closed it again, feeling strangely touched at Hallam's words. "Thank you." She zipped up the bag of belongings they'd assembled. "Let's get this show on the road."

CHAPTER 6

STRATEGY AND CUNNING

"We interrupted something," Kaya said as they ambled back to the family quarters after checking on Aideen and the rest of the Gwilym clan.

"We did," Gryffnn agreed, smiling as he recalled the irritation Aideen hadn't concealed. He reached for Kaya's hand and entwined their fingers, the urge to touch her a siren song whispering through his mind. Her blue hair shone in the light of one of their moons, bright as a blue morpho butterfly. The fragrance of the flowers drifted to him, and he found himself noticing each small sound and committing the moment to memory, his heart full of joy, full of contentment.

Kaya leaned closer and whispered in his ear. "Have we fooled them?"

"We'll know at whitelight," Gryffnn said, his happiness

dimming a fraction. She didn't care as much as him. With time, he prayed that their friendship deepened. "I'm thankful we have you and the Viros royalty as allies. Ransom and I fought with Father over allowing outsiders to visit Narenda. If Father hadn't died, we'd still be a closed planet."

"The benefits are mutual," Kaya said. "As they should be between neighbors."

"Do you think they got away safely?"

Kaya squeezed his hand. "We'll soon learn. Ry and Sable are waiting for us."

Ry gave a brief nod and retreated. Sable smiled and followed Ry.

"It's all good," Kaya said. "How about having an after-dinner drink with Ry and your sister before we retire for the eve?"

Gratitude filled Gryffnn at Kaya's easy suggestion. She hadn't signed up for a war with the Gwilym dragons, yet he feared that might happen. "Are you certain you want to follow this plan?"

Kaya's quick glance held surprise. "You've changed your mind?"

"No."

He didn't need to reconsider because he'd wanted her from the first moment he'd spotted her. He relished her feistiness, her irreverence, her take-no-prisoners-attitude and her inner strength. She was loyal to her friends, and the specters he glimpsed occasionally in her eyes gave her an interesting depth. He suspected the quick visit from her brother and the arrival of a younger sister contributed to the shadows.

Gryffnn winked at her. "I'm craving my next kiss."

"Me too," she said with a cute blink, a sweep of her long blue lashes. She sashayed into the common room, and he enjoyed the feminine rock of hips, showcased by her tight trews and formfitting tunic. Aware he was staring, he ripped his gaze away and followed.

Sable wrinkled her nose. "I can still smell those plants."

"Sorry," Kaya said. "My nose is numb to the stink. I'll have to bathe a few more times before I get rid of the odor."

"They got away safely?" Gryffnn asked, needing the reassurance. Was he doing the right thing? This leadership thing was hard, and once Ransom recovered, Gryffnn intended to offer more help instead of goofing off and doing his own thing.

"Nanu went to the *Indy* straight after we talked at dinner. Niran and his sons transported Ransom and Hallam directly onboard," Ry said. "Mogens, Camryn, and I arrived not long afterward with the children and the luggage. We saw a few of Aideen's crew with their ships. We waved, and when one wandered over, we told him we were traveling back to Viros. They didn't suspect a thing."

"Did it seem to worry them you stayed?" Kaya demanded.

"I caught an older dragon transmitting a message to one of their people here," Ry said. "They didn't seem bothered by my presence."

"It's tom-cycle that will be the problem." Gryffnn rubbed his gritty eyes and sighed. "I'll admit I'm worried. Aideen has enough dragons with her to create a disturbance."

"You have good people," Sable said. "Ransom has trained them well, and you have continued. We'll continue as normal but scrutinize their behavior. We usually have a banquet dinner when guests visit. Why don't we organize one for tom-cycle eve? It's short notice, but our kitchens can handle the challenge. Invite those of standing from our people. They already know to use tact with our visitors."

Gryffnn nodded. "I'll arrange friendly contests. Wrestling. Sword play. Flying and flaming contests. Make out we're pleased with their visit."

"Act like friends and see what bubbles to the surface," Kaya added more succinctly.

"We could arrange an outing to the waterfall and swimming hole," Gryffnn said, considering the various ways to keep them busy. "Arrange a hunt in the valley. If we caught a bovine beast, we could cook it outdoors on the braai."

Ry and Kaya nodded in agreement.

"And if they ask about Ransom? I can't decide what to say." Gryffnn poured a shot for each of them and handed out the slim golden glasses.

"They haven't seen Ransom or Hallam since their arrival," Sable said. "Just tell them Ransom is recuperating with friends. When they ask about Hallam, tell them it was an opportunity for him to visit and see friends, too, so you sent them together. Brother, you don't have to explain yourself. Give them the bare basics and leave it at that."

"Sable is right. Don't dance to their tune," Kaya said. "Write your own music and stick to your plan. They're the interlopers here."

"I agree." Ry lifted his glass in a toast. "If they ask questions, counter with questions of your own. Ask them about their stone deposits. Is it true they're depleted? For all we know, it is Aideen's people behind the theft of your stones."

Kaya paused with her drink halfway to her mouth. "Did you get a close look at their ships?"

"None of them were black," Ry said.

"Do you have contacts on Dalcon who can investigate Aideen's people?" Kaya asked.

"No, but Jacinta is visiting Dalcon en route to the resort at Tiraq," Sable reminded him. "She intended to shop and spend time with her friends."

Gryffnn brightened. Their sister Jacinta excelled at ferreting out secrets. People relaxed with her and suffered from verbal diarrhea. "I'll comm her and let her know what is happening. Sable, that is the perfect solution." He drank the last of his shot and placed down his glass. "Thank you for your help and advice."

Ry clapped him over the back. "Anything you need, just let us know."

"Keep watch for me. Anything out of place or things I miss, tell me. You too, Sable. If Jewel requires aid in the kitchen, ask for volunteers from the village to help. Kaya, are you ready to retire?"

Kaya's pulse did a weird bump and grind at Gryffnn's words. It was funny, but in the turmoil of this cycle, spending time in Gryffnn's bed was the one thing that didn't scare her. She eagerly anticipated the coming intimacies more than she'd ever imagined.

"See you tom-cycle. No doubt early," she said to Ry. "We'll need to be early to stay ahead of Aideen."

"Camryn promised to call me as soon as they arrived on Viros," Ry said. "I'll let you know."

"You make a good addition to the family, Kaya," Sable said with a quick wink.

Gryffnn chuckled and drew her from the room. "How are you enjoying the family excitement?"

"It's like stepping from my family, which is full of drama and surprises, into another of the same," Kaya said drily. "I hoped to escape cut-throat politics and backstabbing."

"Do you want to back out?"

"No, merely pointing out all families have their drama. I've survived mine—so far."

"Do you think you're in danger?"

"I hope my brother is being overly cautious, but I don't intend to stick my head down a hole and ignore the situation. A wise person watches everyone and everything. That way, the surprises are limited."

Gryffnn paused outside his chamber door and smiled down at her. Her heart flip-flopped this time, and eagerness filled her as he claimed her lips. She relaxed against him, falling into the press of mouths and bodies. His smoky scent wound through her senses, way more seductive than the odor of plants that clung to her.

He pulled away and unlocked the door to his chamber by

pressing his palm against the plate. A click sounded. Gryffnn drew her inside and closed the door behind them.

"Alone at last."

She grinned, liking the flash of humor in his hazel eyes.

"I need to contact Jacinta and touch base with Storg, my head of security. Why don't you bathe?"

"All right." Kaya took half a step toward his bathing room.

"Kaya?"

"Yes?" She paused and glanced over her shoulder.

"Don't bother dressing. You won't need clothes for the rest of the eve."

Heat shot through her with the rapidness of blaster fire, and when his smile widened, she guessed her surprise emblazoned across her cheeks. They certainly felt hot enough.

"What happens if we're interrupted?"

"I'll breathe fire first and ask questions later," Gryffnn declared. "I haven't done this for a while, and I'm looking forward to exploring every inch of your luscious body."

Kaya gaped, her mind moving with the slowness of that pancake syrup stuff on a cold day. What did he mean?

A chuckle emerged from Gryffnn, playful and amused. "Go and soak to rid yourself of the stinky plants. I'm certain Sable will have arranged special cleansers for you. Mogens has been teaching her."

"I..." she trailed off, nonplussed by the situation. She, who was seldom at a loss of words.

Gryffnn pulled out a comm and tapped several buttons. Secs later, he was speaking to his older sister.

Kaya wandered into the bathing room and toed off her boots and feet linings. "Lights on," she ordered. Cream tiles with streaks of red covered the walls. There was no cubicle in the bathing chamber. Instead, the area was open, with the water draining through the floor. A large tub, big enough for a male of Gryffnn's size, sat in the far corner of the bathing area near a large window.

During the whitelight, anyone sitting in the tub would have a view of the private gardens, designated only for the family.

The amber floor tiles cooled the soles of her feet as she disrobed. "Water on."

A stream of water hit her from two different directions, drenching her hair and battering her ears.

"Adjust angle," she spluttered.

To her relief, the stream of water lowered and hit her chest. "Overhead water."

A gentle spray came from above, and she reached for the cleanser in a small alcove set in the tiles. A smoky masculine scent floated to her, and she applied the cleanser to her hair and body. It wouldn't hurt for her to smell like Gryffnn. His scent was intoxicating, and now she had the freedom to wallow in the fragrance.

Kaya rinsed off and repeated the process, aware of the rumble of Gryffnn's voice coming from the main chamber. She scrubbed her skin until every inch of her body tingled.

A hand curved around her waist, and she jumped, letting out a squeak that her friend Nanu would've teased her about if he'd overheard.

"It's only me," Gryffnn said. "I decided to join you since I'd finished my calls."

He tugged her against his bare chest, and every trace of spit dried in her mouth. His cock thrust against her backside, and he held her with masculine confidence. Gryffnn angled them away from the water.

"Shall I scrub your back?"

She melted inside at the offer. He wouldn't know it, but this was a great honor on her birth planet. It was a matter of trust since the women killed the males once they'd done with them. Small intimacies of this kind were rare, and she hungered for the close contact. Her other lovers had been her testing her boundaries, scratching an itch, and filling the loneliness of the blacklight.

But Gryffnn... Already, he'd claimed a tiny part of her. She wasn't even sure when it had happened, but he'd filled the isolation she'd felt since Nanu had claimed Jazen. All her friends had moved on while she drifted.

"Kaya?"

"Yes, please."

Gryffnn applied cleanser to her back with an abrasive pad she hadn't noticed earlier. "This pad is made for tough dragon skin, so tell me if I'm pressing too hard."

The smoky scent of the cleanser and a hint of green forests drifted around her in the air. Gryffnn slid the pad across her shoulder blades and down her spine. He left no part of her back untouched. Her back, her waist, her buttocks. Once he finished, he nuzzled her neck and licked the shell of her pointy ear.

She gasped at the arrow of heat that darted to her sex, and her breath caught at the lazy stroke of his tongue. The gentle suction of his mouth at her throat had a moan slipping free. Then, he lifted his head, and a protest rose to her lips.

"My turn," he said, handing her the pad. "You can scrub as hard as you can. It won't injure me or break my skin."

Despite her impatience to get to the good stuff, Kaya accepted the pad and slathered cleanser over it. She'd seen Gryffnn naked before, once after he'd shifted from dragon to humanoid at the training fields. But at a distance. Now, with the luxury to touch, she dallied. His shoulders were massive and full of muscle as were his arms. Kaya rubbed the pad across his breadth, glorying in his groan of pleasure and the freedom to touch. As she scrubbed, his dragon scales colored his skin a fiery red.

Curious, she ran her fingers across the scaly area of his shoulder blade, and he groaned again.

"Will you take me for a ride one day?" she asked.

"Only mates get to ride," he murmured. "Or sometimes children."

"Oh." That seemed to be a solid rule, one they refused to break. She understood, even as she imagined the wind in her hair and the complete freedom of flying through the sky, unfettered by a spacecraft.

She finished his back and hesitated.

"You can't stop now. What about my front?"

Kaya added more cleanser to the pad and turned Gryffnn. His eyes had shifted to dragon slits, giving him an exotic appearance. She ran the pad across his chest, and he rumbled with contentment. The dragon shifter was big all over, from his feet to his frame to his cock.

Eager to explore, Kaya set the pad aside and ran her fingers down his chest. "Not ticklish?"

"My scales make my skin less sensitive," he explained. "Are you?"

"Not telling," she blurted. "Do you...?" She glanced down. "Your cock has tiny scales too."

His eyes glittered with arousal. "Those are for decoration. They appear when I'm aroused."

"Oh." Kaya didn't have a shy bone in her body, yet at this sec, she struggled to keep her composure. This between them was meant to be a favor, for friendship, yet every instinct told her to grasp Gryffnn and never let him go. The thought gave her pause.

"I've been anticipating this." He placed his fingers on her arm, eagerness evident in his curved mouth.

Her heart beat a tad faster because she had imagined their joining since dinner. When she glanced at his hand, the faint redness of the scales shone beneath his skin and contrasted with her own pale blue skin.

"Our colors go well together." He lifted her hand. "You match Hallam."

"Um, I don't think you should mention your son while we're both naked."

"Our son," he said in a husky voice. "Let's dry off and retire. By morn your scent will cover me."

Some of the anticipation dispersed from Kaya, his words jerking her back to the reason she'd agreed to have sex with him. This was friends with very sexy benefits. That was all. Another job for her to complete. Part of her wondered why the idea flattened her mood before she tucked away the troubling vibe.

"And even better, your skin will carry my scent instead of those carnivorous plants."

Her gaze darted up to meet his. "To prove our relationship?"

"Yes."

Yes? That was it? Didn't he intend to add more? Did he like her?

"Were you eager to bed your ex?"

"Way to kill the moment," he said, his tone as dry as the desert on the planet where they'd rescued Jannike and her men.

"And the answer?"

"Yes, I was eager. I fancied myself in love, but I soon learned Aideen and Caley had played me false, stringing me along until they received the funds they desired from my father. Learning Hallam was my son and not another dragon's child was a shock. Caley and I fucked once, the pleasure over before it almost started. I was nervous, lacked control, and spent myself early. Caley laughed and taunted me about her other lovers. I stayed out of her bed after that."

"And since?"

"There have been one or two willing women, but no one recently, and no one I've cared enough about to repeat the exercise."

"Ouch," Kaya said.

"What about you? Has anyone captured your attention?"

Kaya hesitated, wondering if she dared to tell him the truth. She suspected Nanu and her other friends wondered, but she'd never voiced her feelings. "I don't want to disappoint you." Her gaze shot to her bare toes with their pale blue nails. Gryffnn's nails resembled hers, except they bore a red tinge. She frowned. How did he cut them?

"Kaya." A finger under her chin forced her to meet his gaze.

Kaya sucked in a breath, her nakedness, his nudity bringing an even greater sense of vulnerability.

"You don't have to tell me."

"I want to tell you, but I want you to keep liking me."

Gryffnn kissed the tip of her nose. "There is no danger of me taking a dislike of you. Water off. Dryer on."

The water ceased flowing, and balmy air blew across her skin. Her hair fluttered around her head, concealing her face from Gryffnn. A good thing because tears stung her eyes. She, who never blubbered, wanted to howl with the force of an unhappy Lys.

Once they'd dried off, Gryffnn held out his hand. She wrapped her fingers around his, realizing she relished the innocent contact. With other men, she took and skipped anything reeking of affection or intimacy.

Gryffnn led her to his large gel-bed. A servant had turned down the covers and switched on dimmer lights, or perhaps Gryffnn had done it before he entered the bathing room. He lifted her, taking her by surprise.

"What are you doing?"

"Dragon tradition says a male must steal his woman and toss her on his bed." His lazy rumble held a dash of humor that had her own mouth curling. "I'm aiming to get tradition right."

Something in Kaya twisted. Cracked. A little yearning crept free. She'd been running from tradition all her life.

"Now I can kiss you, or we can talk." He set her in the middle of the gel-mattress, and she bounced before stilling.

Kaya swallowed audibly, knowing that for the first time, she wanted to speak with a male, to give of herself. As always, she ran with instinct. It didn't always steer her right, but mostly, things worked out in the end.

Gryffnn settled beside her and pulled her against his chest. Warmth seeped into skin that had chilled, and she cuddled closer. His hand drifted up and down her arm.

"I have had little time for men. If I wanted sex, I found a man and indulged myself."

The fingers halted. "You didn't kill them?"

"No." She barked out a laugh. "But I used them and moved on. Then, I met Ry's brother. We discovered later Talor and Ry were cousins rather than brothers. Long story. Talor was a powerful wizard, and in his desperation to destroy Ry, he sank his claws into me. He bespelled me and used me to keep tabs on Ry and the *Indy*. Because of my actions, Talor almost destroyed Ry. In one of his attacks, Nanu's brother Yep was killed."

"You blame yourself."

"I should've known something was wrong when I wanted to repeat the sexual encounters with Talor."

"You were young, Kaya. He'd never fool you now. We all make mistakes. I hated the mess I made of my life. I wanted to prove myself to my father, but I almost created a war. Ry and the rest of the crew respect you. They trust you."

"Yes, they are true friends. It's myself I have trouble forgiving."

Gryffnn's fingers resumed their up and down strokes on her arm, and her tension dissipated. She hadn't disgusted him.

"After Talor, I was more careful with the men I chose for my bed. Often, I went to the training room or for a drink when I told my friends I was with a male. My stupid pride. A war between my upbringing and the truth," Kaya said.

"What are you trying to tell me?" Gryffnn asked.

Kaya sighed. "That the number of males I've taken to my bed is fewer than rumor might say."

Gryffnn moved, repositioning their bodies to see her face. "Then why did you agree to share my bed? I'm not an act of charity."

"No, of course not," Kaya said, recognizing ruffled male pride when she saw it. "The truth is I've seen all my friends find mates, and I... Goddess, this will sound mean and full of self-pity, but the truth is I'm lonely. I-I like you, and lately, I've been twitchy."

"Twitchy?"

"A word from my home planet. It means my body is craving sex."

"Ah," he said.

"I... Do you still want to have sex with me? Aideen already knows or suspects we haven't been intimate."

"But she knows we intend to do the deed," Gryffnn countered. "Let me ask this. We're friends. True?"

"Yes."

"Our bodies want each other, so why don't we go ahead?"

"But what if something goes wrong? What if we argue? I don't want to lose your regard. One thing my time with Ry has taught me is that friendships are important."

"Even if they're with a male?"

"Ry and Nanu—I would risk my life for them without a blink. Jannike's and Gweneth's mates too. What I have learned since leaving home is that our Sitnam traditional ways are not necessarily right. I value our relationship as it stands, Gryffnn. I respect and admire the way you are dealing with Ransom's illness. Your relationship with your son is special, and I hope I can do half as well with Lys."

"Your points are valid," Gryffnn said, his expression impassive.

Kaya pulled away, disappointed yet a realist. Gryffnn was right to stop this. She'd known it too, which was part of the reason she'd made her confession.

"It would be best if I returned to my usual chamber."

"You didn't let me finish. I am also lonely. We can help each other. I need someone in my corner while I deal with Aideen and Caley."

Another thought occurred to Kaya, one she detested. A sharp pain dug into her chest, the phantom talons coated with a flash of jealousy. "Are you worried about your ex? Do you wish to rekindle your relationship?"

"Hell, no," Gryffnn barked. "Caley is a she-devil coated with dragon scales. I sent my son away to keep him from her clutches. I have no intention of touching her. *Ever again.* She disgusts me, and she doesn't have half the spirit and goodness of you. Not a quarter. We can help each other and stay friends. Please, I need you, Kaya."

Kaya struggled to confirm their agreement because she knew of the Earth curve balls that struck when least expected, the way they hit so hard they pushed everything right and proper off course. She sensed Gryffnn had the power to hurt her, change her like one of these curve ball thingies.

"I won't force you, Kaya. And I won't blame you if you change your mind. Aideen will attempt to overthrow me—no matter which way you decide."

"Huh!" Kaya snorted. "I want to help you. Aideen believes we have a weakness because Ransom isn't available. She's wrong. You'll send her running with her tail tucked between her scaly dragon legs."

Gryffnn's chuckle lightened the tension between them, and she found herself smiling.

"I gave you my promise, and it's still good, but if you end up hating me, I'm gonna poke you in the belly with my pointy sword and say, 'I told you so'."

"Deal," Gryffnn said, and he kissed the tip of her nose again.

He seemed to enjoy doing that, and she found the innocent caress charming.

"Now about this twitchy business. Should we stomp that out?"

Kaya groaned. "I've talked way too much."

CHAPTER 7

PRIVATE TIMES, SEXY TIMES

Gryffnn rolled and caged Kaya between his body and the gel-mattress. He grinned at her, taking in her pale blue skin, her gorgeous bright blue eyes, and her cute nose with the slight upward tilt. Her lips held a tinge of blue, her high cheekbones carrying a deeper blue whenever her emotions got the better of her. Then there was her dazzling blue hair, which was as silky and soft as he'd imagined.

They had much in common with their pasts shaping them and still weighing on their decisions. Except with Kaya, he didn't fear a bad outcome. Every part of him, every part of his dragon cried out to claim Kaya and keep her close. She carried so many qualities he respected. And Hallam liked her.

"One thing before we take things further and cure your twitchiness," he said. "If you're going to do away with me after we have sex, please make arrangements for my son and make my death quick."

"Idiot," she said with a wrinkle of her cute nose. "I don't subscribe to my planet's traditions, and now it's obvious I got this from my father since he's alive and kicking butt, doing secret squirrel stuff with Tayte."

"Secret squirrel?"

"From Camryn's planet. A squirrel is a small fluffy creature that skulks and scuttles around in a furtive manner stealing and collecting nuts."

"These words make sense."

"I suspect my father and Tayte work undercover for important people. I don't ask questions—not that I'd receive answers. And don't repeat this conversation to anyone."

"I know how to be one of these secret squirrel beasties. And this is the reason two men arrived and elderly women left. Can you shift your appearance?"

"No, I take after my mother."

"Should you have taken over from her as ruler?"

"She never asked me, but she muddied the line of command by sending me away. A new ruler will fear my sister or I might return to snatch back power."

"Do you want to?" Her desire to rule might ruin his plans.

She shuddered. "No. If Lys wanted to do it, I'd support her, but the ruling and court intrigue isn't for me. I relish my life now as part of Ry's crew. Exploring new worlds and having dangerous adventures. Excitement. Our lives have changed since we settled on Viros. I never thought I'd enjoy staying in one place, having a base, but it's fun. We go on mostly short jaunts to haul freight or work for your people or for Jannike's men. It can still be exciting even though we're strictly legal now and don't take risky jobs because Ry and Jannike have children."

"You're responsible for children now."

She groaned. "Don't remind me."

Her expression was so disgruntled that he had to smile. She didn't see herself as a nurturer, yet she was. She worried about her friends and was protective of them with a she-dragon fierceness. He dipped his head and kissed her, giving in to the need coursing through him. He'd watched and waited a long time for Kaya Ignatius.

She sighed against his lips, and he deepened the contact, lost in her taste, her scent, her touch.

Lost in Kaya.

She kissed him back, demanding and taking, and he couldn't help the small part of his mind that traveled back to examine memories of his first time with Caley. She'd lay there resembling a glittering, beautiful rock, not showing him compassion or anything except disdain. Pleased to the bone with Kaya's participation, he shoved the viper from his thoughts and concentrated on the beautiful, courageous woman in his arms.

He savored her lips, drawing her flavor into him, the hint of the liquor they'd imbibed earlier and the tartness that was Kaya. He brushed his lips down the column of her throat and pressed them against a rapidly beating pulse point. Her scent washed through him. A trace of the spices and the smoky amber associated with dragons. The plant stink still lingered under the layers, but it was faint. He ran his tongue over the smooth flesh, the dragon part of him demanding he conquer and seize this woman.

Gryffnn knew better. Despite the urge to grab like a greedy thief, wooing Kaya and treating her as the special woman she was would pay dividends later. Even if the sensation of her hands stroking his back and darting lower to caress his buttocks played merry hell with his willpower.

Moving farther down her body, he explored her breasts. They were larger than he'd pictured, the nipples a similar shade of blue to her lips.

"Touch me, Gryffnn. Please. When I said I was twitchy, I meant it."

"I am also twitchy," he said, the idea amusing him.

"Then fix this," she ordered, her brows drawing together in a frown to match her stern mouth. "Turn over. Lie on your back."

Astonished, Gryffnn followed her directions.

"Ah, where to touch first." Her gaze roved his body and her tongue darted out to moisten her lips.

Gryffnn stared, mesmerized by her open inspection of him, the concentration on her face and the lust shining through. Curious, he forced himself to lie still and watch for her next action.

"Your scales are cute. Will you let me see you and touch you in dragon form? I've only seen you from a distance, and we were in a public place. It didn't seem polite to go around stroking the dragons."

"That would get you in trouble," he agreed, trying to imagine the chaos on the training field.

"But you'll let me touch you?"

"Any time."

"No time like the present," she said cheerfully and grasped his cock. "Ooh! You're right. They're softer than I imagined." She ran her hand up and down his shaft as she squeezed and experimented.

Gryffnn groaned, and her gaze flew to his.

"Did I hurt you?"

"No, but you're determined to cure this twitchiness of yours in a hurry."

"Yes." She cupped his balls, examining the minute scales that covered them and squeezed them too. "Interesting. They're changing color."

"Yes," Gryffnn said in a strangled voice. To halt his escalating arousal, he counted, from memory, the items of jewelry in his wealth hoard. One, two, three...

By the time he reached forty-seven, Kaya had clambered onto

him and straddled his hips. Her feminine essence wafted to him, the scent rich and heady. He lost his tally and, grimly, began his count again. All it took was a tiny wiggle by Kaya, and his current total flew out of his head, and his control snapped.

He flipped her off him, flinging her onto her back. Secs later, he pushed his thigh between hers and parted them, pleased—thank every goddess his mother had ever taught him about—with Kaya's obvious arousal.

"Yay!" Kaya said, her blue eyes full of laughter.

Gryffnn released a growl as he guided his cock into position. He pushed his hips forward, the snug walls of her sex squeezing and welcoming. A slice of paradise. With another shove, he rocked until he was balls-deep in her. A groan slipped free as Kaya clasped him to her, lifting her lower body in welcome.

"Yes. Goddess, Gryffnn. Move. Please move."

He needed no urging, every particle of his body ordering him to withdraw and sink back into heaven. Desperate to taste her again, he crushed his mouth to hers, stroking their tongues together. She curled her legs around his hips, her urgency spreading to him, making him increase the pace of his hot, easy glides. Sensations poured through him with each thrust. Pleasure. Happiness. Joy.

Hungry little noises escaped her as he rolled one nipple between his fingers and pushed deep into her.

"Yes. Hit me there again," Kaya demanded.

And he laughed, following her direction because he wanted to please her, and every time he drove into her, it felt so damn good. He withdrew and surged deep. Her channel clenched around him, and Kaya gasped.

"Gryffnn, so good. So, so good." Her fingernails dug into his shoulders as she took her pleasure.

He gritted his teeth and held back until the spasms rocking her tapered off. Her eyes, which she'd closed, flicked open, the same clear blue of the swimming pool beneath the waterfall. Her lips curved.

"I am officially no longer twitchy."

"Excellent, then I can have my turn," Gryffnn said.

"Sounds fair." Laughter shaded Kaya's voice as Gryffnn let lust take him over.

With a convulsive heave of his muscles, he surged into her heat, shifting the angle a fraction to increase the friction as their bodies slid together.

"Again." Kaya sighed happily. "Oh, yes."

Gryffnn nuzzled her neck, his balls drawing up tight until he balanced on a point between pain and ecstasy. Despite the heavy fog of desire clouding his mind, driving him to take his pleasure, he slipped his hand between them and stroked her nub.

She mewed secs before he reached the point of no return. His release rampaged through him, destroying him yet building him back up again. His seed spurted from him as he writhed in the heat of his lover. Each breath emerged in hoarse rasps, his lifeforce muscle pumping extra hard.

Kaya pinched his biceps. "You're more relaxed now too."

Gryffnn smiled and leaned closer for an affectionate smooch. Lazy satisfaction filled him as he withdrew from her and sprawled on his side. He wrapped his arms around her and drew her against his chest. When he inhaled, their scents had blended—not fully, but enough to bring a surge of contentment, enough to warn other dragons that Kaya belonged to him.

CHAPTER 8

THE GUESTS MAKE TROUBLE

"Gryffnn. Gryffnn! Sir, you need to wake up." The muffled demand, along with hammering on his door, dragged Gryffnn from the best sleep he'd had in a quarter of a rotation.

Kaya stirred and peered over his shoulder in aggrievement. "What is that goddess-awful racket?"

Gryffnn slipped off the gel-bed. He ripped open the door to scowl at one of his trusted servants. "What?"

The male servant scanned his body, noticed his naked state, and raised his gaze to Gryffnn's face. "Our visitors are causing trouble. They are trying to enter the family area. They say they are guests and should have access to you and the rest of the family." His gaze slid past Gryffnn to the gel-bed and Kaya.

Gryffnn growled, a low, testy rumble that had the servant redirecting his eyes. "We will dress and come down to handle

Aideen and her people."

As soon as Gryffnn shut the door, Kaya sprang off the gel-bed and hustled into the bathing room. The water started, and Gryffnn strode to the doorway. His woman. Pleasure swept through him as he watched her bathe. He allowed himself a few more secs to soak in her loveliness and her natural sexiness before forcing himself into action.

Aideen awaited, and he couldn't expect his people to deal with their guests' bitchiness. It was time to discover their scheme and squash it before they gained momentum.

He strode to Kaya and ducked his head under the stream of water.

"Is Aideen making trouble?"

"Right first guess." Gryffnn reached for cleanser and scrubbed his chest. Every part of him wanted to grab Kaya and spirit her away to a quiet place where he could spend quality time with her and deepen their ties. It irked him that instead, he had to deal with his ex-clan. He eyed Kaya as she dried and left the bathing chamber.

His brother wouldn't have hesitated.

He always did the right thing.

After scrubbing his body, Gryffnn rinsed off. "Water off. Drier on."

Kaya had set out his clothes when he walked out to the main chamber. "Thank you."

"You're welcome."

He pulled on the trews and a scarlet shirt. "I don't wear dressy clothes."

"These aren't normal circumstances."

Gryffnn mulled over that and agreed with Kaya's strategy. Make Aideen think he was trying to impress her. Make her think he lacked the experience to lead. Make her think she could intimidate him and his people.

He sat to tug on linings and boots, then stood. "Let's do this.

How long until the *Indy* makes a return?"

"I'm guessing Nanu would've pushed the trip back to Viros, but it will still be at least three cycles," Kaya said as they left his chamber and headed for the stairs leading down to the ground floor.

He'd figured on that length of journey but had hoped he'd miscalculated since he could do with the extra help. Strength in numbers and all that.

"Oh, thank goodness. You're awake." Sable bustled toward the stairs before they'd fully descended. "I hope you have a plan because, brother, you need one."

"Where is Aideen?"

"Last I saw of her was when she was stomping around the garden and bitching about the lack of hospitality and pondering if the Drake clan have secrets to hide," Sable said with a trace of disgust.

Gryffnn grinned at his younger sister. "No need to make them too comfortable. After all, we didn't invite them to visit."

"True," Sable said.

"But I'd better calm our visitors. I've decided to organize competitive games between the two clans, followed by relaxation at the waterfall pool. Can the kitchen arrange cold foods to feed everyone once we've finished swimming?"

"I'll make the food happen," Sable said. "The kitchen crew has already started baking extra supplies."

"Excellent." Gryffnn held out his hand to Kaya. "Where is Ry?"

"He went for a walk, or at least that's what he told me." Sable leaned closer. "He wanted to keep an eye on developments. Oh, and there was an argument between our soldiers and Aideen's. Ry ended up refereeing the disagreement. One of Aideen's dragons is complaining about Ry biting him. Ry shifted," she added.

Kaya's brows shot upward. "It takes a lot to rile Ry."

Gryffnn grimaced. "I've never seen him lose his temper. *Frag*, Ry shouldn't have to step in between the clans. I'd better find him and apologize." Gryffnn sucked in a quick breath. "Right, let's do this."

Gryffnn led Kaya outside, and they almost bumped into Aideen and an entourage of guards.

"Where have you been?" the dragon woman demanded, her voice close to shrill.

"Kaya and I slept late," Gryffnn said. "I understand you've broken your fast. Would your people enjoy a friendly competition between your clan and ours? We could start with wrestling and cool off at our swimming hole afterward."

"When am I going to see your brother?" Aideen demanded. "We have traveled all this way to pay our respects."

"Oh, I'm sorry," Gryffnn said. "Didn't I tell you? Ransom is recuperating on Viros. Sable, Jacinta, and I felt that since we had secured the services of a medic on Viros, it would make sense for Ransom to travel there."

"So the rumors are true." Every tense muscle in Aideen released, and her mouth curled into a toothy smile. A sleazy, cunning smile that rubbed Gryffnn's scales the wrong way.

"That would depend on what rumors you've heard." Gryffnn kept his features impassive and waited for Aideen to explain.

"Ransom is on his deathbed," Aideen stated.

"Not true. Ransom is alive and recovering well." Gryffnn watched her closely, experience letting him see the calculation behind her expression.

Beside him, Kaya remained silent, but he felt the tension slide through her frame. He thanked the instinct that had him accepting Ry's suggestion to move Ransom and Hallam. And extra soldiers to bolster their power was a good strategic move. Their men were loyal to Ransom and, by extension, him. He prayed they numbered enough to repel the attack he was certain lurked in the future.

Kaya listened to the words coming from the mocking Aideen and curled her fingers into her palms. Pride in Gryffnn's calm replies puffed out her chest even as she bit her tongue. If Aideen wanted to trample him under her feet, the dragon women should think again. Gryffnn bore a solid core of strength and goodness. He mightn't shine in his brother's presence, but in his quiet way, he got things done. The dragons in his clan respected him, which was why they'd accepted him when he'd had to step into Ransom's role.

Storg trotted in their direction. Kaya nudged Gryffnn.

"They're ready to start the contests," Kaya murmured.

Aideen's lower lip curled in disdain as she deigned to notice Kaya. "What do you care for contests? You're not a dragon."

But she could still take part in the wrestling since she trained with Ry and Nanu. Confident of her proficiency, she still shrugged. "A contest between skilled fighters is always interesting to watch."

"You have no standing here. He might have fucked you, but you're not his mate."

Kaya stayed Gryffnn's retort by squeezing his arm.

"I am, however, his betrothed," Kaya said sweetly. She met Aideen's gaze with an attitude of her own, refusing to cower. Kaya deliberately broke the stare-down and turned to Gryffnn. "I'll get us something to break our fast and meet you at the training fields. I'm starving." She winked at him, and he rewarded her with a quick grin.

He pulled her close to kiss her cheek and nuzzled her neck, his tongue flashing out to lick her skin. Weird but cute.

"I'll see you there." Gryffnn jerked his chin in Aideen's direction. "Aideen, are you willing to have a small side-bet between leaders? I wager you a bottle of Dragon's Breath liquor, the Drake clan will win the most wrestling bouts. What do you say?"

Aideen made a scoffing sound. "I doubt the prowess of your men."

"Shall we shake on our bet?"

"Done," Aideen said, thrusting out her hand.

91

Kaya left them to their bets as she hurried into the family dwelling to hunt down Sable and food.

"Kaya," Ry said, falling into step with her. "Is Gryffnn with the other dragons?"

"Yeah." She shot him a glance and something in his expression had her stomach roiling. "Something wrong? Something Gryffnn should know about?"

"One of the Gwilym ships has left. I watched them load up and take off. Twelve crew."

Not good. "Which direction did they go?"

Ry grimaced. "Toward the mountains."

"Do you think we're hosting our culprits?"

"The notion crossed my mind," Ry said. "If they've discovered a way to negate the resonance, they might be our thieves."

"I'll tell Gryffnn as soon as I get a chance. I don't trust Aideen. She's too smug, as if she knows something we don't."

"I agree." Ry's brows drew together in a scowl. "I'll keep watch from the shadows and skulk around the spaceport. They're aware of how many dragons Gryffnn has at his disposal. If the missing ship has gone to collect more of the clan, Gryffnn will have a problem."

Kaya tapped her chin with her forefinger, thinking. "Is it possible to get aboard their ships and perhaps remove a part or two and slow them down?"

Ry grinned. "That's a sneaky idea, one my crew might suggest."

"*Ha-ha.* I am on your crew."

"You make a captain proud," Ry said. "I'll check on the *Indy's* progress too."

Kaya headed to the kitchens, her belly letting out a rumble at the delicious scents wafting her way.

Sable spied her peeking inside and set aside a large roller, then wiped her hands on her white coverall. "Did you want something to eat?"

Kaya rounded a busy kitchenhand pushing a cart of greens and tubers from the clan gardens. She dodged a bustling Jewel, the dragon's housekeeper as she moved from counter to counter, checking progress. Finally, she reached Sable's side. "Hey, Sable. Sorry to interrupt. Gryffnn and I didn't eat before Aideen rousted us from our chamber. Is it possible to have a snack and a drink? Something that isn't too heavy because I suspect Gryffnn will have to wrestle, or he'll never hear the end of it from the Gwilym clan."

"Here, take a seat," Sable said. "I'll get something ready for you." She paused. "You're good for Gryffnn. He is happier now than he has been for ages."

"Me?" Kaya asked.

"Yes. Aideen and Caley hate that Gryffnn has someone else. I get the sense they expected Gryffnn to fold, to give them what they wanted. Whatever that is. You give Gryffnn strength. Confidence to lead."

"No," Kaya denied. "That's all Gryffnn. It's nothing to do with me."

Sable reached for Kaya's hands. Sable had a Stores, a high-tech artificial arm that functioned as efficiently as her left one. Kaya felt the coolness of Sable's Stores as they clasped fingers. "I have a suggestion. Aideen and her sister won't miss the wrestling. Our female soldiers will fight. Why don't you don a dress and make Aideen believe you're pretty and decorative? We know that's not true. You're a warrior. You're strong and resourceful, but since they consider Gryffnn useless, they'll group you in the same category. If they think you're useless, they'll challenge you for sure."

Kaya gaped in astonishment at Sable, the Drake sister many overlooked. "You think I should fight?"

"Under controlled circumstances. A win on your part will add to Gryffnn's status."

"And earn me an enemy," Kaya pointed out.

"They're our enemies anyway. From what I hear, Aideen and Caley treated Gryffnn abominably. Gryffnn's arrangement was before Ransom brought me to live with them. Hallam is lucky, although he has no idea how low his mother and aunt will sink for currency and prestige. To his credit, Gryffnn has never badmouthed Caley to Hallam. Hallam idolizes you," Sable added.

Kaya thought about Sable's words and nodded slowly. "Hallam didn't show much curiosity about his mother. He accepted Gryffnn's edict to stay away from her, and he was quick to agree to a visit to Viros, especially after he learned he could practice his flying."

"Exactly. This break is excellent for Hallam. He needs to learn about other species and how to deal with them." Sable paused. "Caley hasn't tried to see Hallam either. Gryffnn stayed with them until Hallam's birth and the gene testing, then he took his son and returned home. Father...I heard he wasn't pleased when Gryffnn arrived with a child. There was an argument, and it was the first time Ransom and Gryffnn stood side-by-side, united."

"Ransom and Gryffnn seldom speak of your father."

"He was a good dragon and a strong one, but old-fashioned. I think he drifted after Ransom's and Gryffnn's mother died." Sable reached under a counter for a box and deftly packed it with food suitable to eat on the run. After adding two drinks, she shut the lid with a click and handed it to Kaya. "Take care out there."

"You too." Kaya leaned closer. "We might have to poison their food as a last resort."

Sable blinked her hazel eyes and huffed out a laugh. "You have a weird sense of humor."

"Not kidding. We could put something in their food to confine them to their chambers." Kaya winked. "See you later. Tell me if I can help in any way. These visitors are a demanding lot."

Sable smiled, a rare thing with Gryffnn's youngest sister. "Thank you. You're the first person who has asked after me, apart from

Gryffnn. He also offered help when we last spoke."

"We both mean it," Kaya said. "Thanks for the food."

Kaya left the kitchen via the rear door and took a shortcut through the gardens. The flowering plants were her favorites. The plants in this bed stood taller than her and bore enormous red or yellow blooms the size of a face. The leaves gave off a spicy fragrance that reminded Kaya of Gryffnn's scent. Sort of smoky and rich. Enticing. And best of all, they didn't try to eat her.

When she caught herself smiling one of those dopey smiles she'd witnessed from her friend Nanu, she wiped her face clean and shook her head. Gryffnn had slid into her mind to stay. She had things to do. Places to go.

With brisk steps, she continued through the garden. From the corner of her eye she caught a flash of blue. She stilled, waiting for a repeat of the movement.

Kaya didn't have to wait for long.

Caley slipped through the garden, heading for the private family quarters. Now that Ransom was in Viros, Gryffnn had relaxed security and only two dragon shifters patrolled. Caley had timed her spying mission when the two dragons were at opposite ends of the building, and everyone else had gone to the training field to watch the contests between the two clans.

Kaya set down her meal box and crept after Caley. This woman had hurt Gryffnn and made him the object of ridicule. Because of her, he'd received a reputation as a loser that followed him still, yet Caley had suffered not at all. Kaya bristled, wanting to box the bitch-woman's ears on Gryffnn's behalf.

Caley didn't appear to hear her or bother checking behind her. Dumb beginner's mistake. Was she stupid? Or was she confident in her abilities?

Just as Caley had almost reached the window of the ground floor chamber they'd used as a hospital for Ransom, Kaya spoke. "Can I help you with something?"

Her lips curled up in enjoyment when Caley jumped, the fabric of her pale blue gown rustling against the plants to her left. The dragon woman spun around, her eyes wide for an instant before regaining her equilibrium.

"I wanted to stretch my legs." Caley's lips twisted into a smirk. She smoothed the skirts of her dress and lifted her chin. "I wasn't doing anything wrong."

"You're trespassing in a private area. If you wish to stretch your limbs, you can do that on the training field, the same as everyone else. The wrestling contests are about to begin."

"You're not the boss of me."

Kaya snorted. "A fact that thrills me."

"Exactly. So you can't tell me what to do."

"I am Gryffnn's betrothed, which gives me the power to order you to leave the garden. It's private, yet you persist in spying on us when Gryffnn has made it clear the family area is out of bounds. It's rude to gawk through the windows."

Caley swelled up, her chest expanding, and a weird blue light glowed from her skin.

Oh *phrull*. Kaya studied the dragon shifter with caution. Not good. Caley had let her temper get the better of her and ceded control to her dragon. Kaya retreated one step to give Caley room.

Caley chortled, the sound hoarse and creaky. "Not so confident now."

Kaya's hand settled on her blaster. She didn't pull her weapon but waited, watched.

A curl of smoke drifted from Caley's nostrils, and blue scales rippled over her skin. The seams of her gown cracked with the strain of a larger, more muscular body. They gave without warning, the rent loud and explosive.

"Is there a problem, Miss Kaya?" one of Gryffnn's men asked.

"I caught Caley skulking in the garden. She intended to peer through the windows and maybe enter the family quarters," Kaya said.

Caley's bulk grew, and her dragon side burst over her. She was a paler blue than Hallam, and for a sec, inappropriate humor filled Kaya. Caley was blue, and so was she. It seemed Gryffnn had a thing for blue ladies.

Caley's scales shone under the whitelight while a wicked ridge of black spikes stuck up along her spine. They continued to the tip of her spiky tail. Two horns topped her head, and her eyes shone green with vertical black pupils. Neat ears sat flat against her head. The remnants of her blue gown and undergarments fluttered around her massive blue body.

Caley opened her mouth. No, more of a maw, and sharp white teeth filled it. Those teeth would leave a nasty gash, but the dragon fire could kill her.

Kaya stood her ground, but she had to admit to awe. It was the same wonderment that filled her when she watched Ry or Camryn or Jannike shift to feline. Her body did nothing so remarkable, even though she was a formidable fighter.

Gryffnn's security man spoke into his comm. Two Drake dragons appeared a short time later.

"You need to leave the private garden or we will arrest you," the first shifter said.

"On whose authority?" Caley rumbled.

"Mine," Kaya said. "I am accusing you of trespassing and bad manners. Shift and leave, or Gryffnn's men will escort you to the lockup. I give you to the count of twenty."

The smoke curling from Caley's flaring nostrils increased. "You're not afraid of me. Stupid woman. I could ash you in an instant."

"You could," Kaya agreed. "But you'd start a war. Not a clever move. We outnumber your people."

"No, we have—" Caley broke off to glower at Kaya. She huffed, and a flame burned the plant in the garden, a fraction to Kaya's right.

"That's it," the guard said. "Chain her."

Weapons fired, and instead of spitting deadly ammunition, a fine silver chain shot out, twining around Caley's neck and legs.

Caley issued a pained howl, and the chains smoked where they contacted her skin.

"Move," one of the guards ordered. "The longer you take, the worse the burns from the chains will sear your scales."

"Aideen will hear of this," Caley cried.

"She will," Kaya said. "I will inform her you were trespassing and refused to leave."

"We'll also tell Gryffnn you threatened his betrothed," the nearest guard said. "Move now, or we'll take further measures to disable you."

"You wouldn't dare," Caley growled.

"Don't test us," the guard snapped.

Caley struggled and sucked in a large breath. Before she breathed fire again, one guard produced a different weapon. He shot Caley in the chest, and she let out a pained scream that raised the hair at the back of Kaya's neck. Caley shrunk, her scales fading into her skin with a rapidness that made Kaya blink.

Secs later, Caley wobbled before them, naked and trembling, her skin a pale gray. Tears ran down her contorted features, the suddenness of her shift sapping her strength.

"Take her to the lockup," the security guard ordered.

"No, you can't do this," Caley protested, her voice low and weak, almost broken.

"We can," the guard stated.

"You wait until Aideen hears about this," Caley warned.

"I'll make sure she does," Kaya said. "Thanks, boys. I'd better join Gryffnn. He'll wonder at my delay."

"You'll tell him what happened and what we've done?" the security guard asked.

"I will." Kaya picked up her food box and strode toward the training fields. Cheers of encouragement floated to her, shouts and directions from the opposing clans.

The dragon shifters from both clans surrounded the far end of the training field. As Kaya neared, she saw one of Gryffnn's men wrestling with a stranger. Cheers rang out as the two males grappled. Kaya spotted Gryffnn and made her way to him, her heart beating a little faster as thoughts of the previous night darted through her mind like a fast-playing movie. She sighed with remembered satisfaction. It had been good. Very good. And she couldn't wait to repeat the experience.

Friends, a small voice in her mind reiterated. Yet, her heart didn't seem to care for the warning. It continued to gallop, pushing awareness and arousal to the fore.

Gryffnn sensed her arrival. He angled slightly, saw her, and beamed, his smile wide and genuine. She waved as she squeezed through cheering dragons to reach his side.

"You took longer than I expected. I was starting to worry."

"Are you implying I'm a quitter?"

His eyes crinkled. "Never."

"I ran into Caley in the private gardens. When I challenged her, she shifted to dragon."

"You're not hurt." Gryffnn sobered. He curved his fingers around her biceps and checked her appearance, huffing out relief when he saw nothing worse than the tiny scorch mark on her tunic. "What happened?"

"Your men arrived and fired chains at her. They forced her to shift and are escorting her to lockup."

Gryffnn sighed. "I told you the Gwilym dragons don't respect me."

"Your men acted decisively. The other dragons will think twice before they threaten anyone again. How are the contests going?"

"The scores are even," Gryffnn said. "Which was what I

expected."

"Have you wrestled yet?"

"Not yet. I'm assuming Aideen will choose me as her opponent."

"You'll kick her scaly arse." As Kaya watched the action, two female dragon shifters entered the impromptu ring and sized each other up with mock attacks.

"Do you want something to eat?"

"Maybe later. Come, we'll move closer. You'll have trouble seeing much from here."

"Are you calling me short?"

"You're not short, Kaya. The dragon species are naturally tall and bigger than you."

Kaya allowed Gryffnn to escort her through the press of bodies to a spot on the ringside.

"Ah, you've deigned to join us," Aideen said. "I don't know why Gryffnn has attached himself to you. You can't shift. You wear men's clothes."

Ah, she should've taken Sable's advice and dressed more femininely.

"Only for training," Kaya informed Aideen. "I had intended to walk to stretch out my kinks and exercise."

Kaya almost laughed aloud at the mocking scorn Aideen displayed. Sable had been right. Aideen underestimated her now, and this might become a weapon. Her sneaky *dragon* power.

"Pooh," Aideen said, wrinkling her aristocratic nose. "Walking. Gryffnn, she will not be an asset to you."

"Your opinion has no bearing. It is mine that matters." Gryffnn reached for Kaya's hand and squeezed her fingers. "I have no regrets. Ah, it appears our clan won that bout. Are you intending to wrestle, Aideen?"

"Of course."

Kaya bounced up and down on her toes and clapped her hands

together. "I'm glad I haven't missed you wrestling."

Gryffnn's hazel gaze glittered with knowledge. Kaya was playing at what Camryn called *the little woman act.*

"Who do you wish to wrestle, Aideen?" Gryffnn asked. "A few women haven't wrestled yet, or you can choose a male dragon. Or me."

Aideen scanned the dragons Gryffnn indicated, then turned back to him with decisiveness. "I will wrestle her." She pointed at Kaya with glee, a dare sparking in her visage.

"Me?" Kaya pressed her hand to her chest, pretending consternation while inside, she celebrated. She loved to wrestle and tested herself regularly against Ry and Nanu. At times, she wrestled Gryffnn's men and sometimes Gryffnn. He'd given her pointers and helped her to improve her skills.

"Yes," Aideen said. "I challenge you to wrestle."

Kaya understood this was more than a simple contest to wrestle. Aideen assumed she'd win and wanted to make Kaya appear foolish. If Kaya lost, then by association, that made Gryffnn appear weak. "Oh, but my wrestling skills are limited." Kaya blinked as if in distress. "Can't you choose someone else? I hate to break my fingernails."

"Sweetheart, Aideen has challenged you." Gryffnn's mouth hovered close to amusement. "Aideen, you prepare while I give my betrothed a few hints if that's all right with you."

Aideen nodded but failed to hide her satisfaction. "I will stretch my muscles."

Gryffnn took Kaya's arm and led her away from the group. His clan members watched and whispered amongst themselves. They knew of Kaya's capabilities. Aideen's people laughed, and some of them jeered.

"Kaya, are you sure you want to do this? Aideen is a skilled wrestler, but you're better. After you win, watch your back. Aideen makes a bad enemy."

"Yes," Kaya said. "She is dishonest. Ry said one of their ships left with twelve of her dragons. They flew toward the mountains."

Gryffnn frowned. "That makes no sense. Resonance hits them in the same way as it does us. They're lucky there is no resonance problem on Dalcon. By living here, we build a small tolerance for the resonance, but it would be worse for Aideen and her dragons."

"It makes sense if they're responsible for stealing your precious stones," Kaya said. "We saw someone in silver but didn't get close enough to see if it was a suit or natural armor. My guess is that it was someone in protective clothing. The ship was black, not silver like the ones in the spaceport."

"No. Aideen is cunning, but I don't see her pulling off something like this."

"That is what we will discover. Gryffnn, it might come to a war. Are you prepared for that?"

Gryffnn paled, then straightened his shoulders. "I'll do anything I need to do to maintain control of our people and our home. Anything necessary until Ransom can take over again." He kissed Kaya. "Watch her. She'll fight dirty once she realizes you're experienced."

"Huh!" Kaya said. "Two can play at that game."

Kaya tucked in her tunic and rolled her shoulders before wandering back to the fighting ring. She toed off her boots and padded across the protective gel-mat toward Aideen. The dragon shifter wore her arrogance like a cloak. Kaya didn't know if she'd beat her, but she'd give her a good fight. A fair fight. And as Ry said, that was all any of them could do. Try their best and keep their head held high, which was precisely what she intended to do in this situation.

Kaya grinned when Aideen made *bring it* motions with her hands. This dragon shifter pushed her buttons, and she'd enjoy taking her down. Not that she'd get too over-confident. No, she'd observe and take her opportunities.

Aideen rushed her, and Kaya grasped Aideen's shoulder, grappling and using the shifter's weight against her. Aideen fell to the mat but bounded upright before Kaya held her down. Her gaze had lost confidence, but she didn't hesitate. She charged Kaya, teeth gritted in a ferocious snarl. Her eyes flickered to Kaya as she considered her next move. Kaya held her gaze, experienced enough not to telegraph her thoughts.

Kaya swept out her leg, taking Aideen's balance from under her. She staggered but regained her footing, anger flashing across her face now.

"You think you're smart," Aideen snapped.

"No."

Aideen rushed Kaya, her copper scales in evidence, covering her arms and her cheeks. Kaya let her come and at the last sec, used her momentum to flip her. Aideen landed on the mat with a loud *oomph*. She took longer to get up this time but still avoided letting Kaya pin her.

"Good job, Kaya," Gryffnn shouted. "Do it again."

Exactly my plan. Instead of waiting for Aideen's attack, Kaya advanced, putting the dragon on the defensive. Kaya struck out, chopping her hand across Aideen's left arm. She followed this up with a kick to Aideen's leg and another sweep to trip the dragon. Then, she rushed her and tried to shove Aideen out of the ring.

Aideen veered to the left, and Kaya countered her. She stepped close, using Aideen's momentum to throw her down. Aideen struck the mat, and the air smacked from her lungs by the force of the drop.

Aideen's dragons fell silent, but the Drake clan shouted encouragement.

Kaya pinned Aideen's arms and dropped her bodyweight on top of Aideen, forcing Aideen's back to the mat.

The referee crouched nearby. "One. Two. Three. Bout won by Miss Kaya."

Kaya rolled off Aideen and sprang to her feet. Excitement filled her at the win, although it wouldn't be easy if they ever repeated the bout. Aideen's over-confidence had led to her loss. In the spirit of goodwill, she held out a hand to Aideen to help her up.

Aideen snarled at her, the dragon's shift sliding closer to beast than humanoid. Her teeth snapped a warning to back up the threat.

Gryffnn stepped up beside Kaya. He took her arm and led her back to where he'd stood to watch the match. Someone had retrieved her footwear and left her boots with Gryffnn.

"Best we let her temper cool," he murmured.

"Should I have lost?" Kaya crouched to don her linings and boots.

"Hell, no," he said. "I'm proud of you."

"Good job, Miss Kaya." Storg clapped her on the back but luckily tempered his strength. "I knew you'd kick her arse."

"She was overconfident," Kaya replied. "Another bout might have a different winner."

"Doubt it," the dragon shifter said. "Uh, Gryffnn. It looks as if Aideen is challenging you to a fight."

"But she fought Kaya." Gryffnn turned his attention back to Aideen, who remained in the ring.

"I challenge you, Gryffnn Drake." Her dare boomed across the training field and quieted the excitement of Kaya's win.

"You can take her," Kaya said. "Watch her face. She signals her blows."

"A beginner's error," Gryffnn said.

"Exactly. Go, you've got this. You're fresh while she expended energy and temper on fighting me."

Gryffnn yanked off his scarlet tunic and handed it to Kaya. His chest gleamed in the whitelight, drawing her avid gaze. She'd caressed his hard muscles and enjoyed the strength of him, the private tenderness. His chuckle jerked her from her trance.

"I adore that avid expression," he teased as he removed his footwear.

Kaya felt heat gather in her cheeks. She'd suffered through the flushing thing more this week than she had in rotations.

Gryffnn stepped into the ring to join Aideen, and cheers rang out. Kaya's breath caught as she noted the fierceness of the dragon leader. Kaya had pricked her pride and she wanted payback.

The bout began, fast and furious. They appeared evenly matched, although Kaya thought Gryffnn was holding back. The crowd roared as Aideen rushed him. They grappled, and Aideen flipped him. She failed to hold him down, and secs later, Gryffnn fought free and jumped into a counterattack. He angled his hip and, using brute strength, forced her to the mat. Aideen battled, twisting in his grasp. He pushed her back, her spine hitting the mat.

"One. Two," the referee called.

Aideen struggled free before the final third count ended the bout.

Confidence filled Kaya, but she knew the delicate balance Gryffnn walked. If he embarrassed Aideen in front of everyone, things could go downhill fast.

Aideen twisted her body, using her hip to push away Gryffnn. With a loud roar, she flipped him. It was the move Gryffnn had shown her during one training session many cycles ago. He'd taught her to defeat it, but he let Aideen flip him and pin him for the count of one.

He'd been a youngster when he traveled to Dalcon to mate with Caley. In the rotations since, he'd grown into his body and become stronger. Aideen had made a mistake in underestimating him. To Kaya, it was obvious he was stronger and pacing himself, yet Aideen didn't see this. Her arrogance would be her downfall.

Gryffnn wrapped his arms around Aideen and used his superior weight to shove her to the mat. He forced her back downward, using both arms and legs, and the match ended. A three count against Aideen.

Kaya witnessed the female dragon's fury at her second loss, and a shiver worked through Kaya's body. This was an enemy they needed to keep in their sights.

Gryffnn stood and reached out a hand for Aideen. Despite her testy snarl, he hauled her to her feet and made a respectful bow. "I was lucky," he said. "You almost held me a couple of times. I might not be so lucky on a rematch."

A magnanimous offer on Gryffnn's part and a face save. Not that Aideen appreciated his words.

"We have an obstacle course we use for training," Gryffnn said. "Would you and your people enjoy the challenge? One of my men will go first to show you how the obstacles work since we use both forms while completing the course."

Aideen gave a curt nod. "Acceptable."

"Excellent. Once we finish that, we will break for a mid-cycle meal and refresh ourselves at the pools."

Aideen stomped off to join her dragons, and Kaya saw them wincing and edging a healthy distance from their leader. The shifter waved her hands as she spoke, issuing what Kaya suspected were instructions. She hadn't asked after her sister yet. Interesting. Had she given Caley an assignment to spy on them, or did the two sisters not play well together? Or was it something else Kaya hadn't considered as yet?

"Are you going to run through the obstacle course?" Gryffnn asked, claiming Kaya's attention.

"No, it's best to keep a low profile and let all you dragons play together. I might meet up with Ry and see if Nanu or Camryn have contacted him yet. I want to check on Lys and Hallam."

"Thanks. I miss Hallam. This is the first time we've been apart." Gryffnn scanned the training field and frowned. "Is it my imagination, or has Aideen's party swelled in number?"

Kaya attempted to count the visitors, but they dashed and darted, and she lost her tally. "I'll ask Ry if more have arrived. How many are there on Dalcon?"

"I called Jacinta, and she's heard gossip about an illness in their town."

"You require proof. It might pay to dig a little. The information uncovered might hint at the why of Aideen's visit. Are you going to tell Aideen about her sister?"

"No, not at present."

"Take care and have something to eat. If you're running the obstacle course, you require fuel for strength." Kaya plucked the lid off the box she'd toted around the field and chose a savory meat kebob. She handed it over. "Eat."

A slow smile crept across Gryffnn's face, lighting his features and heating his eyes until Kaya had to force herself to stillness. Her brain wanted her to wriggle and shed the nervous energy, the sensual heat that gathered in her chest and slid stealthily down to her sex. Her ears tingled too.

"Hold that thought," Gryffnn instructed in a soft voice. He leaned closer to ensure no one overheard. "I can't wait to retire with you to my gel-bed."

The ache and pressure in Kaya's chest forced her to breathe, and that cursed heat gathered in her cheeks again. "I...ah, I'll see you later."

"Contact me if there's a problem," Gryffnn said. "Otherwise, I'll see you later this cycle."

"That's a promise," Kaya murmured.

Flustered by the sensual heat in him, his flagrant desire for her, Kaya retreated. She'd thought they were merely friends. Phrull, they *were* friends, but something else hovered between them, something fragile and tenuous, and that unsettled her.

She wasn't sure what to do next.

CHAPTER 9

CLANDESTINE INVESTIGATION

By the end of the cycle, Gryffnn ached with the need to retreat to his chamber, preferably with Kaya and a cold drink to numb the angst roiling in his gut. The urge to thump Aideen nagged at him. Unfortunately, manners meant keeping his hands to himself, except during fighting contests. He'd prayed, prayed so hard for Aideen to pick him as an opponent again.

She hadn't.

Now frustration shoved at him like a rogue wind.

Time had dulled the memories of Aideen and her clan, but this one cycle spent with her and her people reminded him of why he'd hated living on Dalcon, why he'd never second-guessed his decision to bring his son to live on Narenda.

"Gryffnn Drake!" Aideen's thunderous voice scared a flock of bright yellow-and-white birds from their roost in the trees.

Gryffnn turned to face the she-dragon. Her nostrils flared, and wisps of smoke curled upward. Her top lip curled to reveal pointy teeth.

Frag it. She'd learned about Caley.

"Is there a problem, Aideen?"

"Your men have imprisoned my sister," Aideen spat. "I demand you release her."

"My guards caught her trespassing. She refused to leave, then she shifted and spat fire at Kaya. Not only is that rude, it is against the terms I informed you of when you arrived here uninvited."

Aideen bristled at his blunt words. "We communicated with you of our arrival."

Gryffnn ignored the blatant untruth. "I will order Caley's release when she apologizes to my betrothed for threatening her *and* if Caley promises not to enter our private gardens or property again."

"But—"

"Aideen, if I visited your compound and behaved as your people have done, your actions would be far stronger than mine. Cease your bad behavior, and this visit will remain pleasant. Now, I wish to spend time with my betrothed before the start of the communal dinner. Tell your people, Aideen. If any of them misstep again, I won't act with such mercy." Gryffnn strode away without giving her the courtesy of a comeback. The spot between his shoulder blades itched, but he didn't glance back. No more civility. They still wanted to try him, to test him.

He knew his worth, and he refused to bow down to Aideen.

Gryffnn entered the main hall and turned toward the family room, hoping to catch up with Ry and Kaya.

Ry spotted him first. "You need a drink before we tell you what we've discovered."

"By the goddess," Gryffnn muttered, dropping onto a gel-chair with a groan. "I hate the sound of this."

Kaya appeared as solemn as her friend, and Gryffnn's stomach did another dance, the strain of remaining polite increasingly difficult. He accepted the drink Kaya handed him and focused on Ry. "Tell me," he said.

"The missing ship arrived back around two marks ago. Strange thing is that their ship didn't appear on the tracker, not until we spotted them flying in from the mountain range."

Gryffnn spat out a curse. "You think they're coming and going at will because our existing technology isn't spotting them?"

"It's the only possibility," Ry said. "And if they can cloak their ships, it's not a big leap to assume they have other technology."

Kaya tapped her finger on her knee, her gaze distant. "How can they afford this technology? It's not cheap. And why steal your stones? Don't they have their own?"

"The entire visit reeks with the force of a dead odod squawker bird," Gryffnn said. "The more we learn, the more questions I have."

"How do you want to handle this?" Ry asked. "Camryn, Nanu, and Ellard will soon return with reinforcements. I checked with Camryn earlier. I heard Ellard is thrilled because it gives them a chance to train in unfamiliar terrain. It wouldn't surprise me if they want to make this a regular thing."

Gryffnn heaved out a sigh. "I know what I want to do, but politeness and tradition means I must bite my tongue and continue to offer our hospitality until we have solid proof of their deceit."

"Aideen is a bitch," Kaya snapped. "You shouldn't have to put up with this crap."

"Agreed." Gryffnn sighed again and rubbed his hands across his face. "But I don't need a full-scale war."

"You're worried it might come to that anyway," Ry pointed out. "It won't hurt to prepare. Your men are skilled. Why don't you continue with your entertainment plans and keep them busy while

Kaya and I skulk around the spaceport and their ships?"

"What about the men guarding the ships?" Gryffnn asked.

"Make a point of inviting everyone to the entertainment," Ry said.

"If Aideen is here for a friendly visit, why would she leave guards on her ships?" Kaya demanded.

"She has something to hide." Gryffnn said what they were all thinking. "All right. You two discover what you can at the spaceport. Jacinta is already investigating for me in Dalcon. Other than that, I need to wait for Aideen's next move."

"Good plan," Ry said.

Ry's approval meant a lot to Gryffnn since the feline shifter was intelligent and experienced.

Gryffnn's comm buzzed, and he groaned, assuming it was another fire caused by Aideen or her people, a fire for him to put out with tact. He glanced at the screen, and his tension eased.

"It's Hallam." He hit connect and visual-mode, and his son's face appeared on the screen.

"Dad," Hallam said. "Jarlath and Keira said I could call you. It's so much fun here. I like the other boys. We picked berries today, and I helped with the malpacks. They're white, fluffy animals, and they make strange bleats. They look as if they'd be tasty to eat, but Keira said if I toasted them or tried to eat them, I'd have to muck out their quarters every cycle for a whole rotation! I went flying with Keira. She is a crow, and she flies as good as me." His son sucked in a breath, and Gryffnn tried not to smile but failed. He'd missed his son's childish enthusiasm for everything he tried.

"Have you seen Uncle Ransom?"

Hallam nodded vigorously. "We've been busy since we arrived. We visited the city on a flymo before coming to the farm. The castle is real big, Dad. Much bigger than our compound. And the things inside are real glittery. I wanted to touch but Jarlath told me to keep my hands off the pretties. That they belonged to his mother, and breaking them turned her into a real dragon. I thought you said they didn't have dragons in Viros, Dad?"

"How was your uncle?" Gryffnn glanced over at Kaya and Ry and found them both grinning at his son's excitement.

"He's still asleep, but Mogens says he's putting on weight again. Mogens was real happy about that because he turned white all over. We saw the babies. When they play together, they jabber. No one knows what they're saying. Camryn says it's a secret language only they understand and that she and her brother did the same when they were young. They keep the maids and Gweneth and Sheera running around because they're very busy. I said hello to Lys. My sister is pretty, and she laughs a lot. Where's Ma? I mean, Kaya."

"I'm here, Hallam." Kaya came to stand by him, and Gryffnn pulled her onto his knee so Hallam could speak to them both. "I told you you'd have fun. You won't want to come home."

"Is it all right to enjoy both places?" Hallam asked.

"Yes, of course," Kaya said.

"We can visit Viros again once everything settles down," Gryffnn promised. "I want to see this castle myself."

"It's time for you to go to bed," a feminine voice declared.

"Gryffnn, this is Keira," Kaya said.

Keira's pale green face appeared beside Hallam's as she hugged him affectionately. "Hello, Gryffnn." The corners of her eyes crinkled. "Hallam has told me a lot about you."

"Thank you for looking after him."

Keira ruffled Hallam's black hair. "He's a good boy, except when he's eyeing up my malpacks for dinner. It's time for bed. Jarlath is waiting for you so he can start the story where he left off. The other boys are getting impatient."

"Dad, Jarlath tells the best stories. His brother is the king. Did you know? See ya, Dad."

"Behave yourself, son," Gryffnn said. "Good blacklight, Keira."

The screen faded to white, and Gryffnn stared at it for an instant.

"You miss him." Kaya tried to scramble off his lap, but he held her in place.

"I do. He's a good child, although he talks too much, but he has a kind heart and gets on well with everyone. I'm proud of him."

"He takes after you," Ry said. "Our twins are mischievous devils, but everyone loves them. Me most of all. Meeting Camryn was the best thing that ever happened to me, but having the twins has made us even closer. You'll understand, Kaya, once you get to know Lys better."

"I'm frightened I'll break her. Never mind keeping her safe."

"Is Lys in danger? Is that why Tayte brought her to you?" Ry asked.

Kaya settled against Gryffnn, and he loosened his hold now that she'd relaxed.

"There is a slim possibility that someone from my planet will come after her. I'd be more worried if we were closer to Sitnam, but I can't remember the last time I met another being from my home planet, apart from Tayte," she said. "Tayte trusted no one to look after Lys except family."

"I should prepare for the evening meal," Gryffnn said. "Although I'd prefer to spend the time with you."

"I could do the surveillance myself," Ry offered.

"No, it's better if you have a backup," Gryffnn said. "I'll speak with Jacinta again and organize someone to help her too." He hugged Kaya and helped her to her feet. "You stay safe."

Kaya and Ry dressed in black for their mission. While they waited in the family room, they ate the delicious meal of braised ribs and vegetables delivered to them by Sable. Once they were certain the dragons were in the communal dining room, they left via the rear door to the private gardens.

Gryffnn had left three guards on duty, and they stopped to speak to one.

"We're heading out now," Ry said. "I'm not sure how long it will take. We'll return this way. Please don't shoot us and ask questions later."

The guard grinned. "My life wouldn't be worth living if I shot the boss's lady."

Kaya opened her mouth and snapped it shut. Everyone accepted her and Gryffnn as a couple. It was funny, but she was becoming used to the concept. A dangerous path since this arrangement was temporary.

The guard left them with a wave.

"You like Gryffnn," Ry said as they left the private garden and entered the lane that led to town. Hanging lights brightened the way, and she and Ry moved fast, wanting to limit the number of dragons who might observe them.

"He's a friend."

"Pretend all you want. Camryn said it was more, and I can see she's right."

Kaya huffed. "I didn't poke my nose into your affairs."

"Yes, you did. You do," Ry said with an easy grin. "In the same way we poked our noses into Nanu's arrangement with Jazen. If you don't want to discuss Gryffnn, do you want to talk about Lys then?"

Kaya scrunched her brow. "Why are you picking on me?"

"I'm your friend, Kaya. You need to plan for the future."

"I am, and it hurts my head," she muttered. "Can't we—Ry, look over there."

"Isn't that Aideen's head of security?" Ry frowned as Dilan skulked around a corner and out of sight.

"Yeah, did he spot us? This lane is too bright."

"Let's pause in the village and pretend we're shopping," Ry said.

A scoffing sound escaped Kaya. "I bet Camryn has never heard those words coming from your mouth."

"A truce. We'll call a truce," Ry suggested. "No more teasing."

"Today," Kaya said with a grin.

"Works for me."

"Deal. We should check in with Niran and see how he and his sons are getting on. They might enjoy an adventure. It's got to be boring for them keeping a low profile when they're used to busyness."

Ry moved to the center of the lane, giving up his earlier clandestine walk. Kaya matched his travel path, and they strode into the village. The cluster of dwellings and shops was small but prosperous, with smart shopfronts. Cobblestones formed a path on each side of the thoroughfare. Pots brimming with plants bearing purple and red flowers hung from lampposts. They entered a small side alley and headed for a nondescript wooden door.

Kaya grasped the knocker and pounded it to announce their presence.

A lengthy pause ensued.

"Maybe they're not at home," Kaya said.

"They're here. They're using caution and checking on us. Gryffnn told them to take extreme care."

Ry had barely spoken when the door flew open.

"Ry. Kaya," Niran said. The Incorporeal man was tall and thin with long white hair that hung loose to his shoulders. He'd dressed in his normal flowing white gowns and leather sandals. He stood aside to let them enter. "Come in. Please. I hope nothing is wrong."

Kaya followed Ry into the cozy parlor where Niran's two oldest sons sat playing a board game.

"We're conducting a secret mission for Gryffnn. The Gwilym dragons are acting suspiciously, and we suspect his visitors from Dalcon are responsible for stealing the Drake clan's precious stones. Our mission is to get on board their ships to check them out, but we met their head of security skulking around the place. We're not sure if he noticed us, so we're waiting," Ry explained.

Niran's oldest son rose. "Describe his appearance. I can check out what he's doing."

"Can you do it without being seen?" Kaya asked. "We don't want Aideen and her people to realize you're here."

"I've been watching the dragon visitors coming and going from the spaceport. None of them have seen me. Describe this dragon."

"As tall as Gryffnn and a similar build, but he's older. His hair is long and black. He wears it in a single braid that hangs down his back. This eve, he's wearing either dark brown or black trews and a lighter tunic. When we spotted him, he was heading toward the village, but he turned off and took the lane leading to the spaceport," Kaya said.

"I'll check the spaceport," Niran's oldest son said.

The other stood. "I'll go with you."

"Be careful," Niran said. "Do nothing rash. Locate him, learn what he's doing, then return."

"Yes, Father."

"We will, Father."

Both sons bowed solemnly to their father and blinked out, leaving taut silence behind.

"I don't like this," Niran said, breaking the tension between them. "Young Gryffnn is under enough strain with Ransom's illness. It's not right for this enemy clan to swoop in and cause chaos for all of us."

Kaya lifted her chin. "You're right. It sucks, but this is the nature of war—the strong preying on the weak. Except in this case, they've bitten off way more than their arrogant asses can chew."

Chapter 10

Gryffnn is in Big, Big Trouble

"Gryffnn, where is your little pet this blacklight?" Aideen dropped onto the empty chair beside him. She wore a scarlet gown that clung to her fit and curvy body, and she had coiled and pinned her red hair on top of her head in the same style his oldest sister Jacinta often wore. Aideen was an attractive woman, although not for him. Aware of the rot beneath the shiny surface, he'd remain well clear of that trap, not that he'd ever be interested when Kaya had stolen his heart.

He smiled at the thought, looking forward to seeing her again.

Aideen's sly grin shifted to a flirtatious beam, and Gryffnn blinked. *No. Just no.*

"Are you tired of your pet already? Would you prefer a strong and lethal dragon?"

Gryffnn refrained from reminding Aideen that his little *pet* had kicked her arse in the wrestling ring.

Instead of telling her to *phrull* off, he aimed for tactful. "Thank you for the offer, but Kaya and I are happy with our relationship."

"Oh, I thought that was why you'd imprisoned Caley. You wanted to clear the path for me."

Gryffnn couldn't contain his shudder of dislike. Desperate for something to do with his hands, he picked up his drink and drank a good half of the fiery liquor in his goblet. Then, he had an excuse for his involuntary response.

"Caley is refusing to apologize to Kaya. She will remain in the cell until she finds her manners," Gryffnn stated.

"Ah," Aideen said. "I hoped that you and Caley would reconcile. She was younger then and did not act with wisdom."

"She refused my dragon fire and slept with at least two other dragons," Gryffnn said in disbelief. "Why would I give her a second chance when she stomped over my pride and rejected our son?"

Aideen ran a finger down his biceps. Her touch zapped straight to his cock, and he scowled, edging away. What the hell was wrong with him? He drank more of his drink and blinked when the surrounding faces of his clan and Aideen's turned fuzzy. *Whoa!* That kicked harder than he'd realized. He set it down with a thump and somehow misjudged the height of the table. Liquid splashed across the tabletop and over Aideen's hand. "Sorry."

"No problem. Waiter! More Devil's Blood over here," she hollered. She turned back to him once she was satisfied she had the servers scurrying. "I told Caley she had stomped on your pride, and it was too late to go back. I warned her of this before our arrival."

Gryffnn grunted. What the *phrull* was he meant to say? He hated Caley. Aideen too.

A server arrived to top up his goblet. Sable appeared in the lounge doorway where Gryffnn, his people, and their visitors waited with pre-dinner drinks. "Dinner is ready. Please file through to the hall."

"I don't know why your brother brought that woman to your home. She is a half-breed and an abomination with that fake arm."

The cruel words cut through the fog in his mind. "She is our sister and a valued family member," Gryffnn snapped.

Aideen shrugged off his furious words. "She operates your kitchens well. The food is tasty."

Sable was so much more than that, but Gryffnn pushed to his feet. He staggered a step before he regained his balance. Aideen rose and gripped his left arm, her breasts brushing his chest. A shiver of need flooded his body, and horrified, he shook his head.

What the devil was wrong with him?

"I'm starving. The scent of the roasted meats is enticing. Shall we go to dinner?" Aideen fluttered her eyelashes at him.

"Yes, I am hungry too." Gryffnn focused on putting one foot in front of the other. The longer he walked, the more control settled on his shoulders. He'd slept little recently, what with Ransom's illness and worry over Aideen's visit. He'd run out of energy. That was all. He'd feel more himself after he'd eaten.

Storg intercepted them. "Let me escort you to your seat, Aideen."

"I will break protocol and sit by Gryffnn this eve. We have things to discuss." She fluttered her lashes again, and Storg sent Gryffnn a frown of concern.

Gryffnn didn't care where she sat. He wanted to eat, to end this cycle, and retire to his chamber with his Kaya. He shrugged and gestured for Storg to allow Aideen to sit beside him.

Once everyone sat, Aideen thumped her spork on the edge of her goblet to gain attention.

"I want to thank Gryffnn for his hospitality and offer a toast. To forgiveness and friendship between our clans."

Gryffnn had left his goblet on the table in the other room and Aideen signaled one of her people to hand Gryffnn another one. She filled the goblet to the brim from a bottle of liquor her man produced and shunted it toward Gryffnn.

She lifted her goblet. "To closer ties between our clans."

Politeness bade him to drink the toast. He sipped the liquor, not wanting to fog his mind any further. Gryffnn set the goblet back on the float-table. Thankfully, Sable arranged a speedy food service, and they feasted on roasted meats—three different kinds, including his favorite pale yellow meat from the Gerton lizard. Sable produced trays of roasted vegetables and leafy greens, although he noted most of Aideen's people avoided the vegetables.

During his father's time, they had dined solely on meats, but Sable and their housekeeper Jewel had proved to them that a diet of variety aided their strength, and they suffered fewer illnesses.

Sable ended the meal with various tropical fruits from their planet and sweetmeats.

The many toasts proposed by Aideen throughout the meal had his head buzzing from the liquor. Once everyone finished, Gryffnn stood.

"Tom-cycle, we will hold more contests and a scavenger hunt," he announced. "Those who wish to participate should assemble early to break their fast."

Cheers rang out as Gryffnn held his balance by sheer force of will. *Fresh air*. That might buzz the fog from his brain. He angled his steps toward the door.

"Gryffnn." Aideen matched his steps and put her arm through his.

Despite his irritation with the dragon woman, he appreciated her aid this eve.

"I intend to walk in the garden before I retire."

"Would you consent to my company? I have clan matters I wish to discuss with you."

Gryffnn huffed out a draft of air, the force of it burning his lungs and producing a curl of smoke. Alarm grew in him, yet he failed to summon the energy to avoid Aideen. "What do we have to discuss?"

"Let us walk a little yet. I don't wish for ears to flap and our discussion to become gossip."

That sounded ominous.

Gryffnn let Aideen guide him to the garden around the cottage where she was staying. The fresh air didn't do much to clear the clouds in his head, but his balance improved with the exercise.

"We should have closer ties between our clans." Aideen smiled and projected sincerity.

Gryffnn's beleaguered mind screeched at him to use caution. "What are you talking about?"

"I want to mate with you, Gryffnn. Given her behavior, I understand you not wanting to reconcile with Caley." She prowled closer until her breasts brushed his chest. "But us together makes good sense."

Her scent—strangely seductive—wound through his senses. Alarm surfaced at the wrongness of her proximity. He edged away until his back hit a head-high bush, and he could retreat no more.

"You're not immune to me, Gryffnn. I've seen you watching me. We could do great things together, build our clans into a single powerful one that will change the history books."

Heat eased through his limbs and his cock filled.

Wrong. This was so wrong, yet he couldn't seem to halt his body's reaction to Aideen's nearness.

"I...ah...betrothed," he mumbled, a wave of lust striking him so hard his thoughts of loyalty wavered. Every hazy protest faded away, and his cock took over his brainbox. His shaft thrust against his trews with painful intensity. He moaned as pleasure slid over his skin.

"Kiss me, Gryffnn. I know you want to," Aideen crooned.

Her breath feathered over his mouth. Her smoky, spicy scent filled his nostrils. He groaned, a tiny part of him appalled yet helpless to resist. Their lips touched...

CHAPTER 11

KAYA BLOWS A FUSE

"T-thank the goddess I-I've found you! Storg sent me. H-have to come now." The guard panted, trying to catch his breath. Sweat beaded on his broad forehead, and his lungs labored beneath his leather vest.

"What's wrong?" Kaya demanded.

"Don't know." The dragon shifter sucked in a huge breath. "Storg told me it was urgent."

Kaya shared a glance with Ry, and as one, they sprinted through the village and down the lane leading to the compound.

As they neared the private garden entrance, the sound of revelry floated in the air. Laughter and shouting and male posturing competed with feminine titters.

"Where is Storg?" Ry asked.

"Near the cottages." The dragon shifter had regained his puff and kept up with them on the run back to the compound.

Kaya spotted Storg loitering outside the cottage where Aideen was staying. "What is it?"

Storg sagged against the cottage wall on seeing them before straightening and dragging his hand through his hair. Judging by the state of his braid, it wasn't the first time he'd done this.

"Thank the goddess you're here. It's Aideen. I wasn't sure what to do. Gryffnn is inside her cottage. They were kissing—"

"Pardon?" The mental image detonated Kaya's temper. A blast of heat seared her heart and mind and left throbbing fury and hurt. The question *why* hammered into her brain.

She'd thought...

"I'll geld him." She shook the stupidity from her brain and darted a step closer to the door.

Ry grabbed her and jerked her to a halt.

"Wait," he said. "*Think.* Something is wrong. Gryffnn hates Aideen and her sister. He wouldn't do this, not after his suffering at Caley's hands." He turned to Storg. "Are there any of Aideen's guards?"

"One. I've taken care of him. He's behind that hedge, tied and gagged."

Kaya shook away her anger and attempted to force away her surge of jealousy as she listened. "Gryffnn is truly in the cottage with Aideen?"

"Yes," Storg acknowledged, a deep frown etched into his lined features.

"Think, Kaya," Ry repeated. "All I'm saying is we should enter with open minds. Are you ready?" Ry glanced at her, Storg, and the security guard who had alerted them. "Behind me, Kaya," he ordered.

The implacable hardness of his voice had her obeying without question. Gryffnn and Aideen. *Gryffnn and Aideen.* No. No, she couldn't believe Gryffnn would do this to her. Jealous. Goddess,

Ry was right. She *did* care for Gryffnn. She shoved the revelation to the back of her mind and fell in behind Ry and Storg. The security guard entered the cottage behind her.

Throaty feminine laughter floated from the bed chamber. Kaya's mouth tightened at the trail of masculine and feminine discarded garments.

They crept down the passage in single file until Storg froze in the open doorway of the chamber. Ry stepped up beside him. Kaya wriggled past Ry, desperate to see, then wished she hadn't.

Gryffnn lay on the gel-bed, naked, his cock thrusting outward and upward like a sword. His eyes remained closed, his breathing harsh and discordant as he sucked on one of Aideen's breasts.

A naked Aideen straddled his body, the light from one of Narenda's moons highlighting her ample curves.

"Freeze," Kaya snapped and pulled out her blaster, aiming it at Aideen.

"Lights on," Ry ordered.

Illumination flooded the room. It took secs for Kaya's eyes to adjust to the brightness. She glared at Gryffnn, a pounding in her ears. How could he do this? Her hands curled around the butt of her blaster.

Ry's words of caution flooded her mind, and she stilled her urge to fire at both of them.

"You dare interrupt," Aideen said in a haughty voice, the twist of her body pulling her nipple from Gryffnn's mouth. "We were about to have sex. This is a private matter between me and Gryffnn."

Thank goodness! They hadn't done the deed. *Yet.*

"Gryffnn is betrothed to me," Kaya spat. "Which makes this my business. Get off him before I put a hole in you."

Aideen lifted her chin but didn't move. "I am the leader of my clan. Gryffnn leads his, which makes us an ideal match. Ask Gryffnn if he entered this cottage of his own volition. He'll tell you

I didn't force him into this position."

"Gryffnn," Storg said in a sharp voice.

Gryffnn didn't react.

Ry stepped up to the gel-bed and waved his hand over Gryffnn's face. When he still didn't react, Ry lifted one of Gryffnn's eyelids. "Drugged."

They all glowered at Aideen.

"I have no idea what you're talking about," she said, her tone haughty.

"Get off him," Kaya said.

When Aideen raised her brows and sneered at her, Kaya fired her blaster. She didn't aim to hit but to make the point that she could and would next time.

Ry and Storg gaped at the hole in the chamber wall, then stared at Kaya. Behind them, the security man sniggered.

Kaya gestured at Aideen with her blaster. "Off."

Aideen hesitated, and Kaya shot her blaster again, this shot close enough to singe the elaborate coil piled atop the dragon shifter's head. A tinge of smoke rose from the sizzled locks, and satisfaction sank into Kaya's bones.

"Don't make me shoot a third time," Kaya warned.

Aideen grunted and swung her leg off Gryffnn. She ambled over to a looking glass and shrieked on seeing her hair. "Bitch. I'll get you for this."

"I informed you of my intentions. You ignored my advice to move your butt off my betrothed." She glanced at Ry. "Help Gryffnn up and find him something to wear. I'd help, but I still have the urge to shoot something."

Storg and Ry hauled Gryffnn to his feet, but Gryffnn didn't react, his head lolling to the side. They ripped a covering off the gel-bed and wrapped it around Gryffnn.

Once she was certain they had Gryffnn in hand, she followed them from the cottage, her blaster at the ready.

"Follow them," she ordered the security guard. "What is your name?"

"Gregarious," he said.

"All right. Gregarious, follow them until they're inside the private quarters and away from Aideen's people."

Gregarious hesitated. "What are you going to do?"

"I won't shoot Aideen, although I'm mighty tempted. You will find me in the private gardens for a while before I retire for the evening."

He nodded and trotted after Ry and Storg as they manhandled Gryffnn to the family quarters.

Kaya stomped away, long strides taking her to the gardens. The colors and the scents typically left her relaxed and happy. Not this blacklight. The memory of Gryffnn sucking on Aideen's breast and his rampant erection refused to leave her mind.

Usually, she wouldn't care. She'd walked in on a man before, one she'd slept with a few times and thought they'd had a non-verbal agreement. She'd laughed at him, told him his cock would shrivel at the next full moon, and left.

This time...

Kaya stormed past a bed of mauve flowers, their scent sweet and enticing. She stamped back past, her hand slashing out in the burst of temper. Secs later, she stared at the severed flower heads at her feet.

The truth she'd tried to ignore struck her anew.

She liked Gryffnn.

No, she more than adored Gryffnn.

It was why she'd agreed to this pretense. And the sex...

She huffed out a harsh breath as she tested her thoughts, her feelings. She'd enjoyed the closeness with a man. Gryffnn had seemed to care for her too.

Even though it was apparent Aideen had drugged him, this still ached like a betrayal.

Yes, she needed to think.

Gryffnn woke the next cycle, his head pounding with a ferocity that had him wincing at the light blazing through the unscreened windows and slamming his eyes shut. The hammer in his skull continued while his lethargic brainbox fought to recall what had happened and why every muscle in his body acted as if he'd been in a fight.

Cautiously, he slit open his eyelids and turned his head. He frowned at the discovery he was alone.

Where was Kaya?

A knock sounded on his door.

"Enter."

Ry poked his head inside the chamber and stepped over the threshold, closing the door behind him. "You're awake."

"Barely. Windows semi-screen." The automatic screens obeyed the order, and the brightness reduced. His head continued to ache while his mouth craved liquid. He swallowed twice, which did little to ease the dryness.

Ry approached the gel-bed. "Do you remember what happened last eve?"

Gryffnn frowned, casting his mind back. He had nothing. He scanned Ry's somber face, and his stomach twisted into a knot. "What did I do?"

"We found you in bed with Aideen."

Shock kicked Gryffnn in the middle of the chest. His body jerked, the abrupt lurch setting the hammers in his head into a loud cacophony. He stared at Ry, waiting for him to crack a grin. "You're lying."

"Storg and I brought you back to your chamber. Someone

drugged you, and you wouldn't have made the trip without us. You staggered as if you were drunk."

Fear followed on the heels of his disbelief. He swallowed, his sluggish brainbox juddering into action. "Kaya?"

"She threatened to shoot a hole in Aideen."

"She saw me?"

"Naked with Aideen. Yes."

"*Phrull.*"

"If it's any consolation, according to Aideen, we arrived before you did the deed," Ry said.

"Is Kaya...has she left?" *Frag* it, what had happened? He loathed Aideen. He'd go as far as saying he hated her for how she'd behaved before on Dalcon and now.

"No, she's in her normal chamber." Ry glanced at the corner of the room. "Her bag is here."

Profound relief had him squeezing his eyes closed and bowing his head. Could he fix this? "My mind is blank. I remember nothing."

"We're certain someone drugged you. Perhaps a touch of a sex drug. I don't know if you have it here but they market it as rabbit in some of the places we visited before we hit Viros. It makes a person desperate to have sex."

"I've heard of it. You think she drugged me?" Gryffnn didn't have to pretend his shock. That Aideen would stoop to such skullduggery.

"Yes."

"Phrull. Kaya won't want anything to do with me." Misery clamped around his chest, squeezing the spark of panic deep inside him and making it explode and ricochet hard enough to batter his poor head.

"Tell her the truth. She already knows about the drug."

Gryffnn nodded and winced at the shard of pain in his skull. "I'll shower. It might wash the mud away from my brainbox."

"There is more, but I'll see you when you break your fast."

Gryffnn swung his legs over the side of the gel-bed. His aim was to build a life, a future with Kaya, but getting past this...

He forced himself to stand and almost faceplanted.

Ry grabbed him and held him upright until Gryffnn's feet took his own weight. "You'll need help."

"No. Help me into the bathing chamber, and I'll take it from there. I'd prefer you to check on Kaya."

Ry provided the requested aid and left Gryffnn with water pouring over his head. Frigid water to prod him to full wakefulness. As the cold liquid pummeled him, he tried to recall the previous night's events. Ry and Kaya had gone to the spaceport to check on Aideen's ships while he'd eaten with his people and the visiting dragons. After that, his memories grew murky.

Once he shivered from the cold, he issued the order for the water to cease. "Water stop. Drier on."

It was almost an entire mark later before he entered the dining room. Storg, Ry, Kaya, and Sable sat at a float-table, cups of delicate green tay in their hands.

Gryffnn took one whiff of the savory breakfast scents and breathed through his mouth. He dropped onto the empty seat beside Sable. When she poured a cup of tay and pushed it toward him, he mumbled thanks and wrapped his hands around the warm vessel. He took one sip and another, the tay warming him from the inside and moistening his throat. Then, he risked a glance at Kaya.

"I'm so sorry about last eve. I don't understand what happened," he said.

"Aideen drugged you," Kaya said. "Not your fault."

At least she wasn't screeching at him, although she refused to meet his gaze. "I don't know how it happened. Or when. It's a blank."

"Lesson learned," Storg said. "We must watch what we eat or drink, especially you, Gryffnn."

"Is it common knowledge?" Gryffnn asked.

"Aideen is telling everyone who will listen that you seduced her and then put the blame on her. She is adamant Kaya tried to murder her," Storg said.

Gryffnn closed his eyes, his stomach churning too much to consider eating. Great. Just great. How could he look his people in the eye? "Ry, you said you had news for me about your reconnoitering last eve."

"All six of Aideen's ships have special units to render them invisible on your tracking systems. We found boxes of precious stones in the hold of one ship, probably the one I spotted traveling over the mountains," Ry said.

"Aideen is stealing from us?"

"It looks that way, but we need to catch her in the act. None of the boxes we looked through contained unusual stones. If you accuse them of stealing, you might have trouble proving it."

Gryffnn tapped his fingers on the tabletop and stopped when the sound arced through his head. "My man should've almost reached Dalcon by now. Between him and Jacinta, they should garner information to help us. Jacinta hadn't turned up anything more than gossip when I spoke with her, but she said she'll liaise with our man and get back with the info they uncover."

"What are you going to do now?" Kaya asked.

What he wanted to do was take Kaya to his chamber and lock the door until she forgave him. Then, he wanted to make sure she realized he was serious about a relationship with her. He'd take her and Lys to join his existing family of two. Both Ransom and Sable liked Kaya and respected her. Gryffnn lusted after her and felt more for her than he'd ever experienced for Caley.

But none of that would happen until he dealt with Aideen.

"I'll speak to Aideen and persuade her to leave," Gryffnn said. "Surely she won't want to stay here where she's not wanted." He turned to Kaya. "I understand my actions have annoyed you. Hurt you. All I can say is that I'm sorry, and had I been in my right mind, you would have found me in our chamber instead of at the cottage with Aideen. I would…will *never* have an intimate relationship with Aideen."

Kaya gave a stiff nod, and he took heart since she was finally giving him her full attention.

"How do you intend to entertain your guests this cycle?" Ry asked.

"Run one of your flying exercises," Kaya suggested. "It will give you a chance to assess their strengths and if you plot a flight path that goes near the mountain range, you can ascertain how the visitors handle the resonance from the precious stones."

"That's an excellent idea. Even better, the flying will keep them busy for the entire cycle. I'll offer a prize for the dragon with the fastest time." He paused. "Yes, I'll let them choose an item from our finished jewelry."

Sable gasped. "That is a handsome prize."

"Hopefully, it will induce every dragon to run the course," Gryffnn said. "And I won't have to worry about Aideen's dragons taking side trips to steal our precious stones."

"I've heard from Ellard," Ry said. "They're already on the way to Narenda and should arrive before blacklight. Ellard intends to fly straight to the area they're guarding."

"They're on the *Indy*?" Gryffnn asked.

"No, Ellard decided it would make sense to have their own transportation," Ry said. "Camryn and Nanu were preparing to leave when I spoke to them."

"Thank you for organizing this." Gryffnn rose, his head still pounding. He had not a hope of completing the flying course this cycle. He'd organize, record times, and wait at the finish line to judge the winner. "Kaya, would you mind walking with me? I wish to show solidarity in our betrothal."

Alarm surged through him as indecision marched across her pale blue features. He wanted to object, to inform her he had morals and believed in fidelity and faithfulness, yet how could he when she'd discovered him naked with Aideen? *Phrull*, he wished he could remember what had happened.

Finally, *finally*, Kaya nodded and walked at his side as he left the dining chamber.

He led her to the communal dining hall, where their visitors mingled with his dragons and broke their fast.

Silence fell as he and Kaya entered. Gryffnn announced the cycle's plans, but the silence deepened instead of the excited chatter he expected.

Phrull. He'd expected comments about the situation with Aideen, but not this pregnant hush.

"What's wrong?" Kaya's irritation rang out for all to hear.

Aideen stood, and Gryffnn's gaze shot to the Narendanite pendant hanging around her neck. Whispers began, low and persistent. Gryffnn gulped, focusing on the pendant traditionally gifted from the leader of the Drake dragons to his mate.

He forced himself to speak. "The contest begins in half a mark. All those who intend to participate should meet at the training field, where my flight captain will show you the flying course."

"You dare to flaunt your tramp in front of your mate?" Aideen's voice rang out, cutting through the whispers.

He noticed Kaya caress the butt of her blaster, but thankfully commonsense stayed her impulsive action. Pulling a weapon here would start a war. Kaya smirked at Aideen, her attention on Aideen's hair. Gryffnn had no idea why, but Aideen's expression turned icy.

Aideen clutched the pendant in her right hand. "Gryffnn gifted me with this pendant last blacklight, and I accepted his proposal to join our clans."

"No," Gryffnn snapped. "I did not. Kaya is my betrothed. The flying contest begins in half a mark." He grasped Kaya's forearm and propelled her out the door.

"Is that pendant special to your clan?" Kaya demanded as soon as they stood in the private gardens.

Gryffnn didn't understand. "You said the drug incapacitated me last eve, and I was incapable of walking without help."

"Yes."

"There is a family pendant that the leader of the Drake clan gives to his mate. I am not the leader. I am standing in for Ransom until he recovers. Ransom has the family pendant, and I presume he has it locked in his personal safe. I don't have access since only his fingerprint and an eye scan opens the security lock. The pendant Aideen is wearing has to be a fake. Ask Sable if you don't believe me, or contact Jacinta, and she will tell you the same thing."

"What are you going to do?" Kaya asked, her calmness now going a long way to settling the angst writhing through his gut.

"I'll call my people together this blacklight and tell them the truth," Gryffnn said. "I'll speak to those entering the flight contest now." He sucked in a huge breath. "Kaya, I have a confession."

Kaya's expression hardened. "If I learn you've been lying, I *will* fill you with holes."

Gryffnn nodded. "Asking you to act as my betrothed was only part of my plan. I have wanted you for a long time, Kaya. You didn't *see* me, so I grabbed this opportunity to spend time with you. I have feelings for you and want to build a future with you. Lys too."

She stared at him, her emotions screened. Fear tiptoed through him, his mouth drying again as he returned her regard.

Her breath hissed out, and the stiffness left her muscles. "I-I want to believe you. Catching you with Aideen wounded me. It made me realize this wasn't a pretense for me either, that you had the power to hurt me."

Gryffnn stared at her, his throat tight. "We still have a chance?"

"Let's take one cycle at a time. And I would speak with Jacinta."

"Fair enough." Gryffnn pushed a button on his comm and

handed it to Kaya. "I'll be at the training field, organizing the start of the race."

"Once I'm done, I'll bring you your comm."

Gryffnn hesitated, wanting to kiss her. Too soon. He confined himself to a squeeze of her shoulder and a nod. As he walked away, he prayed he'd done the right thing because he'd hate Kaya to leave him.

CHAPTER 12

AIDEEN CONTINUES TO FIGHT DIRTY

L *ater that cycle, blacklight, communal dining hall*

Gryffnn glanced around the hall, and the muted whispers and disgruntled looks sent in his direction had his scales rising to the surface of his limbs. Most of his clan seemed to believe him, although a few wore open disenchantment. Surely Aideen would leave soon? Her presence was stirring agitation he could do without. Phrull, he'd rejected her in front of everyone, yet she continued to maintain they were affianced mates.

She'd informed everyone they'd consummated their relationship, and now that she wore the Drake pendant, all that was left to complete their joining was the exchange of dragon fire.

According to her.

Gryffnn darted a glance at Kaya. Ry and Sable had also joined them in the communal dining hall.

"I demand you get rid of that woman." Aideen jumped to her feet, her voice ringing out. "I dislike how you're flaunting your blue alien in front of me. It's not seemly, and I refuse to suffer the humiliation for any longer."

"No." Gryffnn stood. "For the final time, the sole reason I was in your cottage and in your bed was because you drugged me. I have no memory of last eve. Secondly, I don't know how you got your hands on the Drake pendant, but I am the acting leader. As soon as Ransom returns to Narenda, he will take over leadership again, as is his right. I have no entitlement to the pendant. My family knows I have no access to the safe, so I could not have presented it to you."

Whispers, soft at first, spread from dragon to dragon, each one expressing their opinion to their friends and dining companions.

"Are you calling me a liar?" Aideen screeched.

"Yes." Gryffnn met her scowl with one of his own. "It's late. I suggest you and your people leave tom-cycle before this situation escalates past the point of no return."

In his mind, it had already progressed to that stage, but Gryffnn understood how his brother thought. Ransom wished to keep the peace between the clans and their interaction to a minimum. And as acting leader, Gryffnn intended to follow Ransom's wishes.

"Fine." Aideen stalked from the hall, pausing in the doorway. "With me," she snapped to her entourage.

They abandoned their half-eaten meals, some with dismay, and trailed Aideen.

A burst of chatter came from his people as Gryffnn sat and resumed his dinner. His security team would watch and make sure Aideen kept from further mischief. He didn't even care about the precious stones it appeared they'd stolen. With his new security in place, they'd find it difficult to repeat the theft. Getting rid of Aideen was more important than regaining their property.

After the abrupt end of socialization between the clans, Kaya walked with Gryffnn through the private gardens. One moon was visible overhead, a crescent hanging against the velvet black sky. She'd spoken to Jacinta, Sable, and the security head Storg. All had confirmed Gryffnn's words about the pendant. He'd been drugged—she'd witnessed this herself—so she could hardly fault him for his actions. Still, though, a faint sense of betrayal persisted.

Aideen's fault.

The dragon leader had a game plan, part of which seemed to be to create chaos within the Drake clan. And she kept pushing toward closer relations. Caley getting back with Gryffnn and when that idea fell flat, Aideen had pushed herself into the spot. Was it her imagination? No, for some reason, Aideen wanted firm ties between the clans again.

"Have you thought about us, Kaya?" Gryffnn asked.

She had.

Incessantly.

"I've considered everything you said and am willing to see what happens between us. Wait." She held up her hand when he took half a step toward her, a huge beam lighting his happiness at her decision. "I'll continue to share your chamber, but we won't have sex again. Not yet. I wish to proceed with caution."

Gryffnn sighed, his shoulders slumping. "I understand. I will accept your edict. Am I allowed to kiss you?"

"Yes." She clenched her fists as she tried to convince herself this decision was for the best. The truth. This would hurt her as much as it did him.

Whenever she'd craved sex, she indulged herself. It was true she hadn't dabbled as much in the past rotation, but when she was with a sexy male, she enjoyed physical contact. This truth made her realize Gryffnn was special to her, and she was right to explore where their friendship might lead.

Gryffnn reached for her hand and entwined their fingers. "Let us continue our stroll."

"You're not angry with my decision?"

A heavy sigh escaped him. "After what you walked in on, it's fair. I mightn't want this, but I understand. If I'd been the one to walk in on you with another male, I don't think I would've behaved with the same dignity."

Kaya's lips quivered, and she shot him a glance. "Did you notice Aideen's hair?"

"Yes. What happened to it?"

"I shot her with my blaster when she refused to get off you. Um, there might be a hole in your cottage wall too."

Gryffnn's lips quivered. "I see. I'm glad Hallam isn't here to hear the squabbles and see Aideen's behavior. If he'd been here, she or Caley would've used him to needle me."

"What do you intend to do?"

"Hopefully, Aideen will leave tom-cycle."

Kaya ran her palm over the head of a red flower, releasing its sweet scent into the air. "And the stealing?"

"I'm prepared to let it go as long as she and her people leave. I've been thinking about Caley," he added. "Let's release her now. Then they'll have no excuse to delay their departure."

"Why don't you issue the order?" Kaya lifted her head from the plant to glower at him. "Why do you need to see her in person?"

"I intend to give her a last chance to apologize to you. I'm tired of Caley and her sister. Once the pair leave, they're not welcome to visit again. At least not while I'm acting leader. Ransom can make his own decision." Gryffnn's comm buzzed. "It's Jacinta. Hey, do you have something for me?"

Kaya watched Gryffnn as he spoke to his sister. Affection

shimmered in his voice and his easy manner displayed their comradery. It was the same when he interacted with Ransom and Sable. His son too.

"They what? The entire clan? I'd heard the rumors of the stone deposits giving out, but I wasn't certain if they were true. I hate to question Aideen—she'd take my queries as a challenge. You're certain?" Gryffnn listened to his sister. "Thank you, Jacinta. You'd make an excellent spy. Tell Pade he can take two cycles rather than rush back. Sure, you can journey back together. See you soon, and thanks."

"Have you discovered something helpful?" Kaya asked once Gryffnn ended the call.

"Everyone from Aideen's clan is here on Narenda." Gryffnn replayed everything he knew about Aideen and the Gwilym clan and shook his head. "They're all here because the rest of her clan perished from a mystery epidemic. And that's not all. Rumor says their precious stone deposits are depleted. Jacinta and Pade will visit their lands and observe if the rumor about their wealth is true."

"That's a big step—walking away from an existing settlement. Aideen is looking to build a future for her clan."

"Yes, at our expense. She wants to grab a mate from our clan or steal our resources to start afresh somewhere else."

"If that's the case, she has achieved part of her goals. What are you going to do?"

"I don't know. I empathize with her people, but it pisses me off that she sneaked around and try to use my inexperience as a leader to take advantage. Why didn't she front up and tell the phrullin truth?"

Kaya shrugged. "I don't know. Pride, maybe?"

"If our people were in trouble, if they were sick, or our resources were running out, we'd try to fix the problem. We'd find another way to survive."

A snort escaped Kaya. "The woman is a *me-me-me* parasite. I don't trust her, and I can't wait for her to leave Narenda."

"I'll be happy to see the back of her," Gryffnn agreed. "Let's release Caley. Then, tom-cycle, if they refuse to leave, I'm booting their asses off Narenda."

"What about Aideen's people? What if they don't want to follow Aideen?"

"An excellent point. What would Ransom do?" he asked.

"I don't know. You have a better idea of how he might react."

Gryffnn pursed his lips, his brow crinkling as he considered that. "I know he was angry on my behalf. Father blamed me."

"*Pfff.*" Her unladylike snort drew a smile from him and created a flash of a dimple on the right side of his mouth, one she hadn't noticed before. Kaya found herself leaning toward him to place her lips on the dent and made herself stop.

"I'll think about whether to offer them a place here. Aideen has skilled craftsmen who work in a different style to our clansmen. Whether I can trust them is another matter."

"Aideen's people. Enough said, I don't envy you your decision."

Gryffnn led her to the end of the garden. Before they left the privacy of the tall plants and muted lighting, he drew her to a halt. "Can I kiss you now?"

Without hesitation, Kaya stepped into Gryffnn's personal space. She breathed in his amber, smoky scent, and her heavy thoughts faded. Despite the drama of earlier cycles, she wanted this. Gryffnn cupped her face with his hands, his eyes more elongated, the pupils more dragonlike than she'd seen.

"Thank you for giving me another chance," he whispered before he covered her mouth with his.

Kaya closed her eyes and relaxed against his broad chest, enjoying the caress of his lips, his closeness. Also, a tiny part of her—the bitchy part—enjoyed his apology and his careful treatment of her. He wasn't taking her for granted and was prepared to fight for her.

He nibbled on her bottom lip and she opened to allow a more intimate contact. Their tongues twirled together, and a slow burn of pleasure coasted through her.

Finally, Gryffnn parted their mouths, his quiet sigh of regret at having to stop echoing inside Kaya. He smoothed her hair away from her face and clasped her hand.

"I guess it's time to face Caley again."

Hand-in-hand, they entered the area where they'd incarcerated Caley.

"Gryffnn, sir." His security team member straightened to attention.

"Everything all right?"

"Caley has been quiet since I delivered her meal. Her sister visited her, and they argued, but the shouting didn't last long," the guard said. "I was about to collect her dishes and check if she needs anything."

"Do you have the cell keys? I've decided to release Caley. She'll be leaving Narenda tom-cycle," Gryffnn said. "You can clear the cell once she's gone to her allocated cottage."

Kaya followed Gryffnn deeper into the area they used as a prison. The thick stone walls held the cycle's heat at bay, the temperature cooler than outdoors. Kaya shivered, preferring the tropical temperatures. A strange scent drifted to her as they walked deeper into the building.

Gryffnn cursed and took off at a run, sprinting along the dim corridor to the cell at the far end.

"What is it? What's wrong?" Kaya called after him, lengthening her steps to catch up with him.

He skidded to a halt, cursing.

Kaya pulled up beside him.

Caley sat slumped on a chair, a pool of blood beneath her.

Gryffnn cursed again and unlocked the door. He slid it across and hurried to Caley's side.

"Is she dead?" Kaya stepped closer, studying Caley. The blood came from her mouth rather than a body wound. "Poison?"

"I think so," Gryffnn murmured. "It must've been something quick acting. Her dinner plates are empty, so it might be something she ate. But I doubt it. I'd bet my left wing that if we search, we'll find an injection site."

"Aideen?"

"That's my best guess." Gryffnn's jaw tightened until his expression turned moody. "Aideen will blame me. She'll allege I killed her sister."

"She'll refuse to leave tom-cycle."

"She might even issue a challenge."

Kaya guessed from his tone that this wasn't good. "Which means?"

"We fight in dragon form, and the winner takes everything. If Aideen bests me, she'll take over the clan because Ransom isn't in any condition to exert his leadership rights."

"But you didn't kill Caley. I've been with you the entire time. The guard said Aideen was here, and she and Caley argued. He didn't check on Caley again after Aideen left. I mean, why would he? They're sisters. You wouldn't expect Aideen to kill her family."

"Perception is everything," Gryffnn said.

"Ry is here. He'll help."

"He's not a dragon," Gryffnn said. "Crap, this just gets worse. Can you speak with the guard and get him to call Storg for me? Tell them to come to the cell. I don't want to shift Caley without witnesses. Once we record her surroundings and position, I'll get Storg to start an official investigation."

"What about Aideen?"

"If she is our killer, she'll be waiting to see how I handle this situation. And she'll toss accusations, placing the blame squarely on me."

CHAPTER 13

MURDER AND A FIRE

G ryffnn tracked Aideen down at her cottage. "Stay with me," he murmured to Kaya and Ry, who had accompanied him. "Don't let Aideen get me alone."

"We won't," Kaya said.

Gryffnn knocked and asked to speak to Aideen.

"Ah!" She broke into a broad beam. "You've come to your senses and see the benefits of a closer relationship between our tribes. Very sensible. We shall make a formidable team."

The dragon woman held delusions if she believed he'd ever consider them a team.

"No, it's not that." He paused, waiting for her to invite them inside. When she didn't, he straightened. "I have bad news. I'm sorry, Aideen, but Caley is dead."

He watched her closely, and he sensed Kaya and Ry doing the

same thing at his back.

"Caley is dead? How? Why? No, you're joking." She patted her chest, a small laugh escaping—a sound of disbelief. "She can't be dead. I spoke with her recently. She was in perfect health."

Was that a hint of calculation? *Frag it!* If someone informed him of a family death, he... No, he didn't truly understand how he'd act.

"Kaya and I found her. I'm so sorry, Aideen, but Caley is dead." Gryffnn watched Aideen's reaction again, attempting to decipher her expression, her feelings on hearing of her sister's death. She wasn't giving him much. Disbelief, yes. But not a shred of guilt.

"You killed her!" Aideen surged forward and thumped him solidly in the middle of the chest.

He took a rapid step backward, out of the range of her flailing fists. "No, I did not. Kaya and I visited Caley because I intended to release her ready for your departure tom-cycle."

"I demand satisfaction," Aideen spat.

"I—what? No! I did *not* kill your sister. My head of security is investigating as we speak."

"They'll find in your favor," Aideen accused. "Any investigation will be flawed."

"I. Did. Not. Kill. Your. Sister," Gryffnn roared. He jabbed his finger at Aideen, a muscle ticking furiously at his jaw. "I didn't." His nostrils flared, and fiery heat spread through his chest as his scales rippled across his skin. A black curl of smoke spiraled upward, escaping from between his gritted teeth. He glowered at Aideen and stepped into her personal space, doing nothing to halt the rise of his dragon. "You were with Caley before she died. You argued. I have a witness."

"That's a lie." Copper scales rippled up her throat, her dragon equally aggressive.

"Gryffnn," Ry murmured, tugging on his arm. "Back away. You need to calm the fuck down."

144

Gryffnn let Ry pull him another step back. His dragon side didn't approve, and heat seared his throat. A curl of smoke drifted from his nostrils. He lifted his top lip into a sneer and planted his legs in a solid stance, refusing to stir from the spot until he said his piece to Aideen. "I'm tired of your accusations, Aideen. I'll inform you of our findings during the investigation. You'll receive an update at whitelight."

Gryffnn forced himself to retreat despite the crazy urge to challenge Aideen. Ry was right, and honesty bade him to acknowledge Ransom would never approve of a challenge. There was nothing more he could do this blacklight.

Ry's comm buzzed. He took the call, spoke quietly, and returned his comm to the clip on his hip. "Ellard and his men are in position."

"Thank you."

"What do you think Aideen will do?" Kaya asked.

"She's hard to predict." Gryffnn scowled at the slam of the cottage door and the high-pitched shriek that battered his ears. "The only certainty is this will not end well. No matter what I do, it will be wrong."

"Is there anything I can do to help?" Ry asked.

"Assassinate Aideen," Kaya answered before he could speak.

Gryffnn barked out a laugh. "I wish, but my conscience refuses me that option. Kaya, I will check in with Storg. Can I meet you at my chamber?"

"Sure." Once Gryffnn strode away, Kaya fell into step with Ry. "What do you think about this situation?"

"Gryffnn is right," Ry said. "It's a bomb waiting to explode. Watch your back, okay?"

"I am. I trust Aideen about as far as I could throw her."

"I'm considering telling Camryn and Nanu to stay away."

Kaya barked out a laugh. "That will go well."

Ry sighed. "I know, but it's worth a try. At least all the kids are safe on Viros."

"You really think Aideen or Gryffnn will snap?"

"It's not a case of *if*. It's when," Ry said.

"That's my reading," Kaya agreed.

They parted in the private family wing. Kaya pressed her palm to Gryffnn's identification plate. The door slid open, and Kaya walked into his chamber. Unable to settle, she prowled the perimeter. During her third circuit, the door opened, and Gryffnn entered.

"I want to do more than kiss," Kaya blurted. "If you and Aideen end up fighting together and something happens to you—" She clenched and unclenched her hands. "I'm still angry. My head knows Aideen staged the situation, and it wasn't your fault. You were drugged, but my heart wants to pummel someone."

"Me?"

"I can't get the vision of you and Aideen out of my head." A shudder ran through her, and she knuckled her eyes until she saw colors behind her closed lids.

"Have you changed your mind?"

"No." She straightened abruptly, her hands falling to her sides. Their gazes caught, magnetic and searching, and the tension slid from Kaya's muscles.

Two giant steps had Gryffnn at her side. An instant later, he swept her off her feet and into his arms. It was a speedy trip to the gel-bed, and she scarcely bounced before he covered her, their chests sliding together. Satisfaction slashed his mouth, and his eyes glowed as he stared down at her.

"I'll take that," he murmured.

His lips slammed against hers, the fit wrong at first. Then, he realigned their mouths and sank deeper into the kiss. His hands skimmed her body. He unfastened clothes, pushed off boots, ripped her undergarments until she lay panting and naked beneath his hard body.

Kaya groaned against his mouth and admitted this was precisely where she wanted to be. He nuzzled her neck and gave her a hint of teeth while she burrowed her hands beneath his tunic. Skin. She needed skin.

His scent filled every breath as he kissed and teased and nibbled her neck, her collarbone.

"More," she demanded.

He laughed, his humor a burst of warm air against her breast. "Your blue skin is so pretty, but do you know what I noticed first about you?"

"My sparkly personality?"

His chuckle echoed through the chamber. "No. You gave me attitude and peeked at my brother's butt."

"I did not."

"You did," Gryffnn confirmed.

Laughter bubbled up in her. "Well, to be fair, Ransom has a superior backside. But I've come to appreciate yours," she added with a sassy wink.

"You look pretty when you smile. Your eyes sparkle." He kissed her eyelids and pulled back to grin at her. His gaze drifted to her mouth, and sensual tension slid over both of them. "I noticed your cute pointy ears the first time we met." He ran a gentle finger around the rim of her ear, and she shuddered.

Urgency surged through her at the delicate touch. Few men commented on her ears or even noticed them. Lots of aliens had pointy ears. She pushed at his chest and grasped his tunic. "Off. I want you naked. Now."

Gryffnn rolled off the gel-bed and hurriedly stripped. Desire flared in his eyes as he joined her again.

They fell together in a tangle of arms and legs, urgency making them clumsy. Laughter filled the air, along with heated sighs and moans. He nudged her knees apart, and the scent of arousal drifted around them, rich and heady.

Gryffnn wasted no time. He lined up his shaft and pushed deep, stretching her in the perfect way. Kaya clutched his shoulders, moving with him. She kissed his neck, his jaw. Flicked out her tongue to taste the salt on his skin.

And as they pleasured each other, peace flooded her mind. A sense of rightness clicked into place. Every instinct inside her told her to cling to this man, this dragon with a huge heart.

Gryffnn surged into her and hit the perfect spot, driving her thoughts back to the present. She clung, aiming a kiss at his mouth. Although she missed, it didn't matter as bliss swirled through her like a rogue wave. She shattered, her fingernails digging into his broad shoulders. Secs later, Gryffnn roared out his enjoyment, the flash of heat generated between their bodies weird but not unpleasant.

When their hearts ceased their violent pounding, Gryffnn withdrew from her and rearranged her limp body in his arms.

"Kaya, I..."

Alarmed, she slapped her hand across his mouth to hold the words inside him. While she cared for him, she wasn't ready for declarations.

His eyes glowed above her hand, and his tongue flickered out to tease her palm.

It tickled, so she moved her hand out of range.

"I intended to say that I'm glad you changed your mind, and I appreciate the support you and Ry gave me during the meeting with Aideen. I almost lost it, and that would've been a mistake."

The corners of Gryffnn's eyes crinkled, and suspicion rose in her as she stared at him. The man had guessed her thoughts. They'd amused him. But it told her something else. Gryffnn understood her in ways no other man ever had.

"I'm glad Lys and Hallam are safe on Viros," she said before she confessed to something else.

"Me too," Gryffnn said. "If anything happens to me—"

She stopped his words with her hand. "They'll be safe. Always. The feline shifters are good people. Decent. They'll look after our children and Ransom too."

His eyes crinkled again. "You said *our* children. I might be wearing you down."

"What are you blathering about?" Kaya wiped the expression from her face but feared she fought a losing battle. Gryffnn had claimed a corner of her heart, and it terrified her.

"Shush. I don't mean to scare you. I'll wait as long as necessary. Go to sleep," he ordered. "I suspect tom-cycle will try us all."

Unsure of how to reply, Kaya closed her eyes and tried to relax. Gryffnn seemed to have the right words to confound her and keep her off balance.

Loud thumps on Gryffnn's chamber door woke her. She must've fallen asleep despite her busy mind.

Gryffnn bounded off the gel-bed and hurried to answer the summons. "Lights low." He ripped open the door. "What's wrong now?"

Kaya sat up and clutched the covers to hide her nudity. She didn't see who it was, but she heard the answer.

"Fire in the village. Storg has organized a crew to put it out."

Kaya stood and dressed rapidly. "Is Niran okay? His sons?"

"They raised the alarm," the man said.

"I'll be down shortly," Gryffnn replied.

Kaya handed him clothes. "A suspicious fire?"

"Not sure yet. We'll find out soon enough. At least Storg is on the job. We're used to quick action when it comes to fire."

"I guess it's a familiar hazard for dragons."

"Yep."

Kaya clattered down the stairs after Gryffnn. They met Ry and Sable at the bottom of the staircase. Niran and his two sons shimmered into sight.

"Niran. Thank the goddess you're all right," Gryffnn said.

"Our dwelling is not as healthy," Niran said drily. "The smoke woke us, and we shimmered to safety and raised the alarm. The fire spread fast. Suspiciously fast."

"So you think someone lit it?" Gryffnn asked.

"I'd suspect a fire since the visiting dragons seem intent on baiting you," Ry declared.

Kaya agreed.

"I'll prepare chambers for you here," Sable said.

Gryffnn nodded. "Please. You are welcome to stay with us. I don't want Aideen to see you, though, so please keep a low profile."

"You could go to Viros," Ry suggested. "Spend time with Leeam and Sheera. They'd love to see you."

"I refuse to let someone drive us from our home," Niran stated. "Besides, we might prove helpful to you."

Gryffnn scowled. "I don't understand why someone would light a fire in the village."

"You suspect the fire in the village was a diversion?" Kaya demanded.

Gryffnn reached for her hand and squeezed it. He didn't release it despite the interested glances from everyone present. "Let's say I'll feel better once I check on our compound buildings to set my mind at rest."

"We'll help," Ry said.

Kaya nodded.

"Thanks. Most of the guards will be fighting the fire. Please keep the windows screened. Aideen might seize the opportunity to do some spying."

Kaya exited the family dwelling with Gryffnn and Ry.

"I smell smoke," Ry said.

CHAPTER 14

A CUNNING, CLEVER PLAN

G ryffnn lifted his head and dragged in a huge draft of air. "That's not coming from the village."

He raced in the direction of the smoke. The building where they'd placed Caley's body. He should've guessed. At least Storg would've left a guard there. Pushing himself, he sprinted toward the burning building. Despite being made of stone, much of the framework was combustible, and if someone had doused Caley with flammable liquid or foam, she and the building interior would burn.

"*Phrull!*" Gryffnn flew forward, airborne, after tripping over something in the middle of the path.

"It's the guard," Kaya said. "Go. I'll take care of him."

Gryffnn picked himself up and raced toward the burning building. It was separate from the main buildings and used as a medical center. Their healer had died three rotations ago, and Mogens used the building to treat the Drake clan if any dragon required medical aid. They were mostly a healthy bunch, so Ransom hadn't recruited a replacement.

Gryffnn skidded to a halt in front of the medic building, his breaths rasping through his nostrils. *Frak it!* Scarlet and orange flames licked along the roof of the medical building, which told him they were too late. He edged closer, but the intense heat forced him back.

The fire had done its work, burning Caley's body and destroying any evidence that might point toward her murderer.

Shouts came from behind him, and the thunder of racing feet. Storg and his men. They swung into their practiced fire-fighting routine. Gryffnn pitched in to help. Ry joined them, working at his side. Soon the smoking remains presented no threat to other buildings.

"This was deliberate," Storg rumbled, frustration in his voice. "It proves someone poisoned Caley and wanted to hide the evidence."

"Aideen won't see it that way," Gryffnn said. *Phrull, could this situation become any worse?*

Kaya aided a wobbly guard to their sides, her arm around his waist to keep him upright.

"I'm sorry," he said, apology etched into his cheeks. Lifeforce trickled from a wound on the dragon's head, and his face was paler than natural in a hot-blooded dragon. "Someone hit me from behind."

"You didn't see them?" Storg demanded.

"Not their normal face. Whoever it was screened their face with a mask," the guard said. "I glimpsed a black face and cat whiskers before they hit me."

"Huh, cat whiskers," Ry said. "It looks like I'm meant to be the fall guy."

"Fall guy?" Gryffnn asked, figuring it was one of the strange words Ry and his crew had gathered during their travels.

"Aideen is trying to blame Ry," Kaya explained.

"Did you get the tests done?" Gryffnn asked Storg.

"Yes, but all the samples we took burned along with Caley." Storg scowled, his heavy brows edging closer together. "This has Aideen's touch all over it."

Gryffnn's summation too. He scanned the area and noted a few of Aideen's people, but they appeared curious and concerned rather than guilty. "Keep alert. Pass the word—if any of Aideen's people attack them in words or physically, they're to back away. Aideen is pushing for a reason to attack. Call me if you have any further problems."

Storg nodded and set about dispersing orders to his team.

"I don't like this," Ry commented as he and Kaya accompanied Gryffnn back to the family quarters.

"Me neither," Gryffnn said. "I'm prickling as if I have a target on my back."

Gryffnn slept fitfully during the marks to whitelight. His mind churned, his thoughts darting hither and thither. He arrived at no conclusions apart from one fact.

Aideen lay at the root of his troubles.

She was busy controlling his actions from behind the scenes, leaving him in the vulnerable position of having to react and put out dragon fires. He mightn't know for certain, but he could make an intelligent guess as to the reasons. She wanted to take over the Drake clan and its resources, and with the number of her people available, she had a fair chance of success.

Their modern ships worried him. A notion occurred, and he nudged Kaya awake.

"What is it?" she murmured, sounding more asleep than awake. "Wanna sleep."

"It's time for me to tilt the odds in our favor," he said, nudging her again. "Fancy a clandestine jaunt?"

Kaya yawned and rubbed her eyes. "It's blacklight. If that's your best flirtatious line, then it's no wonder you're still single."

Gryffnn grinned and slid from the gel-bed. "You're the only one I'd ever try that line with. I'll wake Ry."

Kaya sat up with a groan. "Why are you waking Ry?"

"We're going to check out the Gwilym ships again."

"Oh. Maybe you should ask Niran and his sons if they'd help. They must be pissed at their home burning to the ground."

Not a bad idea. If Aideen succeeded in her coup, they'd have to choose whether to relocate or work with the Gwilym clan. "Meet me at the base of the stairs."

Gryffnn slid from his chamber and set about rousting his guests.

Niran didn't hesitate. "I want to help, even though I take your point about the danger. I hate that I had to send my people away for their safety."

"Aideen is responsible for the secret mine in the mountains and the traps we've discovered," Gryffnn said. "The evidence is pointing that way, but I need certainty before I can act. It's what Ransom would do."

Niran patted Gryffnn's shoulder, his fingertips cool against Gryffnn's higher body temperature. "Ransom will be proud of you when he sees how well you've looked after your clan."

"Thank you." The praise meant a lot when it seemed as if, in most cycles, he was running after his tail.

"We're helping," one of Niran's sons declared. "Our friend died in one of those traps. Painfully."

Gryffnn nodded, understanding their need for revenge. "Just take care. I suspect things are about to get real ugly at whitelight."

Ry and Kaya clomped down the stairs to join them.

"What's the plan?" Kaya asked.

"We'll remove the stolen stones to our warehouse. Also, I want to check out the technology on the ships, the weapon capacity. If possible, I want to disarm the weapons because if Aideen leaves and fires on us, we won't be able to defend ourselves," Gryffnn said.

"She'll have guards on her ships," Ry said.

"Yes." Gryffnn quashed his conscience. "I figure she knocked out my guard, and I can do the same to her security force."

Kaya fluttered her lashes. "I like a man with a plan."

Ry grinned. "It's what I'd do. It seems only fair."

"We'd better leave at intervals to avoid detection. Ah, here's Storg. I asked him to join our excursion," Gryffnn said.

Ry and Niran set off first, then Niran's sons with Storg.

Gryffnn used the wait time before he and Kaya left to further his plan to keep Kaya. "Do you want children?"

Kaya cocked her head, her dark blue brows rising halfway to her hairline. "Children aren't something I've ever considered. Although my race values offspring, their methods of ensuring the race continues and adding variety to the gene pool put me off the idea. Seeing Ry and Jannike and now Nanu find their mates..." She shook herself. "I don't know. I must decide about Lys."

"Are you still worried about breaking her?"

"*Phrull*, yes. I'm lucky that Camryn was willing to take Lys with her."

"I miss Hallam. When Caley and I got together, I was young. The sex part was enjoyable—on my side at least." His grimace held irony. "The first time I saw him, he was so tiny. He curled his little fingers around my thumb, and he laughed. I fell in love with him. The rotations have gone so quickly. Now, he's flying and learning to control his fire. It's time for us to leave." Gryffnn placed a hand at her hip, subtly herding her toward the exit.

They kept to the shadows, and although part of him expected to spot Aideen's people, he sighted no one until they reached the rendezvous point at the spaceport.

"We've seen three different guards, but their paths seem regular,"

Ry said.

"They don't expect trouble." Gryffnn pressed his lips together, irritated anew at the Dalcon dragon's arrogance. "Let's have some fun. We'll take them out one at a time. Each team can have a turn. Disable rather than kill. I wish to question them later. We'll stash our prisoners in our private quarters."

"My sons and I can transport them one at a time for the short distance," Niran volunteered.

Ry and Niran captured the first guard, taking the young dragon by surprise when Niran popped up in front of him. Ry stalked him from behind and slapped his hand over the dragon's mouth to contain his unmanly *eep* before he hit him hard enough to knock him out.

A short time later, they had all three dragon guards bound and unconscious but still breathing.

"Aideen posted younger, more inexperienced guards," Kaya commented.

"Her arrogance will be her downfall," Ry said. "Gryffnn, Storg, can you sense the resonance from the stones on the ship?"

"No. These youngsters had no problem. Do you think it's the ships' design or something else?"

"We'll have a better idea soon," Ry answered. "They have the stones packed in boxes. Kaya and I opened a few and shut them again."

Gryffnn nodded and glanced at each member of his small team. "Do we know which parts to remove to render the ships unusable?"

"Kaya and I will take care of that," Ry said.

"What if we steal the entire ship? The one with the precious stones onboard?" Kaya asked. "It will be easier than physically shifting the boxes, and we'll get a better idea of the ship's capabilities."

Gryffnn grinned at the audacious plan, admiring the devious

mind that had produced it. Sexy and intelligent. "I like it. Let's load the three dragon guards and take them, plus the ship, to the other side of the planet where Ellard has set up camp. Ry, Kaya, can you get the ship started?"

Kaya beamed. "We'll give it a try."

"Gryffnn, you and Storg had better approach carefully in case the resonance from the stones is too much for you." Ry picked up a dragon and arranged him over his shoulders. "Let's do this."

Life on Narenda ran smoothly, or at least after Ransom took over the leadership role. They trained, made their jewelry, and sold it at huge profits, amassing an impressive dragon hoard of wealth. Gryffnn hauled one of the captured dragons over his shoulder and followed Ry. Recently, adventure and purpose filled his cycles, leaving him more alive and fulfilled than he'd been in rotations. Their seclusion from other planets may have added mystique, but it had made their cycles monotonous. If he felt this way, other dragons would too. Something to consider and report back to Ransom.

The spaceport was a huge open area with bays or gates where visiting ships parked. Since they regulated visits to their planet, it wasn't necessary to man the spaceport during the blacklight.

Ry's and Gryffnn's boots echoed in the cavernous space. Due to the clandestine nature of their task, they didn't turn on illumination but used their shifter traits to guide them through the darkness. A hand tucked into the waistband of his trews. *Kaya*. He recognized her scent. Satisfaction filled him as he smelled a layer of dragon on her now. Any dragon shifter would take note and the possessive side of his nature thrilled to this fact.

Gryffnn and the others followed Ry.

"It's this one." Ry bypassed the bays containing the first five ships and stopped at the sixth. "The ships are sealed, but Kaya has a knack with locks. We got inside easily last time."

"I require a little light to do my magic," Kaya murmured.

Niran approached, his charcoal gray robes rustling with each step. "Let me have the honor," he murmured.

An instant later, a small lamp glowed in his hand, highlighting the mischievous expression on his usually placid face. Gryffnn realized then the Incorporeal people also needed a purpose, and he made a mental note to speak with Niran later about changing the way they did things, or at least discussing change with their people.

"Hold the lamp near the lock," Kaya instructed. She pulled a small pouch of tools from a pocket and extracted several.

She bit her bottom lip and muttered as she plied her tools. Despite the passing time and the danger of discovery, Gryffnn enjoyed seeing this part of her. Competent. Brave. Determined.

His warrior.

He heard a faint click, Kaya slid her hand into the innards of the control and secs later, the main door slid open.

"I'll stay out here and keep watch," Storg said. "Give me a shout when you're ready to take off."

"I can shut the door after us," Kaya said. "You don't need to keep watch. If anyone comes, they'll wonder about the missing guards, but hopefully by that time, we'll have absconded with their ship."

"Oh," Storg said, and the sound held bemusement.

Gryffnn hid his glee as he placed his captive on the floor of the main cabin. His head of the guard wasn't used to females telling him what to do. A crusty bachelor, Storg spent his days ordering around his men.

"Everyone take a seat and buckle in," Kaya ordered and winked at her captain. "Ry and I need to concentrate."

On the bridge, Ry and Kaya scanned the instruments.

"Anything look familiar to you?" Ry asked in a low voice.

"No, but we have a secret weapon. I figure we can comm Nanu and show him the controls."

"They should be almost ready to leave Viros, if they haven't left already," Ry said.

"Well, we need to do something. I thought it would be easy to steal their ship, but I've seen nothing with this tech." Kaya commed Nanu and switched to visual.

"What?" a grumpy voice demanded.

Kaya's eyes widened at how his hair tendrils swayed around his head. Then, she took in his naked chest. "Sorry, did I interrupt something?"

"Yes," Nanu said. "My sexy dream about Jazen."

"Sorry," Kaya said. "We have a problem. We're on a ship and want to steal it, but the controls aren't familiar. Ry and I need you to talk us through takeoff—at least until we can familiarize ourselves with the controls."

"Show me," Nanu ordered.

Kaya pointed her comm at the various instrument panels.

"Why are you stealing a ship? No, wait. I'm sure you have a good reason," Nanu murmured, his tone a little absent. "There don't seem to be controls. Maybe it's voice-activated?"

"Coded to a certain pilot?" Ry asked.

"That wouldn't make sense. I'm sure there is a safety control so the ship won't fly for anyone. It might be as simple as whoever sits in the pilot seat controls the ship."

"Which one is the pilot's seat?" Kaya asked.

Ry shrugged. "Let's both try and see what happens. *Controls on.*"

Kaya ran through the launch sequence they used on the *Indy*. Nanu always made sure his passengers strapped in for safety. Aideen didn't care about her people. She used them. She hadn't had a problem murdering her sister.

"Commencing launch sequence," Kaya said.

Lights sprang to life on the control console.

"Whoa," Nanu said. "I can't wait to check out these ships. See you soon."

"You are not the usual pilot," a masculine voice boomed.

Startled, Kaya glanced around the bridge. Ry shrugged, so she went with instinct. "Trainee pilot, Kaya."

"Another one." The masculine voice sounded disapproving.

"I am ready to learn," Kaya said. "What is your name?"

There was a pause. "No one has asked me that before. My name is Solon. It means wise one."

Kaya and Ry exchanged another speaking glance.

"Solon, my orders are to take off under blacklight conditions and to fly over the mountain range." She remembered Ransom and added, "At a high altitude before landing on the far side. What procedures should I undertake?"

"Flick the two buttons beneath the armrests on your chair." Solon sounded bored.

Kaya fumbled for the buttons and discovered two raised nubs. She pushed both at the same time.

"Take off procedures initiated," Solon said. "Should I follow my last flight path?"

"Yes, please," Kaya agreed. She held her breath while the ship rumbled to life.

"Would you like me to give you verbal control for future flights?"

"Is this common?" Kaya asked. It was a little weird discussing procedure with the ship.

"Normally, I bond with one pilot. My previous pilots have died," Solon said.

"How do you know this?" Kaya asked.

"I ask. Where is my previous pilot?"

"I am the trainee pilot. No one has informed me of a death. My boss ordered me to learn to fly this ship." Kaya held her breath, hoping that the intelligent ship wouldn't boot her out of the driver's seat.

"Two pilots," the ship said. "I could choose my favorite."

Kaya gulped. "Can we take off, please?"

"State your order," Solon boomed.

"Ready for takeoff," Kaya snapped out. She could do firm and assertive.

The ship's thrusters powered up.

"I love this new technology," Nanu said and envy sounded in his voice. "Is the ship as quiet as it seems?"

"Yes. We're flying to meet Ellard," Ry said. "I'm unsure whether we'll unload and return the ship or stay with Ellard. We're winging it at present. You'll be able to check out the ships when you arrive. Aideen has several."

"I can't wait. You'll be fine now that Kaya has control," Nanu said. "See you soon."

"Lift off," Kaya said, continuing to go with whatever seemed logical.

"You are better than the other pilots," Solon stated. "You give precise orders. Your body temperature is reading normal. You're not sweating on my seats."

"Ah, thank you," Kaya said. It was the lack of information—or consequences—that had her calm. She didn't know enough to fear the outcome of this flight.

The ship rose vertically until it cleared the spaceport.

"Set course to destination," Kaya ordered.

Ry leaned closer. "At least if the ship's computer follows the last route, we'll have conclusive proof of theft."

Once the flight path leveled out, Ry unfastened his harness. "I'll give Gryffnn an update."

Kaya turned her attention to the vista outside the spacecraft. The moons offered little illumination, making the ship's computer necessary for navigation. "Can you show me the view outside even though it is blacklight?"

"Panoramic scene coming up on screen," Solon informed her.

The view on the screen bore a greenish light, but it was enough to see the training fields, the jungle beyond and the jut of the distant mountain range.

"Where were you designed?"

"On the planet Dalcon," Solon said.

"How many troops can you hold?"

"Each ship can carry one hundred medium-sized beings," Solon replied.

"Great job," Gryffnn said as he dropped onto the copilot's chair.

"Do you have an accurate count of Aideen's people?" Kaya asked.

"Two hundred and ten," Gryffnn answered promptly. "A big enough complement to worry me since most are males. They're young, though. Have you noticed that? Aideen is one of the oldest amongst the group."

"We're getting closer to the mountain range. Any hint of resonance? I can take the ship up higher."

"No, nothing," Gryffnn said. "I should, right? Whenever I need to go to our reserve of stones, that affects me. I'm always glad to leave the warehouse."

"Solon, what materials is the ship made of?" Kaya asked.

Gryffnn jumped when Solon boomed out an answer, one too technical for Kaya to understand. "The ship talks," he whispered to her.

"It does. If Aideen has six ships of this caliber, why is she waiting to attack? Why would she plan for Caley to pick up your relationship or throw herself at you?"

"If Jacinta is right, and this is their entire population, perhaps she wanted to keep her people alive. She can trust her people, while if she took control of Narenda, she'd have to destroy our infrastructure and face losing some of her dragons. Perhaps she went for easy first."

"If she thought you'd be a pushover, she's wrong," Kaya said. "You're strong and decisive and firm with your orders. People from your clan approve of you as much as Ransom."

"Do you think so?"

"I do." Kaya glanced at the screen that showed their progress. "We're directly over the mountains now. Any hint of resonating?"

"No." Gryffnn stood. "I intend to explore the rest of the ship. Holler if you need anything."

"Will do." Kaya turned her attention back to the view. "Ah," she muttered. "That's the area they mined." She glanced at the velocity gauge, blinking when she noted their speed. These ships were sleek and modern and fast.

How had Aideen acquired not only one but six of the ships?

Perhaps she'd ask.

"Solon, how long has your owner had you?"

"Twenty mins," Solon said.

"Huh?"

A thin rod thrust out from the instrument panel. The end glowed a deep red. Kaya screamed and struggled with her harness.

"Cease!" she shrieked.

The rod kept coming, and Kaya tried to ward it off with her arm.

"Perfect," Solon said as the hot rod made contact.

Ry and Gryffnn charged onto the bridge as she screamed again, the smell of burning flesh accompanying the searing pain on her arm. To her relief, the rod retreated, and she scrambled out of the pilot's seat, her breathing coming in harsh pants.

"What the frag just happened?" Ry demanded.

"I have no idea!" Kaya studied the throbbing mark on her arm. It was a brand. "Property of Solon?" she demanded. "Really?"

Gryffnn growled, his red scales in evidence, while Ry had his blaster out.

"At last," Solon said, and the ship sounded gleeful. "I have a bonded pilot."

"What does that mean?" Gryffnn snarled.

"Explain," Kaya snapped, surveying the brand on her forearm.

Maybe she could have it removed.

"We are intelligent ships. Each of us bonds with our pilots."

"You mean I grow and attach to you?" Kaya asked, horror slithering through her veins.

"No. It means only you can fly me now," Solon said. "I will not perform for another pilot."

"Why did you choose Kaya?" Ry asked. "You have flown with other pilots."

"She asked me my name," Solon said. "She flies with sensitivity and admits her lack of flying knowledge. Every other pilot has tried to dominate me. With Kaya, we were one."

Cautiously, she fingered the brand. "Thanks, I think."

Gryffnn calmed and grasped her arm. "Let me see," he whispered. "It's pretty. The brand could pass for decoration at first glance with the delicate scrolls, and it matches your skin."

The indigo blue of the brand was a shade darker than her skin. Thankfully, the throbbing had subsided a fraction. "Will it stop hurting?"

"Soon," Solon promised. "The brand is not intended to incapacitate you. You will now have voice control over my entrance door. You will not need to use your pointy instruments next time."

"Um, okay," Kaya said, biting her lip to stem her laugh.

Ry scowled, his brow crinkling as if in deep thought. "What happens if I purchase a ship of this type and the ship refuses to bond with me?"

"We're meant to bond, but some of us didn't. A programming fault they couldn't fix," Solon said cheerfully. "Instead of losing their investment, our makers sold us off cheap."

"Ah," Gryffnn said. "That solves that mystery."

Kaya shook her head and grinned. Solon sounded giddy with excitement.

"I have told the other ships I have found my one," Solon said.

"None of them are bonded either?" Ry asked, exchanging looks with Gryffnn and her.

"No," Solon replied. "Arrival at destination in ten mins."

"I didn't suffer from the power of the mountain range," Gryffnn said.

"We are constructed of a material impervious to most pollutants," Solon declared.

"Do you know much about the woman who purchased you?" Gryffnn asked.

"She is a bitch," Solon said.

Kaya chuckled. "You're not wrong there."

"Kaya, my pilot, should I start normal landing procedures?"

"Yes, please, Solon. Everyone strap in for landing." Kaya eyed the pilot's chair with caution. "Do you have more surprises for me?"

"No, Kaya, my pilot," he crooned. "We shall fly beautiful missions together."

CHAPTER 15

AIDEEN DECLARES WAR

Kaya landed the ship without issue and powered down. Although it was still blacklight, she could see the mined area and the gentle slopes leading down to the dry creek bed, thanks to Solon.

"What now?" Gryffnn asked, his mind racing with the possibilities. If they could get the other ships to bond with his men, they'd cut off Aideen's ability to steal from them. And if she thought to attack from the air with machines, they'd stop that before she acted. Of course, then he'd cut off her transport options, which might prove problematic. "I wonder if it's safe for me and Storg to exit the ship?"

"I have standard-issue hazmat suits," Solon said helpfully. "They are in the locker on the storage deck."

"Thank you, Solon," Kaya said. "We will not stay here for long.

We're unloading the cargo and returning to the town."

"Very good, my pilot."

"I don't like the possessive note he uses when he says *my pilot*," Gryffnn whispered, moving closer to ensure private conversation.

"It is creepy." She swept her tongue over the rim of his ear, and a shudder went through him. "My lover."

Gryffnn huffed out a laugh at her sly humor. This unpredictable woman worked deeper into his heart with each passing cycle. The urge to mate with her fully was a siren whisper in his ear, but he had no right to his impulse. Phrull, he had no clue if she'd survive his dragon fire, which made his longings screwed up. What kind of man was he to risk the woman he loved? Yeah, loved. Now that he'd admitted it to himself, he needed to front up and tell Kaya.

As soon as he'd sent Aideen packing.

He'd explain the dragon fire concept to her, tell her the risks and the rewards... He held her closer and stole the kiss he craved, even with their audience.

"My pilot," Solon said, and his tone emerged steely. "Is this male hurting you? Should I evict him without a hazmat suit?"

"No, my ship," she said smoothly. "Gryffnn is my mate."

Gryffnn tensed and drew away from Kaya while Ry's eyes widened. This could go very wrong if Kaya didn't handle the ship with care. *Phrull*, the ship rivaled Kaya for attitude. They'd make a formidable pair.

"Ah, if you are set on keeping him, then I will endeavor to get along with him."

Gryffnn relaxed a fraction while Kaya winked at him. "This is not funny," he murmured. "We shall discuss this later."

"Kaya, my pilot. Do not forget to take my owner's bracelet. It pairs with your brand and will enable us to communicate while we are apart."

A compartment Gryffnn hadn't noticed opened, and a shiny silver bracelet nestled inside. Kaya glanced at him and Ry, silently asking their advice. Ry shrugged and finally, Kaya reached for the bracelet and slid it onto her right wrist.

"Testing. Testing," Solon said cheerfully. "Ah, perfect. Please remove it when you are exchanging happy fluids with your mate. I do not wish to hear that."

Ry's eyes widened further, and he slapped his hand over his mouth. His broad shoulders shook as he made a rapid exit.

"Yes, my ship," Kaya said in a choked voice.

It was wrong—weird—to experience jealousy toward a ship. Kaya had confirmed she was his mate in front of others, and he intended to hold her to that. He had to remember the ship wasn't truly alive. Biting back his growl, he whirled and stomped to the cargo level. "With me, Storg," he barked.

His head guard fell into step with him. "Is something wrong?"

"No." Yes. He was jealous of a ship. "We can't leave the three dragons here. Without hazmat suits, the resonance will present a problem. We'll have to take them back with us. Also, I need volunteers, dragons who wish to become pilots. Can you suggest any?"

"Pilots? Our dragons prefer to fly and enjoy the wind against their scales. I am the same way. I never enjoy riding in a ship. It's our dragon nature," Storg said. "Crap, can you hear the singing of the stones? I couldn't hear a thing until we landed, but now my head is ringing."

Gryffnn's head was buzzing unpleasantly. "Yes, we should hurry."

They clomped down a narrow metallic staircase and entered a huge space. Boxes filled the far end of the cavernous deck. The boxes of stones. Strangely, he didn't experience the pull from them, which he should, given the number.

He studied the boxes closely, the hard sides made from a material he'd never seen before. He scanned the rest of the space. "Ah, this must be the locker Solon mentioned." He pulled it open and saw half a dozen silver suits hanging from a rail. He handed one to Storg and donned another.

"Amazing," Storg said. "The suits cut the singing from the rocks."

"But we're silver blobs. Ry mentioned seeing beings in silver. Obviously, Aideen's people wearing hazmat suits." His mind returned to the ships. "Perhaps I will consult with Niran and Ry. Five ships are sitting at the spaceport. The ships are intelligent and bond with their pilots. They haven't bonded with any of Aideen's people." Gryffnn explained about Kaya and the ship that had chosen her as his permanent pilot.

"That is creepy," Storg said, his voice deeper because of the suit.

"Tell me about it," Gryffnn agreed in an undertone.

They walked to the cargo exit and glanced out. Kaya, Ry, and several other men busily shifted the boxes of cargo off the ship. Niran and his two sons were busy helping too. He and Storg pitched in, and soon, they had one hundred and twenty boxes offloaded.

"They stand out," Ellard said, scanning the boxes once they'd finished. "I'll get my men to blend them with the surroundings."

"Thank you." Gryffnn had met the big feline shifter several times and trusted him. "I appreciate the help you're giving us."

"It's good training for my men," Ellard said.

"Kaya, my pilot. Your prisoners are awakening."

"Whoa," Ellard said, gaping at Kaya. "That's the ship?"

"Yes," Kaya said, frowning at the bracelet that blinked like a warning light. "Thank you, Solon. Please tell them we will be there soon and not to panic."

"The first thing I'd do on hearing the ship speak to me is panic," Ry said.

"Exactly," Kaya said with a gamine grin. "Aren't I mean?"

"They might know of the ship's capabilities," Gryffnn said.

"Our purchaser is not aware of our full capabilities," Solon's voice boomed from Kaya's arm. "We thought it wise to wait and learn."

Solon was quick enough to bond with Kaya. *His mate.*

Gryffnn grimaced, once again aware of the incongruity of envying a ship. The sooner he learned if Kaya wanted to accept, *could* accept his dragon fire, the better because the he-beast in him wanted Kaya, and he didn't intend to share.

The first signs of whitelight were surging over the horizon when they landed back at the spaceport near the compound.

"What will you do with the prisoners?" Kaya asked.

Gryffnn had considered that. "They're young. Now that I've learned the truth of Aideen's clan lands, I will offer them a place with us. If they accept, we'll watch them and attempt to integrate them with our flight."

"And if they object?" Ry asked.

"I'll send them on their way with Aideen."

"Are you going to speak with her now?" Kaya asked.

"I'd intended to, but I'm curious about what she'll do when she discovers her men missing and the stones have vanished." Gryffnn yawned. "I think I'll retire to my chamber for a rest."

Kaya yawned too. "An excellent plan, except Solon won't let anyone onboard without my permission. Aideen won't know the stones have gone missing. I'm beat."

Gryffnn grinned and leaned closer to nuzzle her neck. "We can rest together."

"*Eew!*" Solon screeched.

Ry's eyes widened—he seemed to be stuck on that reaction—and he slapped his hand over his mouth. Gryffnn could see the mirth dancing in his friend's eyes.

"How long until we reach base, Solon?" Kaya asked. Her voice held a gurgle of amusement, but Gryffnn failed to see the humor.

"Twenty mins at top speed," Solon informed them.

They arrived at the spaceport twenty mins later.

"Camryn and Nanu are back," Ry said on spying the *Indy*.

"Is that your ship?" Solon asked. "She is a big monster."

Ry did that wide-eye thing again, and Gryffnn wasn't sure how to react to Solon's lustful tone.

"Ry and I and our friends all own a share," Kaya said.

"Will you introduce me?"

"The *Indy* isn't an intelligent ship," Kaya said.

"A pity," Solon replied. "I do admire her lines."

"I...um...Camryn," Ry said, unfastening his harness. He almost sprinted off the bridge.

"Should I let him out, my pilot?" Solon asked.

"Yes, please," Kaya said. "Can I place my bracelet on privacy mode?"

"That might be wise," Solon said after a pause.

"Kaya, could you arrange for Solon to allow Aideen entry if she wishes to get aboard?" Gryffnn asked. It wouldn't matter if Aideen discovered the missing stones. She'd stolen them from him and his people in the first place, so she could hardly complain when he stole them back.

"Kaya, my pilot. Is that your wish?" Solon asked.

"It is," she said. "Thank you for your help this cycle, Solon. We appreciate it."

Solon made a harmonious humming sound. "You are welcome."

By the time Gryffnn had spoken to Niran and his sons and told them about the ships, dealt with the three prisoners, and secreted them away, whitelight had fully arrived. The early morn heat beaded sweat on his forehead, and fatigue settled over him. Despite that, satisfaction filled him at all they'd achieved and learned. He strode over to the *Indy*, where Kaya, Ry, Nanu, and Camryn were in discussion.

Camryn grinned at him. "Ry told us about the ship that has designs on Kaya."

"Is your bracelet switched off?" Gryffnn asked.

"Yes," Kaya said.

"I can still hear you," Solon trilled. "You're in the spaceport."

A broad grin danced across Nanu's face. "I can't wait to tell Jazen."

"What do you want us to do this cycle?" Ry asked. "Watch Aideen and her people, of course. Anything else?"

"Rest. I intend to before I face Aideen. Take Camryn to the pool and enjoy your cycle. Storg's men will watch Aideen and report back on any problems," Gryffnn said. "We'll see you later. I want to check on the people living in the village before we return to the compound."

"Fine with me. Is Niran still staying in the family quarters?"

"Yes, until we rebuild for them. They wish to consult with their family before we proceed since they require a different floor plan now that there are more of them. Using their energy, they could manufacture a new building, but they do better if they have a permanent residence."

Gryffnn took Kay's arm and led her from the spaceport. They turned left toward the village. The burned buildings appeared worse in the whitelight.

Kaya stared at the charred remains of where Niran and his family used to live. "What if you rebuilt the entire block with shops in the front and perhaps another level above for family quarters? Make them lighter with large windows, and you could make a wide, covered verandah area so they might display their goods outside to entice shoppers inside, yet keep out of the bright whitelight."

"All good ideas. I'll tell Niran." His comm buzzed. "It's Jacinta."

"Gryffnn. We visited the Gwilym compound. It's been razed to the ground. Something bad happened. Anger and sorrow vibrated in the air," his sister said.

"The rumors are true then," Gryffnn said.

"It seems so," Jacinta agreed.

"Thank you for getting back to me."

"Is everything all right there?" Jacinta asked, worry in her tone.

"So far." Gryffnn grimaced. "Although the situation will go to hell when I speak with Aideen."

"Take care, brother. She is the sort to knife a body in the back while smiling to their face." Jacinta disconnected, and Gryffnn thrust his comm into a pocket. A blur of movement in the sky above grabbed his attention, and he frowned as three dragons arrowed toward them.

Even though they were far away, he recognized the copper dragon in the lead.

Aideen.

"If Aideen breathes fire, run as fast as you can," he ordered, his gut tensing with fear. Kaya didn't have the protection his scales afforded him. His attention remained on the dragons as he commed Storg. "Aideen is heading my way in dragon form. I require backup."

"Might be a problem. I walked into the middle of a full-scale battle."

"Kaya, speak with Storg." He tossed her his comm and rapidly stripped. He called up his dragon, the shift rushing through him. "Find out what happened." His voice emerged lower and garbled. Hopefully, she'd understand.

"Why didn't someone call us?" Kaya demanded.

"They blocked all communication," Storg said. "Gotta go."

Kaya contacted Ry. "There's trouble. Stay clear of the compound. Go back to the spaceport. I'll call Solon to let you onboard."

Ry hung up before she could say more. Niran and his sons materialized with Sable.

"What's happening?" Kaya asked tersely, her gaze on Gryffnn as he sat on his haunches and prepared to take off.

"From what I can make out, Aideen made a surprise attack before whitelight," Niran said.

"She issued a challenge," Sable said, her blue eyes full of fear. "Oh, Kaya. I'm so sorry."

"What are you talking about?"

"She's challenging you for Gryffnn's hand. As Gryffnn's mate you have to accept. It's an ancient law. If you don't... If you don't, your life will be forfeit and Aideen has the right to claim Gryffnn as her mate."

Gryffnn roared at Sable's words, his fury ringing out for all to hear.

In the sky above, Aideen let out a triumphant shrill.

Kaya used her bracelet to buzz Solon. "I need you to let my friends on board. Anyone who Ry approves of. You have met him. Please follow his orders until I tell you otherwise."

"Yes, my pilot."

"Niran, I need my sword. It's in Gryffnn's chamber underneath the gel-bed. Would you get it for me?"

Her mother had given her this sword and blessed it under the goddess's gaze. Her mother had told her the blade had been forged in magic, and to believe in its magic when she needed it most.

Niran disappeared and reappeared a short time later, her sword in hand.

Kaya accepted it from him, her gaze on the approaching dragon. "Tell Ry to guard Lys," she said. "Take Sable and your sons to the new ship. Ry and the others should have arrived by now."

"Kaya," Sable whispered. "You can't do this. Aideen will kill you."

"I refuse to let Aideen take Gryffnn. She'd make his life hell. Your clan would suffer too." She more than liked the dragon and wanted to keep him as her own. She—the perennial good-time girl—wanted to make a family with Gryffnn, Hallam and Lys. The thoughts that had drifted through her mind at odd times, crystallized into full-blown plans.

Their future.

"Go," she said to Sable.

When the young dragon hesitated, Kaya gave her a swift hug. "Go to Ry. He'll keep you safe."

Once Niran disappeared with Sable, Kaya turned to Gryffnn.

His red scales glowed, and his dragon eyes radiated fury. She strode to him, approaching him head on. Massive in his dragon form, he stood on four tree trunk legs while his long red tail lashed back and forth in agitation.

She stopped in front of him. "Gryffnn."

He roared, the heat from his breath unpleasantly hot.

"Gryffnn, listen." She stood on tiptoes to place her hand on his huge beating heart. "I have a plan."

CHAPTER 16

A FIGHT TO THE DEATH

A plan?

Gryffnn wanted to roar to the heavens. *Phrull*, nothing about this situation would work to a plan. Aideen wanted a place in the Drake clan, and the only position she'd accept was leader. He'd never in a million rotations expected her to reach for an old law to win.

It wasn't ethical.

Yet it was sneakily brilliant since if he stepped away from this challenge, he'd lose everything. Ransom and their people would lose everything, and he'd lose his love, Kaya...

Fear rippled through him, clutched at his mind, and squeezed his heart painfully hard. How could Kaya win against Aideen, given the obstacles in her way?

Aideen held every advantage.

Heartsick, he watched Aideen and her two guards land. No, not guards. Escorts. They carried the ceremonial pouches on their backs, which would hold the ritual silks to make the challenge official. Aideen was following the correct protocol and adhering to the ancient law. One escort from her clan and one from his.

Aideen stood her ground, her victorious, toothy dragon smile showing she thought she'd won. She might well be right. A sour taste filled his mouth as he slapped on an impassive expression. Too late to seize Kaya and flee to safety. Besides, he couldn't leave his clan at Aideen's mercy. His instinct to wring Aideen's neck and unleash his dragon on her arse tore him deep in the gut and ripped at his chest. A snarl escaped him, and Aideen's smile widened further to reveal the jagged points of her teeth.

The two escorts shifted, dressed in the red-and-black silks, and after a brief consultation and a word for Aideen, approached Gryffnn and Kaya.

"Gryffnn, pay attention," Kaya snapped, battering her fists against his chest. His heart turned over in despair. Even using her full strength, her fists merely tickled him. How could she hope to best Aideen?

Full of anguish and unsure what to do for the best, he lowered his head and rubbed against his love. She seized his head in determined hands and hurriedly whispered her plan into his ear.

"Gryffnn Drake," Aideen's man said. "Aideen Gwilym hereby offers a challenge for your hand. I have consulted with the spokesman from your tribe, and he agrees the challenge is legitimate."

Gryffnn bit off a pithy curse and lifted his head to scan both dragon shifters. His clan man tugged the hem of his silks and cleared his throat. Regret shone in his slanted eyes, along with determination.

"The challenge has been issued according to our ancient law," his man said. "All is in order. You have declared Kaya Ignatius your mate before your clan and the Gwilym clan. Aideen Gwilym wishes to dispute the mating and offer herself in exchange. Do you accept the change of mate?"

"No," Gryffnn roared.

"No, he does not," Kaya declared.

"Very well," Aideen's man said with a trace of glee. "I shall inform Aideen of your acceptance of her challenge. You have ten mins to prepare. Your representative will remind you of the rules of engagement." He retreated to join Aideen.

Gryffnn glowered at the she-dragon, battling his instinct to throttle her. If—*when* Aideen injured Kaya—she would pay. He didn't care about rules and ancient law. Kaya was the mate of his heart, and if she died, he'd grab his revenge and walk into the light to join his love.

"I'm sorry, Gryffnn," his clan man said. "Aideen attacked at the onset of whitelight. We held our own, and when she saw our strength was enough to repel her forces, she issued this challenge, citing the murder of her sister as the reason for invoking the ancient law. I consulted our law books, and she is in the right. If you hadn't publicly claimed Kaya, you could fight Aideen."

Sable appeared from behind a bush, carrying a bright red suit of the exact color of his scales.

Ah, protective armor. An excellent idea, but he didn't think it would safeguard Kaya. Her plan... His head slumped, the heaviness in his heart dragging him down, mind and body. He didn't see a way to beat Aideen.

"Give her a little dragon fire," Sable ordered. "It will make Kaya stronger and less vulnerable to Aideen's fire.

What? No! What if his fire killed her? Kaya wasn't a dragon. He decided to live with Kaya as his mate without worrying about the last stage. He trusted Kaya implicitly. She'd never betray him, and they could have a good life together, raising their children and making a family. Once Ransom recovered, he'd had more options, and he and Kaya could travel.

"Gryffnn." Sable marched up to him and shook her fist at him. She struck him much harder than Kaya, her half-dragon heritage giving her strength.

"Gryffnn," Kaya snapped. "Stop imagining the worst. It's puncturing my ego and making me nervous. If your dragon fire will strengthen me, we need to try. *Now*." Her puny fists thumped his scales again.

His skin rippled, and he inched away before he laughed. He'd never suspected he was ticklish in his dragon form. *Gryffnn. Control yourself.* He shook his head when a voice that sounded awfully like Ransom's echoed through his mind.

"It might kill you," he protested, his voice emerging in a low, rough growl.

"Aideen intends to do her best to kill me anyway," Kaya said drily.

"Do it," Sable ordered.

"If Aideen kills you..." Gryffnn couldn't bear to finish the thought.

But Kaya pushed, her chin lifting in challenge. "If Aideen kills me, what?"

"I'll follow you to the afterworld."

"*No, you will not.* You will discover a way to best Aideen and send her scaly butt running, then you will raise our children. But I will try hard not to fail. I find I am very attached to you." She planted her hands on her hips. "*Give me the dragon fire now*."

"Change into the fire-retardant suit first," Sable said. "Hurry, time is ticking."

Kaya yanked off her boots and stripped to her underwear.

His favorite red ones. Heat built in his chest, along with lust and a wave of love. It was then he decided to risk giving Kaya his dragon fire. His lover was so brave. A true warrior.

SHELLEY MUNRO

He'd give her a taste of his fire. If Kaya's plan had even a chance of working, Sable was correct. They needed the edge the dragon fire would give them.

"Time is up," one of the escorts called.

Kaya thrust her arms into the form-fitting red suit and wriggled her hips to get the tight fabric to sit correctly. She twitched at the fire-retardant material, then thrust her feet into her boots.

Fully dressed, she stomped over to him. "Fire me, baby."

He blinked, impressed by her courage, her attitude, her fearlessness. Then he scanned her blue, blue eyes and noted she wasn't as confident as she projected. Good. It wouldn't do to fall into arrogance. Aideen was a formidable opponent.

"One kiss," he rumbled.

Kaya's knees knocked together before she firmed them to hold her weight. *Attitude was everything*. She recalled her mother saying that when she'd been a mere youngster learning to wield a sword.

She strode to Gryffnn with barely a hitch in her step, cupped his big head and stared into his slanted dragon eyes.

Gryffnn took a deep breath before nuzzling her mouth. Guilt—she saw it in his eyes. A hint of indecision. But this was bigger than her. Bigger than both of them. If Aideen continued unchecked, the entire Drake clan would suffer.

"It's time," she whispered and pressed her mouth to his much bigger one. She smelled smoke and amber.

"Don't do this, my pilot," Solon shrilled from her bracelet.

But she didn't hesitate. She opened her mouth and waited without having a single idea of what taking dragon fire might mean to her.

Gryffnn breathed out, the heat of his breath searing her mouth and throat. Her brain demanded she pull away, but she disregarded the act of self-preservation and clung, trusting that Gryffnn wouldn't hurt her. Heat built in her chest, harsh and painful. Her

180

lungs labored, wisps of smoke curling from where their mouths joined. Her closed eyes streamed, tears running down her cheeks.

Secs later, he pulled away, and she staggered, still struggling with the heat that writhed through her limbs, threatening to burn her from the inside out. Her knees buckled, and she dropped to the ground. Harsh pants. Sounds of distress escaped her blistered mouth. Groaning, she wrapped her arms around her body and curled into a ball.

It hurt.

She hurt.

Heat. So much heat. It blistered her throat, her lips, her chest. Even her stomach.

Goddess, what had she done?

"Time's up," the Gwilym escort yelled. "If you don't come out now, Aideen will win by forfeit."

Kaya attempted a tiny breath. When that eased the pain knotting her muscles, she took another. She had to stand. No alternative. She pushed to her hands and knees and moaned as her lungs labored. It was raining, and the wetness made hissing sounds when it connected with her skin. Coolness flowed from the point of contact, easing the searing and debilitating heat.

"Kaya. Kaya!"

She sucked in a third, deeper breath and levered open her eyes.

"Kaya."

Someone was calling her name, the sound so wretched and full of despair, her heart ached. She pushed upright and staggered a fraction before gaining her balance. Gryffnn stood over her, his big red head bowed, tears streaming down his face and dropping to the ground and striking her skin. She ran her fingers over his scales and collected his tears with a shaky hand. She transferred them to her burning face and sighed at the blessed relief.

A roar came, and instinct had her smoothing Gryffnn's tears over her arms. Her sword. *"Where is my sword?"*

"Kaya?"

"Gryffnn? What is happening? Why can I hear you?"

"The dragon fire worked. Goddess, it worked." Jubilation and excitement filled his voice, and he straightened from his slump. *"I didn't think it would. I thought I'd killed you."*

"Your sword," Sable said, presenting it to Kaya.

"Are you all right, my mate?"

"Unsteady on my feet," she replied as she attempted a step.

A second roar—a definite challenge—reverberated through the air.

"Quick. Climb on my back. Are you sure this plan will work?"

"No," Kaya said, her legs shaking with every step. She didn't think she'd remain upright, let alone climb and gain her balance enough to wield her sword. But she had to try.

"Oh, you intend to use Gryffnn to meet Aideen on equal terms. Excellent plan. Let me help you." Sable darted forward and used her strength to shove Kaya upward. Kaya straddled Gryffnn's broad back, just behind his wings, and clung when he shrilled and lifted into the air. Kaya panicked at first, slipping and sliding until she clasped his tough body with her thighs.

"Can she do that?" Aideen roared.

Kaya gripped Gryffnn, only loosening her hold when her hand tingled. She watched the two escorts confer and concentrated on staying upright.

"As long as Gryffnn doesn't use his claws or fire, she can use his power of flight," the escort from the Gwilym clan shouted.

"Hang on to my wing joints," Gryffnn instructed.

"Fly straight and level. I need my hands to hack at her with my sword."

"It will bounce off her scales. Dragon scales are strong and durable."

Aideen had taken off before them and now, she dive-bombed them at a frantic speed, front legs extended, claws protracted with glittering menace.

"*Get as close as you can while avoiding her claws. I need to hack her soft underbelly.*" Somehow, she needed to fight off the lethargy caused by Gryffnn's fire and regain her usual energy. Yeah, an easy assignment. *Right.*

Aideen bellowed. Fire shot from her great, gaping maw. Panic roared through Kaya as flames flashed in her direction. She leaned right, and Gryffnn flapped his wings, darting in the same direction. The abrupt course change surprised her, and only her fierce, panicked grip stopped her from toppling off Gryffnn's back.

Still, the flames raced across her left-hand side before Gryffnn guided them out of the path. Kaya let out an almighty shriek as if she were in pain. It was only half pretense.

"*Are you all right? Kaya.*" Gryffnn's anxious inquiry blasted through her mind.

"*Not so loud. The suit protected me. Quick, turn back and fly under her. It's a blind spot. She won't see us straightaway. She thinks she hurt me. The dragon shifter is arrogant, and that will be her downfall.*"

Gryffnn turned and arrowed upward with a speed that took Kaya by surprise. She yelped, clutched at his wing joint and hung on for life. The air rushed through her hair, tangling it into a mess. Her eyes streamed from the lingering result of the dragon fire and the speed at which Gryffnn zapped through the sky.

"*Concentrate, Kaya. You can do this.*" She swiped the back of her hand across her eyes, gripped her sword tighter, and waited for an opportunity.

Aideen, in full flight, was a magnificent sight. Her copper scales glittered as did her teeth and claws. Kaya swallowed. Fear gripped her. Her heart beat faster. Her mouth dried. She wanted to look away from the dragon hurtling toward them. A dragon who wished her dead.

Gryffnn flew at Aideen. At the last sec, he ducked her extended talons and flew beneath her.

The opportunity Kaya was waiting for. She thrust with her sword. Her arm jerked, then it felt as if it might wrench from the socket. *Her sword.* Gritting her teeth, she clung to the hilt and used her entire body weight to yank it free. It came with a *whoosh*. Rain showered her and struck her upturned face. No, not rain. Black blood.

She wrinkled her nose at the sooty stench then Gryffnn beat his wings, and they glided away.

Aideen roared, her wings beating strongly, her grimace scary as she stared at Kaya.

Kaya gulped at the death-promise in Aideen's eyes. Now she'd poked the dragon—literally.

Aideen turned her big body so fast that Kaya blinked. Her heart banged against her ribs, panic rippling down her spine. Aideen let out another roar and charged. Goddess, her speed. She came at them, talons extended. Gryffnn waited until the last sec before ducking out of the way. His big body tilted at an angle that challenged Kaya's balance. *Phrull it.* She was an encumbrance. How had she ever thought she could best Aideen?

Aideen breathed fire, and it hit both her and Gryffnn. Her eyes watered. Heat blistered across her face and the smell of burning hair filled her nostrils.

"Remember that dragons have limited fire and must recuperate. The more often she fires flames at us, the weaker this skill will become."

Fine for Gryffnn to say. Kaya's left side throbbed, and her face had a bad case of what Camryn called sunburn.

"All right. Let's do this. I want to harry her and hack at her with my blade. Try to keep level because I need to stand. Don't worry about me falling off, but if I do, make sure you catch me because I will come back and haunt you. I'll scare away every woman who dares to look at you. If I die because you drop me, you will live to regret it!"

"Yes, my love."

"I mean it."

"Aideen is preparing to attack again."

"Bring it," Kaya muttered. With unsteady hands and legs, she forced herself to stand. Ah, if she hooked a foot under Gryffnn's wing joint, that might aid her balance. For an instant, she took her eyes off Aideen to position her foot. She spread her feet and forced herself to face Aideen's charge, her eyes wide open and her shoulders straight.

Kaya thrust her sword, but it glanced off Aideen's scales. This time, she didn't throw fire. Kaya hacked blindly with her sword again and got Aideen's tail. Her blade sliced out a hunk of flesh, and Aideen roared. Black blood splattered Kaya, obscuring her vision. She swiped the blood away with a quick hand.

Gryffnn banked with speed, and Kaya wobbled, losing her balance. She struck hard with her knees, Gryffnn's scales like coarse gravel. A curse escaped, and her heart battered against her ribs as she absorbed the pain. Aideen screeched, and gasping, Kaya scrambled to her feet.

Aideen flew at them, her copper wings a blur. Her mouth opened, and the roar she unleashed came from deep in her belly. Flames followed, searing and hot. Gryffnn dodged, and Kaya toppled off his back. Aideen screamed triumph and swooped toward Kaya's falling body.

Goddess, she was going to die.

Aideen came at her with talons outstretched.

Kaya flailed, forced herself not to think about falling, and presented her blade. This time, her aim was true. She thrust her sword into Aideen's breast, right between her front legs.

Kaya grabbed for Aideen's claws, and her free-fall halted. Her arms wrenched, pain rippling through her shoulders. Kaya grunted. Her breaths sawed in and out. Her sword.

Regather your blade.

With gritted teeth, she swung her legs up and pushed all her weight on the sword. It moved a fraction. Aideen's roar of pain deafened Kaya. Her ears rang, but she doggedly wrapped her hands around the hilt of her sword and used her full weight to inflict harm.

A gurgle came from Aideen.

"Kaya!"

Kaya turned her head. Gryffnn hovered at a safe distance.

Aideen let out a roar and unleashed fire. The spurt of flames was weaker than the earlier ones, but it still burned Kaya's hair and face. Aideen's own belly scorched with the heat, and grimly, Kaya yanked on her sword. It started to come free from Aideen's chest with a horrid sucking sound.

With an almighty groan, Aideen dropped like a stone. The wind whistled through Kaya's hair as she, too, fell. The ground looked way too close.

"Jump, Kaya. I'll catch you."

Kaya leaped before she second guessed herself, trusting Gryffnn to catch her. She glanced downward. The trees grew closer. She made out Sable. Ry, Camryn, and Nanu looked up at her with horror. Goddess, she might die this time.

Aideen hit the ground and didn't move. Kaya closed her eyes, the wind frisking her face and making her eyes water.

"Kaya."

Her eyes popped open. Gryffnn plucked her from free fall just as she reached the level of the tallest trees. He squeezed her tight, and it hurt, but her panicked breath evened out, and she sent a prayer of thanks to the Goddess for granting her the boon of life.

"Kaya, are you all right?"

"I want to land. I want to stand on the ground."

"Yes, my mate."

Gryffnn landed near his sister and Kaya's friends. He set her down, and Kaya wobbled, her hand trembling so much she dropped her blade.

"Kaya!" Nanu shouted, sprinting toward her.

Camryn ran, carrying a first aid box, while Ry and Nanu brandished weapons.

Aideen's escort and the one from Gryffnn's clan raced toward Aideen. The dragon woman wasn't moving.

The escorts consulted, and the Drake one walked toward them. "Aideen is dead. You have won the challenge."

"Kaya, your hair. Your face." Camryn's hands fluttered upward, stilled, and settled back at her sides. Her wide eyes held concern.

"Nanu," Kaya croaked. She didn't care about her appearance. She was alive, and that was all that mattered.

"Yes?"

"Flying on a dragon didn't live up to my expectations. I don't want to do it again."

"Kaya." Gryffnn lurched to a halt in front of her, now in his humanoid form. He gently traced his finger over her hot cheek.

Kaya forced a smile and loosened her death grip on her blade. "Did that just happen?"

"You don't wish to fly with me?" Gryffnn asked.

"That was more excitement than I needed."

"Oh, Kaya. I forgot to tell you," Ry said. "A ship has landed carrying three women. They look as if they are of your race."

"Three women?" Kaya's hand wrapped around the hilt of the sword. "How did they clear security? Why are they here?"

"They must have applied for landing status," Gryffnn said. "If security passed their application. Is there a problem?"

"Are you Kaya Ignatius?" a voice boomed from behind her. "Queen Gleneese's daughter?"

Kaya bristled as she rotated to face the three warriors. She took in the three women at a glance. Definitely from Sitnam. Their pale blue skin glowed with health while their blue hair hung in shiny curtains to their shoulders. Each wore the traditional warrior uniform—tight trews and a form-fitting tunic. The fabric offered the wearer ease of movement while fighting.

"What do you want?" Kaya demanded, although, with a sinking heart, she guessed their purpose. They wished to remove her from the line of hereditary chain. Next, they'd go after Lys.

Phrull, Tayte. He'd told her no one would find her and implied she wouldn't need to deal with this crap.

The woman standing in the middle of the threesome sneered. "You're Queen Gleneese's daughter? I wouldn't have believed it. You have none of her beauty."

Because she'd just fought a freakin' dragon. "Yes, Gleneese was my mother," Kaya spat. "What of it?"

"I challenge you for the right to rule Sitnam."

"What is the point? I will never return to Sitnam," Kaya said, forcing her exhausted body to stay erect. This would not end well. "I have no interest in ruling our people."

"I can't take that risk," the woman said. "I challenge you for the right to rule." She pulled her sword from the scabbard at her hip.

Kaya sighed, her gaze on the sharp tip of the blade. Her fingers tightened and released on the hilt of her sword. She lifted her head to stare at the woman challenging her. Her jaw had set in determination.

"No, Kaya. You can't fight her now, my heart. You must rest and recover." Gryffnn sounded apprehensive.

He was right to worry.

"They don't care and won't play fair. If I turn my back now, they will try to kill me by other methods. Lys will never be safe and will spend her entire life running. Watch the other two warriors and make sure they don't interfere."

"I accept," Kaya said. "Let me have a word with my friends, then we shall begin."

Kaya strolled over to join her friends, forcing herself not to limp or show any hint of how badly Aideen had knocked her around.

Gryffnn hovered at her side.

"These women are from my home planet," she said. "Somehow, they have tracked me down and insist on challenging me. I am a risk to them because my mother used to rule on Sitnam. They think I wish to take her place. I don't, but only a challenge will settle this."

"Kaya, no," Camryn said. "You're injured."

"They don't care." Numbness seeped through Kaya, her limbs heavy weights, rooting her to the ground. "I have to do this. If anything happens to me, please keep Lys safe."

Sable nudged Gryffnn. "Give Kaya more dragon fire."

"No. She's too exhausted to take more of my fire."

"Just a little. Trust me on this, brother. Less than you gave her before. It will give her an edge."

"Gryffnn, if your fire will help me, then please. I need every advantage I can get," Kaya said.

Gryffnn nodded and stepped away. He shifted rapidly, and Kaya went to him. She pressed her forehead against his lowered head and breathed in his familiar smoky scent. The sooty fragrance of Aideen still filled her nostrils. Every muscle in her body throbbed and ached. How could she fight again without falling on her face?

"Okay, Kaya. Are you ready?"

"Yes, my mate."

"I love the sound of that. You truly want this? A future with me?"

"I do," Kaya said without hesitation. Gryffnn made her happy.

Gryffnn inhaled, and his eyes glowed. She steeled herself for pain as she waited. He huffed out his breath, and heat warmed her throat and down into her belly. Surprised, she clung to him, the fire not hurting as much this time.

Gryffnn parted their mouths and took a step back. *"Try not to die, please, Kaya."*

Kaya smiled and turned to face her challenger. She strode toward the trio and jerked her chin while forcing every ache in her body to the back of her mind. She could fake it with the best.

"Your sister warriors will stand over there with my friends," Kaya said in a decisive voice. "There will be no interference or stacking the odds in your favor."

The woman sniffed.

"You haven't even had the courtesy to introduce yourself," Kaya snapped. "You know who I am."

"I am Greerita, daughter of Manx."

Ah. That explained things. "Why isn't Manx issuing the challenge in person?"

"Our mother is sick. Her last wish is for me to take over as the ruler."

"Be my guest," Kaya said. "I don't wish to rule. My life is here with my mate and my friends. I have no intention of returning to Sitnam."

"I don't believe or trust you." Greerita sneered. "Not that any of our people would willingly follow you. You are ugly. Your hairstyle is weird. You look like a male."

Kaya's lips twisted, and even that hurt. She prayed she didn't fall on her face. Even now, her sword hand trembled. "Is that your worst shot?"

"I'm surprised you caught such a strong mate."

Tired of the insults, Kaya lifted her sword and charged. She got in the first blow, but Greerita blocked with expertise that told Kaya this wouldn't be an easy fight. Her best bet was to make this quick. She advanced, attacking with gritted teeth. Each blocked blow reverberated up her tired arms. She huffed out a breath, and the resulting curl of smoke distracted her.

What the phrull?

"Concentrate, Kaya!" Ry shouted when Greerita's blade whizzed past her left biceps.

Kaya fell into the routine she often trained with Ry or Nanu or Jannike before Jannike's pregnancy. She attacked, forcing her limbs to fall into the well-practiced steps. Thankfully, her body recalled each motion, and her limbs flowed into the attacking sequences. Greerita was talented with her sword but wasn't prepared for Kaya's frenzied attack. She blocked and blocked again. The clash vibrated up Kaya's arm. She gasped a breath and blew it out before going on the assault again. Heat collected in her belly, her mind set and determined on driving this usurper away.

"I don't care a frag about ruling on Sitnam," she shouted at Greerita. "You're stupid if you think I crave the power."

Greerita fought back, her blade spearing along Kaya's arm. The flame-retardant suit didn't pierce easily, and the blade caught this time. Kaya pushed Greerita off and huffed out a breath. A thin flame flew from Kaya's mouth and struck Greerita's face.

The woman let out a shriek and fell back, her shoulders heaving.

Kaya stumbled and caught herself, her chest heaving from the exertion. Aware of the other woman's uncertainty and shock at the flames—hell, Kaya had surprised herself—she was warier now, less confident of her abilities. Kaya attacked, using the last of her energy reserves. This time, she drew blood, the pale blue drops running down Greerita's arms. Kaya pushed close, and they parried, the blades hissing as they danced together.

"You will not win," Greerita sneered, her breathing harsh and uneven.

Kaya didn't let down or guard or bother to reply. She dragged in a breath and blew it out. Another thin arrow of flame flew from her mouth and struck Greerita's throat. Kaya slashed. She chopped. She thrust her blade into the wide opening left by her shocked opponent. Kaya's blade nicked Greerita's arm and drew more blood.

She fell, and Kaya thrust her sword at the woman's throat, holding it close enough to draw blood from the shallow wound, but not kill Greerita.

"Finish it," Greerita hissed, her blue eyes full of hatred.

"Did you kill my mother? Or did Manx?" Kaya demanded.

"Not me."

"Your friends?"

Greerita swallowed, and the blade moved with the minute motion. "My sisters, No, they didn't kill the ruler."

Kaya's shoulders rounded for an instant. "I do not wish to rule. I have a mate. A son. They need me." She didn't mention her baby sister since that would complicate the situation further. "On Sitnam, I'd have to kill them."

"You've grown...s-soft," Greerita sneered with bravado.

"Not that soft," Kaya said, keeping her tone even. "I beat your arse."

"You haven't t-thrust your blade home."

"No." Not as brave as she pretended. Kaya came to a quick decision. She shifted her blade and crouched beside the smart-mouthed woman. "Here's the deal. I let you and your sisters leave Narenda and never see you again. You go back to Sitnam and tell anyone who asks that you killed me, and your mother and your line are now the rulers."

"You say that now." Greerita pushed herself up to a sitting position. Her chest rose and fell rapidly as she recovered her breath. "How do I know that you'll keep your word?"

"My home is here with my mate and my son. I repeat, I have no interest in ruling a planet of women. I adore men and have no problems dealing with them on a cycle basis."

Greerita gasped. "You would belittle yourself by dealing with men."

"I told you I have a mate. I have male friends, and we work in partnership." Kaya thrust her face into Greerita's space. "For the last time. I. Do. Not. Want. To. Rule. It's all yours, sister."

Kaya pushed away from Greerita and took a calculated risk, turning her back on the woman and striding to Gryffnn, to Ry and her other friends. Every determined step sent agonizing waves of pain soaring through her limbs and up her back. Only pride and sheer guts kept her upright. Soon. Soon, she could retreat to their chamber, but until then she'd remain upright if it killed her. Appearances were everything. Something else her mother had taught her.

"Ry, can you escort them to their ship? Please make certain they understand that if I see them in this region of the solar system, I will shoot first and ask questions later. Make sure she and her sisters understand that I *will* keep my word." She sent the terrified and cowering women a disgusted glance and continued to speak to Ry. "Next time I see them, I'll kill each sister without hesitation."

Nanu stood beside Ry, his copper-colored hair tendrils hissing and swaying around his head. "I'll be the bad guy. I can scare them into keeping their word."

Gryffnn remained silent at Kaya's side, letting her say her piece. Her mate. It was still strange, yet the cold spot in the middle of her chest had disappeared, replaced by warmth and possibilities. A sense of rightness and completion. When he saw her sway, his muscular arm curled around her waist, and he stood as silent support while she issued orders.

"Steady, sweetheart. You're doing great. The women from your planet won't return. They look terrified."

"Good. I didn't want to fight them. I never wanted to rule and spoke the truth to them."

"Kaya, you need medical attention. Let me treat you back at the compound," Camryn said, her brow furrowed with concern.

"Thanks, but first, Gryffnn and I need to speak with Aideen's people."

"Kaya, sweetheart. I can do that. The two escorts will inform everyone of the challenge results." He traced his finger down her nose, a gentle caress.

"No, I'm your mate. We should do this together," Kaya said, wavering on her feet. Goddess, she hoped her body didn't defeat her will and determination.

Camryn planted her hands on her hips. "Fine, but I will stand at your side to make sure you don't fall flat on your face."

"My hero." Kaya made her eyelashes flutter, and even that hurt. She staggered when she tried to take a step, and Gryffnn steadied her.

"This is my fault," he said.

"It's not," Kaya snapped, her temper prodded by his stupid words and the throbbing pain in every muscle. "It's Aideen and the women from my planet. You have done nothing except try to protect your people. Your brother will be proud once he learns of all you have done and the challenges you have faced." She forced her legs to take another step and tripped, the effort to lift her booted feet too much.

"Kaya, I'm carrying you."

"No."

"Don't listen to her," Camryn said. "Stubbornness is one of her least attractive attributes."

Despite her argument, Gryffnn lifted her into his arms, and she groaned with relief when she no longer had to hold herself upright.

"Where are we going?" Camryn asked.

"Everyone will be at the training field," Gryffnn answered.

"You can put me down once we get there," Kaya said, her eyes closed. His scent and proximity relaxed her and allowed her to catalog her aches and pains. Hot skin—burns probably. Hair—singed. Bruises—many. Bones—sore. Breathing fire—she'd think about that later.

"Sweetheart, we're almost at the training grounds."

Loud shouts and chatter clued her in to this without Kaya needing to open her eyes. *"Put me down. I will walk."*

"Kaya—"

"Please, Gryffnn. I need to show my strength and stand at your side as your mate."

Chapter 17

Kaya Draws Respect

Pride spread through Gryffnn as he set Kaya on her feet. He continued to hold her arm, and she allowed this. It took long secs for her to take her first step, and the paleness of her blue face beneath the red-and-black burns inflicted by Aideen told of the toll this sheer stubbornness was taking. Admiration at her strength of mind and body filled him. His mate. He still couldn't believe she'd taken his fire and lived. No mate in their recent history had held bloodlines other than dragon.

He'd lusted after her ever since he'd first seen her, and that initial attraction had grown to liking and respect. Now, his heart filled with love and joy and humbleness because a strong woman such as she had accepted him.

Kaya tripped—only his quick intervention saving her from a face-plant. Camryn cast him a concerned look, and he sent her a nod in return. They'd make this quick.

Storg saw them coming and raced to meet them. The head of security paled when he saw Kaya, and Gryffnn understood the dragon's shock. Wiry tufts of blackened hair and a burned scalp were all that remained of Kay's pretty blue mane. Her right ear bore nasty burns, and her red suit appeared charred. Her flesh showed through holes in the fabric. She limped, her weight on his arm greater than earlier.

"My mate and I wish to make an announcement," Gryffnn said.

Storg—an older and experienced warrior—visibly swallowed his instinctive protest and nodded. He marched onto the middle of the field and bellowed. "Silence."

Heads craned and turned, measuring their progress as Gryffnn guided Kaya to the spot where Storg stood. Chatter and comments flew from dragon to dragon, but silence fell when he and Kaya reached Storg.

"I wish to present my mate, Kaya Ignatius," Gryffnn called. "This cycle, she accepted a challenge from Aideen Gwilym. The challenge officials will have informed you Kaya defeated Aideen. To Aideen's people, I offer you a deal. You may leave Narenda this cycle without persecution or prejudice. For those who have nowhere to go, I offer you sanctuary on Narenda, but first you must swear fealty to the Drake tribe and acknowledge my brother Ransom as your leader and myself and Kaya Ignatius as your temporary leaders. You have the rest of the cycle to decide your fate. Those who wish to stay, present yourself here at the training field this eve to make your pledge of loyalty. Those who wish to leave, assemble at the spaceport. I expect your departure by the end of this cycle. Do not return because my patience with the betrayal of your clan is at an end. An unauthorized return will not end well. For those of you with questions, present yourself at the compound in three marks. My staff will show you into the audience room to air your queries."

Gryffnn glanced at Kaya, his concern growing. Only her force of nature kept her upright. "*We shall leave now, my mate.*"

Loud shouts, cheers, and chatter broke out at the end of his announcement. Gryffnn didn't eavesdrop or try to discern which way Aideen's people would decide. He didn't care. All he wanted was to get Kaya to his chamber where they could treat her and give her something to make her sleep and begin the healing process.

Many men would quail at her appearance and worry about scars and her lack of hair. Not him. He looked at Kaya and saw bravery and courage greater than a battalion of soldiers. He saw strength of character, and although she kept her heart buried beneath layers of sass and attitude, her love for the people she cared for shone through. Even better, he was one of her favored.

His mate.

Despite himself, he smiled. "Show a Drake clan welcome for my mate," he shouted.

Cheers, whistles and stamping feet rang out. Lively applause.

Kaya wavered on her feet again, and Camryn shot him a concerned glance.

"Come, my mate. We shall leave my people to celebrate."

Kaya tripped again, and he ached to sweep her into his arms, but one glance at her set expression told him to wait until they left the training field. Sable joined them and flanked him. Storg fell in behind, and their tiny procession made their way off the field at Kaya's speed.

Gryffnn ached for her and wanted to rail at her stubbornness, yet he knew this show of strength would fuel the tales told around dinner and during celebrations for many rotations. In her wisdom, Kaya knew this too, which made her an excellent strategist. His clan would never see her as weak or decry her lack of dragon blood.

Finally, *finally*, they reached the outskirts of the field. Gryffnn snatched Kaya into his arms and strode toward the family quarters. Sable trotted after him while Camryn kept pace, opening gates and doors as they made their way to his chamber.

"I'll fill the bath with cool water," Camryn said. "You strip off her suit."

"I'll comm Mogens and consult with him regarding suitable treatment," Sable said.

The two women set about their tasks, leaving Kaya with Gryffnn. He set her on her feet and held her for a fraction longer until he was certain she'd remain upright.

"Where is my sword?" she murmured. "It is the only thing I have left of my mother."

"Nanu has your sword," he said. "But that is not true. You have your mother's heart and courage, and you have your sister who, if she grows up to half the woman you are, will be a formidable force."

"Lys and Hallam can come home now."

"They can," he agreed. "Ransom and Niran's people as well."

Gryffnn reached for the blade he carried whenever he entered the jungle. He slit the suit down the middle and peeled it from her skin.

"Not my underwear," she snapped.

Gryffnn smiled since this tiny burst of temper told him she'd recover. While she might wear the scars of her encounter with Aideen, they represented her courage and bravery. "I promise to leave your underwear intact."

The suit had helped deflect some of the damage from Aideen's fire, but her face, hair, and right side bore burns.

Kaya yawned as he removed her underwear. Once she was naked, he carried her to the bathroom. He placed her in the cool water, and Kaya sighed.

Someone knocked on his chamber door.

"I'll take care of Kaya," Camryn said.

Nodding, he answered the summons to find Ry, Nanu and Sable. He ushered them inside and closed the door.

"How is she?" Ry asked.

"She was snapping at me about her underwear while I cut off her suit," Gryffnn said.

"A good sign," Nanu said, his hair tendrils settling against his head on hearing this.

"Her face..." Gryffnn sighed. "And her hair. I don't know."

"I have spoken with Mogens, and he has advised me." Sable carried a bag of potions and salves. "Nanu, activate the float table for me, so I can set out everything. I have a salve for her face. A potion that Mogens said will soothe the burns inside from the dragon fire and her hair..." She pulled a face. "Mogens has no remedy for her hair. He needs to see the damage before he can recommend a course of treatment."

"Sable," Camryn called from the bathing room. "Do you have shears?"

Shears? Gryffnn hurried after Sable as she sped to Camryn and Kaya.

"What are you doing with shears?" he demanded.

"I will cut Kaya's hair to remove the damage."

"But she won't have any hair left," he blurted.

"Will you reject me now that I'm ugly and bald?"

"Never," he snapped. "You are not ugly to me. I don't wish to hear you repeat that ever again. You are my courageous, beautiful, big-hearted mate, and I stand at your side no matter what."

"You'd better. I refuse to suffer through recuperation only to see you canoodling with another woman." Kaya looked fierce, her stubborn chin lifting in pure attitude.

"I gave you my fire. You've always had my heart."

Sable squeaked and clapped her hands together. She broke out in a broad grin that sat well on her normally sober features. "You're mind-speaking. True mates. Oh, I can't wait to tell Jacinta and Ransom."

"Is that true?" Camryn asked.

"Yes," Kaya whispered, her voice hoarse.

"Shush, don't speak, sweetheart," Gryffnn said as he crouched beside the tub.

Camryn snipped Kaya's hair, and by the time she finished, Kaya had none left. "Lucky for you, your face is a nice shape."

"Your ears are cute." Gryffnn pushed the words past the blockage in his throat.

"Drink this. It will soothe your throat and stomach." Sable handed her a goblet full of a thick purple liquid.

Kaya reached for it and almost dropped it into the water.

"She needs a straw. A drinking tube," Camryn added. "How do your infants drink liquids?"

"Ah!" Sable said. "I shall retrieve something suitable from the kitchen."

Gryffnn took control of the goblet. "I'll hold it for you. Try to drink a little."

They let Kaya soak in the cool water then dried her carefully, treated her wounds, and placed her on the gel-bed to rest.

Gryffnn lingered and placed a kiss on her cheek as her eyes closed. In his big bed, she seemed tiny, yet this cycle, this warrior woman of his had slew a dragon for him and his clan. He'd not forget her act of selfless bravery nor the claim she had on his heart.

Unwillingly, he left her to sleep. Sable had promised she'd return to watch Kaya until he'd dealt with whatever shit came from Aideen's clan. At least with Aideen and Caley gone, he might have a chance with her people.

As he entered the communal dining room, silence fell. The dragon who had stood as Aideen's official rose and pressed his hands together as he bowed at Gryffnn.

"The dragons of the Gwilym clan have discussed your offer. We wish to offer our fealty and pledge to serve you."

"Will you betray me?" Gryffnn barked.

"No, sir," the man replied.

"Who murdered Caley Gwilym?"

The dragon hesitated and glanced at one of his peers. Finally, he turned back to Gryffnn. "I cannot say for sure, but I believe Aideen murdered her sister."

"Your clan stole from us," Gryffnn said in a harsh voice.

"It's true," the dragon replied. "But I know the location of the stolen stones. I can retrieve them for you."

"Fine," Gryffnn said. "My investigations show your clan has deserted your homelands. Rumor also says your wealth of precious stones is depleted—the reason you stole ours. Explain why I should trust you."

Once again, the dragon glanced at the members of his clan. An older dragon stepped away from the mass of dragons and joined them. Gryffnn recognized the dragon by sight but didn't recall his name.

"You're right," the dragon said. "You have no reason to trust us, but the truth is we have nowhere else to go. Aideen invested all our currency in the ships. Although Aideen was our leader, it was the tradition for the leader to take advice from the elders of the clan. We tried to tell Aideen she should take a different path, but she refused and listened to not one of our arguments. I, for one, intend to swear my allegiance to your clan and will work to gain your trust. You'll find our other clan members are of the same mind."

"I hope so," Gryffnn declared, not in the mood to sugarcoat his doubt. "I will see you in the smaller adjoining audience chamber. One at a time." Gryffnn strode away without a backward glance.

For the next three marks, he interviewed the Gwilym dragons. Each pledged their allegiance without hesitation. Gryffnn considered their talents, and he and Storg assigned them tasks to complete for the coming cycles. He split the Gwilym dragons between his own men.

"Storg, I'm heading back to check on Kaya. Contact me in the event of problems. Ry and Nanu have offered their aid should we require it. I expect it will take time for the new arrivals to assimilate with our people. There will be problems. I want to stomp on any niggles straightaway."

"Will do," Storg agreed.

Kaya was asleep when he reached his chamber. He stared at her, his heart twisting at her vulnerability and her sizzled hair.

"How is she?" he whispered.

"Mogens told me to give her a sleeping draft," Sable replied. "You rest. I've finished for this cycle. It's been a long one."

Sable gave him a quick hug before retreating. Gryffnn sighed when he scanned Kaya again. Then, he stripped and crawled into bed with her. Although he closed his eyes, his mind refused to let him rest. Kaya...he loved her so much, and this cycle, he'd almost lost her.

He tossed and turned and tossed once again.

"Gryffnn, I can't sleep with you fidgeting as if you have insects crawling over you," a hoarse voice croaked.

"Kaya?"

"Were you expecting someone else in your bed?"

"Never entered my mind," he said, rolling over to face her. "It's always been you."

A faint smile curved her lips. "What happens if my hair doesn't grow back?"

"We'll get you a kick-arse wig." Unable to help himself, he reached out and skimmed her mouth with his finger. "You can have any color you want."

"I've always wondered about pink. Can I hold your hand?"

Gryffnn's throat tightened, and his gaze blurred as he wove their fingers together. He cleared his throat, but the lump of emotion, his fierce love for her unmanned him.

Her mouth worked and not a sound came out. She tried again. "Are you sure about this? Us being mates? I know you said you wanted me, but as a mate. We're tied together now. I can sense the bond. We can't undo this, and I look...well, I haven't seen my face yet. After seeing Camryn's face when she cut my hair, I decided not to look."

"Why would I want to change our mating? You have provided our storytellers with rotations of tales. I'm nothing like Caley, Kaya. Look into your heart. You know this." It was understandable she had doubts. This...their mating had happened so fast and under pressure. He hadn't had the time to court her as he'd wished. "Don't ask me this again. No man enjoys his woman, his mate, doubting him."

"But I live on Viros. And I work with my friends."

"I'm hoping you'll live here with me. You must recover before you return to work. I need to make sure things run smoothly here on Narenda, but it won't be forever. Ransom will regain consciousness soon. Once Ransom takes over again, I'll be free to travel with you. If you, Ry and the others want me."

"You don't expect me to stay on Narenda?"

"I won't enjoy being apart from you, but you're my mate, not my prisoner. Do you think Ry would mind swinging the *Indy* via Narenda to pick you up? Or, you have your own ship now. It's not that far between Viros and Narenda."

Kaya's wide smile brightened his mood. "A fine plan. I admit, it worried me—the idea that now we were mates, you'd expect me to change."

"I relish your determination and sassiness, your smart-arse attitude. You challenge me to be my best."

"Nanu calls me a pain in his arse."

Gryffnn chuckled. "You can be. But I can deal with that personality quirk. Now go to sleep. You need to heal so I can make love to my mate."

"I'm not a patient person. My temper will become nasty."

"Are you trying to scare me away?"

"No. Yes. Maybe."

"Give it your best shot, sweetheart. Nothing you do will make me change my mind about you."

CHAPTER 18

THE AFTERMATH—LOVE AND HAPPINESS

W hen Kaya woke the next cycle, every muscle in her body throbbed. Her face smarted, and coldness prickled across her scalp. She turned her head and noted Gryffnn was awake and watching her. They still held hands and numbness from remaining in the same position had her groaning.

"Kaya." Gryffnn bolted upright. "What's wrong? Where does it hurt?"

"Everywhere, but my arm has gone to sleep." She rolled toward the edge of the gel-bed and gingerly stood. Her legs folded, and she hit the floor. *Ow!*

"*Kaya!*" Gryffnn scrambled around the edge of the gel-bed, his expression distraught. His hair stood up in funny tufts, and his eyes turned as round as one of Jazen's pies.

She wobbled out a smile, trying to reassure him when she

couldn't decide how to move to inflict the least amount of pain on her aching muscles.

"You're all right."

"I ache. Every part of me hurts, but I'm alive. I'll heal." She concentrated on lifting her arm to explore her decimated hair. "My head is cold. Help me up so I can see the damage."

Gryffnn scowled. "You need more rest."

"I need to see my face. No matter what you say, I intend to see my face."

Gryffnn's features blanked. "All right. Let me help you."

Kaya gritted her teeth as he lifted her to her feet. She crossed the chamber with tiny shuffles until she reached the looking glass. Foreboding built in her chest. A touch of fear. She held her breath and forced herself to study her reflection.

It was worse than she imagined.

Instead of her pale blue cheeks and jaw, the entire right side of her face was black and bright red. A deep indigo bruise covered her swollen left cheek. She sucked in a careful breath and struggled to hold back tears. Her beautiful hair.

Her throat worked in a swallow. "Do you think my hair will grow back?"

"We discussed this last eve." His fierce gaze locked with hers. "We will speak with Niran and ask him if he'll make you some kick-arse wigs. You said you wanted pink."

"Did I say that?" The earlier cycle had taken on a dreamlike quality, and if it weren't for her battered body, she'd never have believed what her mind told her.

"You did. Let me help you back to bed. I'll apply more of the healing salves. How is your throat? Does it still feel raw?"

"Yes."

Gryffnn kissed the tip of her nose and lifted her. In secs, she lay on the gel-bed. Her eyes closed as Gryffnn tended her, his touch gentle while the salve softened the sting on her flesh.

"I want you to take this sleeping potion," he said once he'd finished. "Mogens told Sable that you should sleep and rest for at least three cycles."

Kaya wanted to argue, but her eyelids kept drifting down, and soon, she gave up the struggle.

Gryffnn's heart ached. He loved this courageous woman so much, yet he didn't think she was ready to hear this truth. Although, their strong mating bonds must give her an idea as to the depth of his feelings. His relationship with Kaya bore no resemblance to his one with Caley. For Kaya, he'd lay down his life.

He donned the first garments to hand and left his chamber. He found everyone breaking their fast in the family dining room.

"How is Kaya?" Camryn asked. "I thought about coming to check, but I didn't want to wake her if she was sleeping."

"She's sore. I get the sense it's worse than she admits. Her lack of hair upset her, and she complained about a cold scalp. I applied the salves and gave her another sleeping draft."

"We have a solution for her cold head," Sable said. "Mogens suggested a different salve and a head wrap. We need to reapply the salve every three cycles."

Gryffnn nodded and sank onto a chair. "There is so much to organize."

"You've made an excellent start," Ry said. "Storg has assigned all of Aideen's dragons tasks, and he's given them new accommodations, so they're living with your own people."

"Yes, it might aid in their assimilation, and it will aid us security-wise since my people can watch them," Gryffnn said. "I'd like to bring Hallam and Lys home now that the danger is over. Niran's people... I'm not sure if they should return yet. I want to watch for problems first."

"I get the sense that most of the Gwilym clan welcome their change in circumstances," Ry said.

Nanu nodded. "I agree. I can fly back to Viros and pick up Hallam and Lys. It will give me a chance to check in with Jazen. I'll need someone to watch the two kids on the return journey."

Camryn exchanged a glance with Ry. "I'll go with Nanu. Our twins are probably running riot, and our nursemaids will threaten to leave if they're terrorized for too long."

Sable set a plate of food in front of him. "Eat, Gryffnn. You're worried about Kaya, but you must stay strong. The clan depends on you." She poured him a hot cacjuice. "Will you bring home Ransom too?"

"No, not yet. The security is better for him at the castle. It's too dangerous to have us both together right now." Gryffnn had struggled with this decision. In his comatose state, Ransom was vulnerable, and with things unsettled, he preferred to keep Ransom safe. Only family and their close friends knew of Ransom's location. Yes, it was better that way.

He took a bite of his meal and pushed it away, picking up his cacjuice instead. The bright purple liquid slid down, soothing his throat and the dryness of his mouth. "I must speak with Niran. Call if Kaya needs me."

"We'll leave for Viros this morn," Nanu said.

"Thanks," Gryffnn said.

"I'll help Storg." Ry stood, walking with Gryffnn from the dining room. "You're worried about Kaya."

Gryffnn didn't hide his concern. "Yes. She seems calm, but I thought she might cry when she saw her hair."

"You love her."

"I have for a long time. I wanted to court her, but as usual Aideen phrulled that up for me."

Ry clapped him over the back. "Kaya isn't an easy woman, but once she gives her loyalty she never falters. Things will work out for you."

Easy for Ry to say. He wasn't as invested as Gryffnn.

208

Twenty cycles later

"Ma. Ma. Ma!"

Kaya turned to scowl at Hallam. "Did you teach Lys to say that?"

Hallam's bottom lip quivered and his eyes twinkled, making him resemble his father. Her breath caught since her position of parent still amazed her, but the responsibility had become more natural.

"No, of course not, Kaya." He leaned closer with a conspiratorial grin. "You should blame Camryn and Jannike. Their twins call them Ma. Lys learned it from them."

Lys beamed at Kaya and clapped her hands together before springing at her and grabbing a handful of pink hair. Kaya's wig couldn't withstand the infant's strength, and with the next frantic tug, the hairpiece slid away from her scalp.

Hallam stared at her and mortified, she made a grab for the wig. Lys thought it was a game and issued a delighted chortle.

"Ma!"

"Your hair is growing back," Hallam said. "It's the same color as my scales. Not one blue, but many shades. You don't need your wig any longer."

"But it's ugly," Kaya snapped.

"My scales aren't ugly."

"I didn't say that," Kaya said hastily. While Hallam acted with maturity, he was still a youngster. "Are you sure it looks all right?"

"It matches the cobweb scar on your cheek. Your right ear has the same color variation. Kaya, It's beautiful." Hallam radiated sincerity, his cheeks turning a deep red when she gaped.

"Oh." Kaya didn't know what to say, but warmth filled her chest. She'd always enjoyed Hallam's company—his curiosity and eagerness to learn, and now she genuinely appreciated the dragon child.

Lys crawled closer and grabbed another handful of pink hair. This time, Kaya didn't fight her sister's eagerness. Instead, she grinned at Lys and winked at Hallam.

Hallam stared at her hair and cocked his head. "I'll ask Dad to cut my hair short so we match."

A wave of affection for him filled her chest, her throat and stole her breath.

"That is a fine idea. I need a haircut, too," Gryffnn said from the doorway. "How are you?"

Kaya wrinkled her nose. "I'm tired of lazing away the cycle."

"Excellent, because I have a plan. Hallam, will you look after Lys for three marks? Sable is here. She will help you."

"Lys." Hallam held out his arms to Lys. She cooed and dropped the pink wig, then let Hallam pick her up and carry her from the chamber.

Gryffnn strode across the space between them and crouched in front of Kaya. "I've arranged an outing."

Kaya lifted her hand to her hair. An instinctive response because—she admitted it—her lack of hair filled her with self-consciousness. Her skin prickled as if everyone was staring at her and judging her appearance lacking. The scar on her face attracted attention. She'd heard the other dragons whisper about her.

"Hallam is right. The new colors in your hair match your face and ear. Your hair is still short, but it is growing. You mightn't believe me or Hallam, but the truth is people will stare because your looks are striking."

"You're telling the truth."

"I never lie to you."

She cupped his solemn face, his intent and happiness radiating through their mate bond. "Where are we going?"

210

"It's a short flight to a private spot where no one will interrupt us."

"A flight. Uh, hell, no!" She scrambled backward as fast as a green scooting insect. "No flying. You are talking about dragon flying, right?"

"Of course."

"That's a big, fat no. I can fly Solon there."

"There is no landing area for Solon. Kaya, trust me."

She gulped, the idea of whizzing and swooping through the air filling her mind with memories. They flickered like a fast-running battle, bringing terror and pain. Her limbs ached as she shook her head.

"You're hurting my feelings," Gryffnn said. "You're implying I won't keep you safe. It's a short hop over the jungle. We'll swim at the pool and relax. I've been busy ensuring Aideen's clan settles while you heal. It's time to return to normal. If you don't leave the family rooms, I'll assume you're not ready to return to work with Ry."

Kaya's mouth dropped open. "But you said—"

"I didn't think you'd hide away."

Kaya snapped her teeth together. "Are you calling me a coward?"

Gryffnn didn't reply but offered her an even stare. It held a challenge. *A dare.*

She knew what he was doing and sensed he was trying to help even as his maneuvering annoyed her intensely. But he wasn't wrong. The one time she'd ventured into the communal dining area, everyone had stared, and whispers—catty gossip—had filled the hall. Something she'd dealt with before but it had hurt and made her self-conscious.

Eavesdroppers never hear good of themselves. She'd experienced her mother's wisdom with painful clarity. Hallam might speak favorably of her scarred cheek and ultra-short hair. The clan women pitied her and wondered how Gryffnn looked at her.

She swallowed as the overheard words pounded her brain, still as painful now as when she'd first heard the whispers.

Kaya lifted her chin. "No dropping."

"I shall hold you in my arms," he promised.

"Arms?"

"My talons," he explained. "Come. Let us go now." He scooped up the pink wig and handed it to her.

She stared at it for an instant, took it from him, and after an even longer pause, set the bright pink wig aside. "I'm ready. Let's go."

Gryffnn seized her and stole a kiss before he hustled her from the family common room.

The stares and the nosy interest struck Kaya as she and Gryffnn stepped outside and wandered to the training field.

"Why are we walking to the training field?" she whispered, uncomfortable at the scrutiny.

"I want to prove to them all that you are my mate in all ways."

She frowned at his words, not understanding his meaning.

"She is bald," a female dragon whispered. "So ugly."

The words carried since the dragon woman had spoken during an inconvenient hush.

Kaya didn't ignore the insult this time. She swiveled and prowled over to the dragon, fire blazing in her heart. Gryffnn was right. She needed to face this pettiness and stomp on it. She was a warrior, but she was behaving like a victim. The dragon woman stood a head higher than Kaya but took half a step back when Kaya confronted her.

"Gryffnn is my mate, and my hair doesn't bother him. Your opinion matters little."

Gryffnn stepped to her side and slipped an arm around her waist. "If I hear nasty words about my mate again, I'll let Kaya loose with her sword."

Storg, who had been instructing a group of young dragons on the finer points of flying, stepped up beside Kaya. "If it wasn't for Kaya, Aideen would be in charge of our clan. Don't you understand the close call we had? Because of Kaya, we're free to continue our lives in the usual manner. Apologize."

"It's all right." Kaya bared her teeth. "Anyone else who insults my hair or appearance will meet the pointy end of my sword. That is a promise. Gryffnn, shall we leave now?"

"Yes, I'm ready." He pressed a quick kiss to the top of her head and sauntered away to a clear space on the training field. He stripped and shifted to his dragon form.

His change occurred quickly, and his red scales soon shone in the whitelight, glittering as brightly as the jewels prized by the dragon shifters. In his dragon form, he towered over her, making her feel dainty. Like the other dragons she'd seen, he had stubby antlers and his eyes were more almond-shaped in his dragon form. His teeth were white, sharp weapons, while his black talons glittered as much as his scales. As she perused his folded wings, his long scarlet tail lashed from side to side.

"Are you ready, sweetheart?" His eyes gleamed in a challenge.

"Bring it." She lifted her chin and stalked toward him, his dare helping her gain her equilibrium and shove her fears aside.

But her legs still trembled as he scooped her up, his giant talons curving around her in a protective yet gentle hold.

He laughed, his dragon glee deep and throaty. Secs later, he lifted into the air, his giant red wings flapping. The wind rushed past her ears and made her eyes tear. Trepidation clawed at her chest, and she swallowed rapidly once, twice as they rose higher into the air.

"See? I promised to keep you safe."

"We haven't arrived yet."

Gryffnn chuckled at her tart reply. In truth, she did feel safer gripped in his talons, and she relaxed a fraction.

Soon, the training field, the clan compound, and the staring dragons became tiny, and she could see the jungles and the ridge of mountains in the distance.

"Where are you going, my pilot?" The wind tore at Solon's voice.

"She is spending free time with her mate," Gryffnn growled. "Do not interrupt. Kaya will speak with you tom-cycle."

"Kaya, my pilot?"

"I will attend to you tom-cycle," Kaya shouted.

"Is it wrong to be jealous of a ship?"

"He is worried about me. Solon fears losing his pilot when he's only just found me. I'll have a word with him. It will be easier once I put him to work."

Gryffnn continued to fly toward the jungle with its profusion of green trees, red vines and noisy birds that squawked in alarm when he skimmed over the canopy.

"I feel safer when you're holding me."

"I told you so."

Kaya grunted. Nobody enjoyed a smug smart-arse. Now more secure with her balance and welfare, she took in more of their surroundings. They followed the path of a silver river as it twisted and turned through the jungle. She glimpsed several grayish animals that squealed and tore into the protection of the trees.

"Do you hunt here?"

"We do, but not this cycle."

He swooped downward, surprising a squeak of alarm from her. While she knew he'd never willingly drop her, she recalled the terror of free-fall during her battle with Aideen. She bit her lip to halt a further girlish screech. She'd given Gryffnn enough entertainment this cycle.

"There's a clearing near the lake. We're landing there."

Kaya pushed out a shaky breath. She closed her eyes as they approached at what seemed a crazy speed. Then, an instant later, the rush of wind in her ears ceased.

"You can open your eyes now, sweetheart."

Laughter shaded his voice, and she pulled a face as she opened her eyes to see his naked form. "That was better than skidding and slipping on your back."

"That was the only way to fight Aideen. I'm surprised she stuck to the challenge and didn't injure us both."

Kaya rolled her eyes. "Now he tells me."

"You had enough to deal with. Come." He grasped her hand and tugged her to him. "I don't wish to discuss Aideen now. She is in our past."

"Aren't you going to get dressed?"

Gryffnn grinned at her tart tone. "We have total privacy. None of our clan will dare to interrupt us—not after I informed them I'd skewer them myself and then let you loose on them."

Kaya sniffed.

"We haven't made love since before the battle, Kaya. You're healed now, and I wanted to spend time alone with you without interruptions from our children or the rest of the clan. Things are more settled, and Sable can deal with Hallam and Lys. Storg will contact us should there be a major problem." He took her hand, as he often did, twining their fingers as he led her over to a shady spot.

The green tree bore long, droopy strands for leaves and cast shade on what was a hot cycle.

"Shut your eyes and don't peek," Gryffnn ordered. "I wish to prepare my surprise."

"You have a surprise?" That strange warmth filled her chest again. No one else had ever cared for her or spoiled her like Gryffnn did.

"Are you peeking?"

"No." She shut her eyes. Intriguing rustling caught her attention. "Can I look yet?"

"Not yet."

So she waited, the warmth spreading to fill her mind with contentment. She was happy. Her breath caught at the realization.

In the past, she'd grown bored and moved on, pleased that her job with Ry gave her a reason to leave. But she wanted to stay with Gryffnn and not solely because of the mating bond.

"You can look now."

She opened her eyes to find Gryffnn closer than she expected. His eyes glowed with tenderness, and enticed, she reached for him. His strong arms wrapped around her, their mouths met, and everything in her world solidified. He made her feel safe. Valued. She'd always thought giving her heart to a man was a show of weakness—the teachings of her people—but Gryffnn stood at her side.

Their lips parted, and he gave her another quick kiss and stepped back, clear satisfaction on his sexy features.

"Oh!" Kaya stared at the soft rug and the picnic he'd arranged beneath the tree. "Thank you. That's perfect." She'd needed this—a slice of special—to jolt her from her funk. The uncharacteristic self-doubt and moping.

"Should we swim first or eat?"

"Swim," she said.

"Last one in is a rotten egg."

She wrinkled her nose at him and sat to remove her boots.

"Should I help?"

"No. I can tell by your twinkle that your way of helping will include ripping and yanking. I refuse to fly back half-naked."

Chuckling, he walked to the edge of the silvery lake. She took a moment to ogle his muscular backside before removing the rest of her clothes. He ran the last two steps and jumped with a gleeful shout.

Kaya grinned at the enormous splash he made, a chortle escaping because he resembled his son. *Their* son. With a smile still on her face, she hustled to the water's edge, conscious of the web of scars on the right side of her torso.

"You have cobwebs on your body too."

She scrutinized Gryffnn's face, searching for a hint of distaste. She found none.

"Come and swim with me. The water is refreshing."

"That's code for cold."

"A little," he agreed. "But I'll keep you warm."

Her skin heated under his avid gaze, her breasts prickling to tight peaks. She inched into the water, sucked in a harsh breath at the chill, and plunged beneath the surface.

She popped up with a screech. "It's freezing."

Gryffnn was at her side in an instant, his arms coming around her as he drew her against his chest. His body heat seared her pebbled skin as he grinned down at her.

"You're beautiful, Kaya. Never try to hide your scars. Hallam was right when he said they're delicate cobwebs."

"How long were you eavesdropping?"

"A while," he said, his lips curling. "Ma."

"*Pffff!*"

He cut off her snort with his lips. Before, his kisses had held playfulness, but this time passion spilled over. Sensual intent. Her heart beat a little faster, awareness and need firing to life. The kiss went on and on until she trembled. He trembled. They broke apart, both breathing hard.

"Kaya," Gryffnn whispered, pressing his forehead to hers. "I've missed you."

"I'm sorry. I-I...after Aideen—"

"You have no need to apologize. You needed to heal, to deal with the aftermath of the battle. I wanted to give you that time because my clan owes you so much."

"Our clan."

Gryffnn stroked her cobweb cheek, affection shining in his dragon eyes. "Our clan," he agreed.

Without warning, he scooped her up and carried her from the water. He set her on her feet and sprawled out on the rug.

"Come and join me," he whispered, his voice husky.

He was enticing her again, and she couldn't resist him.

She ambled toward her mate without giving her limbs the order. She knelt beside him, and he smiled, his features full of approval. His arms came around her. Safety. Security. Love. His touch gave her all these things.

"I want to love you."

"Yes." Kaya kissed his jaw and leaned against his warmth. He took her mouth, and she wrapped her arms around his neck, clinging. Gryffnn hummed, then he licked her bottom lip and slipped his tongue past her parted mouth. The scent of smoke and amber filled her, and she gave in to the increasing urgency of his caress.

Hands stroked. Lips nuzzled. Tongues licked. Chests rubbed together.

"You're back," he murmured secs before he nibbled her neck.

She wriggled away from the ticklish sensation. "I've been here."

"In body. Not in mind or spirit."

She paused, her palm pressed above his beating heart. He was right. She'd checked out during her recovery. "I'm sorry."

"Unnecessary." He lowered his head to blow across one pouting nipple. They both watched the dark blue peak draw tight. "I'm glad you're here with me. I've missed my mate."

In a way, she'd punished him and herself. The battle with Aideen. The sword fight with the Sitnam woman. Everything had bombarded her, then there were her injuries. She admitted to a touch of vanity when it came to her looks. Men had always taken notice of her, even though she'd given up glancing back in return. No, she'd needed to get her head straight, needed to heal and she'd distanced herself to do this. No more, she promised herself. *No more.*

She moved down Gryffnn's body, her hand curling around his erect shaft. It was velvety soft, despite the tiny scales. Fascinating.

She licked the head and gloried in his groan. She got in one more lick and a sly suck before he forcibly lifted her away.

"I'm too close," he said, rolling so their positions were reversed. "I want this time to be for both of us."

Desire flared in her, eagerness and impatience. "Yes."

He nudged apart her thighs with his knee and loomed over her, sensual intent etched into his face. This time his kiss carried possessiveness, and instead of pissing her off, she enjoyed his silent statement of ownership. One hand branded her hip, then moved downward to skim her sex. Liquid arousal met his touch, and they both groaned.

"Now," Kaya said. "Please. Now."

"I don't want to hurt you. I wanted to go slow, to make love to you. To show you my feelings for you."

"You'd never hurt me." Conviction rang out in her voice. Her palm stroked his face, her throat tightening with love and hope and happiness. "I know how you feel about me. You show me every cycle. Please, I need you now."

For a short time, their gazes dueled, then he nodded.

She held her breath as he lined up his cock and pushed past her entrance, filling her in a seamless thrust. It was magical and perfect. She gripped his broad shoulders, her moan of pleasure loud enough to send a cautious bird skyward.

"More."

"I can tell I'll need to get used to your bossiness." Gryffnn stroked into her, his shaft stretching her in a decadent manner. In a silent demand for more, more, more, she lifted her hips and took him even deeper.

Gryffnn laughed. "Impatient much?"

"Yes."

"Excellent." He withdrew in slow increments, tormenting her and sealing her protest with his lips. One big hand teased a nipple, and her next breath was deep and unsteady, the arrow of heat stoking her hunger.

"I've missed you, Kaya." He pushed back inside her, his strokes faster now and driving her pleasure.

"I'm here now." Kaya clasped him tight and skimmed her hand down his back. The faint roughness of his scales thrilled her now that she'd become used to them. Her hand came to rest on his muscular buttocks as she strained upward to achieve the perfect angle.

Her orgasm struck without warning. Fast and deep, the pleasure reverberated through her, streaking to her toes and rippling across her upper body to frisk her breasts. Her flesh spasmed around his shaft, and Gryffnn thrust harder and faster, his strong strokes extending her orgasm.

One final stroke, and he stilled his roar of pleasure startling yet another bird. Kaya kissed his neck, his upper chest and sealed their mouths together while Gryffnn trembled in her arms.

His heart drummed against her breast as he kissed her back. When their kiss ended, he rubbed their cheeks together, smooching with her.

Finally, he parted their bodies and drew her into an embrace.

"Gryffnn," she murmured.

He lifted his head, his brows rising as he waited for her to continue.

"I love you," she blurted.

"I knew from the moment our mate bond snapped into place," he said with a trace of smugness. "I was waiting for you to realize."

"Aw, Gryffnn." She sighed. "I've never felt this way. So happy. Contented and satisfied with my path."

"You're an incredible woman, Kaya Ignatius. I've loved you for a long time. I've been waiting for you to catch up."

"Nanu says I'm hardheaded and stubborn."

Gryffnn's hand played across the scars on her torso, and she didn't even flinch. "He might be right, but you're my hardheaded and stubborn mate, and I never wish to change you."

"I know. You like me as I am. Do you know how rare that is?"

He tweaked her nose. "You're an easy woman to love. Will you return to work soon?"

"Is that all right with you?"

"Ry keeps the trips short, and matters here at the compound will keep me busy. I need to decide what to do about Ransom and if we should seek further treatment. Should I give our newest people more freedom? I must decide if they're trustworthy enough to work with our precious stones."

"Mogens said Ransom seems to be regaining weight."

"Yes, but he's still unconscious and resonating on some cycles."

Knowing of Gryffnn's concern for his older brother, Kaya changed the subject. "I have a suggestion about the jewels. Why don't you issue each dragon with a stone and hold a contest to design a piece of jewelry? Allow them to create whatever they want. That will showcase their skill and their desire to work. Offer a prize. You could allow the youngsters to design as well. I've heard Hallam mention designs. He complains that he'll croak if he has to make another practice pendant."

Gryffnn huffed out a laugh. "Sounds like our son. I like your idea. It will allow each dragon to use their imagination and possibly benefit us in the future."

She beamed at him. "Are you intending to feed me?"

"Yes, and Nanu gave me a celebration bottle. He called it bubbles."

Kaya's brows rose. "Nanu parted with his last bottle of champagne?"

"He suggested I woo you before you ran away from the best thing that has ever happened to you."

"Hah! You two had quite the conversation before the *Indy* left."

"Nanu is your best friend. I asked his advice."

"Did it help?"

"You're here with me." His smile held smugness. "We love each other."

"That's true." Her stomach gave an ominous grumble as she considered his words. Warmth and emotion spread through her, a sense of peace and rightness. Companionship. Definitely love.

Gryffnn chuckled and opened the basket. He pulled out a pie and cut two generous slices. "Meat pie. Sable got the recipe from Jazen." He set out two plates and placed the pie on them. Next, he produced the champagne and two decorated goblets. "I'll let you open the bottle," he said, handing it to her.

Kaya did so and poured the champagne. "A toast."

Gryffnn cocked his head and accepted his goblet, curling his long fingers around the vessel.

"To you, my mate." Kaya lifted her goblet. "*I love you.*"

"*About time.*" His eyes glowed, and his dragon peeked at her from Gryffnn's slanted eyes. "I promise to love you and our children. I will honor you and care for you in sickness and in health. You are the mate of my heart, and with you at my side, I am the luckiest dragon on Narenda."

Heat rushed to her cheeks, his sincere words tugging at her heartstrings. "Hey," she whispered as he raised his goblet in salute. "I wanted to do the speech."

"You wouldn't be here with me if you'd decided we didn't suit."

"Once you asked me to pretend to be your mate, I started to think of you as more. After the dragon fire exchange, everything clicked into place."

"But these last cycles, you've been so distant."

"I'm sorry," Kaya said. "I told you. I needed to get my head straight."

"You're worth waiting for, sweetheart. Never doubt that." His eyes held the same contentment that filled her heart.

"So are you," she whispered.

They lazed away the cycle, eating, drinking, taking another swim and loving each other.

"This must be what my mother felt for my father. I mean, she went against tradition and didn't kill him after breeding," Kaya said. "She must have loved him."

Gryffnn sat up and frowned at her. "Don't kill me. I won't appreciate it."

Kaya chuckled. "I take after my mother. Part of why I refuse to return to Sitnam is that I'd need to follow tradition. I dislike the waste of life." She shuddered. "I and everyone else thought my mother had killed Tayte's father and my father. Tayte knew, and I'm a little irritated about that skullduggery."

"When things calm down here and with your brother, we could visit him. I've only traveled to Dalcon, and after hearing of your adventures, I'd enjoy seeing more outside Narenda."

"I've never spent much time on Slyvia. That's an excellent idea. I wonder if Olivia is still there."

"Olivia? You haven't mentioned her." Gryffnn glanced up at the sky. "Blacklight isn't far away. We should go." Gryffnn packed the basket and rose. He offered her his hand and pulled her to her feet. With quick efficiency, he folded the rug and placed it inside the basket. "Can you hold the basket on the flight back?"

"I can."

During the return flight, Kaya paid more attention to the scenery. Narenda was a beautiful planet and a place she'd be happy to call home.

When they landed, Hallam, Lys, and Sable were at the training field to meet them.

"Anything wrong?" Kaya asked once they'd landed.

"Not a thing," Sable assured them. "I hoped to tire Lys, so she'd sleep through the blacklight."

Lys threw up her arms and shrieked at Gryffnn. It wasn't fear but excitement.

Hallam laughed. "She likes dragons. Take her for a flight, Dad."

"Is that all right, sweetheart?"

"Go for it, but please don't drop her. Tayte will use his pointy blade on both of us."

Gryffnn accepted Lys from Hallam and cradled her in his talons. He lifted off and everyone laughed at Lys's excited chortles that drifted to them as Gryffnn did a slow lap of the training field.

When Gryffnn landed, Hallam said, "Now we truly are a family. Lys has flown with a dragon. She's allowed because she's part of our family."

Touched, Kaya wrapped her arm around Hallam's shoulders and kissed his cheek before taking Lys from Gryffnn.

A family. Kaya ambled toward the family quarters with her mate, her two children, and her sister-in-law. She'd never thought to have a family, had thought the ties would stifle her freedom. Now she understood her friend Nanu and why he'd fought for Jazen. She'd skewer anyone who dared place her family in danger.

Contentment settled on her like a favorite cloak as she glanced at Gryffnn.

This emotion that squeezed her heart and made it hard to breathe was love, and she couldn't wait to walk into the future with her mate and family at her side.

Marks later, after a meal in the communal dining hall, she and Gryffnn headed for their chamber. Her comm buzzed as they entered their private rooms.

"See how you distract me? I left my comm sitting here."

"And that is a problem why?"

Kaya laughed. "Ry might have a job." She picked up the comm, tapped a button, and spoke. "Hey, Camryn. What's up? Wait. What? Okay. I want Gryffnn to hear." She clicked another button, and Camryn's voice shot into their chamber.

"Ransom has regained consciousness. Mogens said he sat up and shouted that his mate was stealing his precious stones."

"He's woken? That's great news! But I don't understand. Ellard is patrolling the area. He has reported nothing out of the ordinary," Gryffnn said.

"Ransom was insistent. He wanted to know where the devil he was, and he set the curtains on fire. Your brother-in-law is one determined, arrogant dragon."

Kaya glanced at Gryffnn. "Did he hurt anyone?"

"Not once we promised to return him to Narenda," Camryn said drily. "We're on our way. I wanted to warn you before we arrived." A roar sounded in the background. "Gotta go," Camryn said hurriedly, and the comm connection went dead.

"I'll check in with Ellard," Gryffnn said.

Kaya listened to the conversation and relaxed once she learned all was well.

"Did Ransom mean Aideen?" she asked.

"Ransom hated Aideen because of what happened to me. He'd never consider mating with her. Goddess, I can't believe Ransom has regained consciousness. I'm so relieved."

"Well, we can't do anything now," Kaya said with a wink. "What do you say we hit the gel-bed?"

Gryffnn's frown faded, the slow curl of his lips and the light in his eyes showing approval. "Mate, I adore the way you think."

And with that, he seized her and kissed her breathless. Kaya melted against her mate and settled in to enjoy the blacklight with her dragon.

Are you curious about Ransom? I have the perfect heroine waiting in the wings for him. Check out Star-Crossed with Scarlett to learn more.

https://shelleymunro.com/books/star-crossed-with-scarlett/

ALSO BY SHELLEY

Middlemarch Shifters
My Scarlet Woman
My Younger Lover
My Peeping Tom
My Assassin
My Estranged Lover
My Feline Protector
My Determined Suitor
My Cat Burglar
My Stray Cat
My Second Chance
My Plan B
My Cat Nap
My Romantic Tangle
My Blue Lady
My Twin Trouble
My Precious Gift
My Grumpy Wolf

Middlemarch Gathering
My Highland Mate
My Highland Fling
My Elusive Mate
My Valiant Princess
My Highland Wedding
My Highland Billionaire

House of the Cat
Captured & Seduced
Claimed & Seduced
Merry & Seduced
Stranded & Seduced
Seized & Seduced
Hunted & Seduced
Festive & Seduced
Betrayed & Seduced
Enticed & Seduced

Dragon Investigators
Blue Moon Dragon
Blood Moon Dragon
Black Moon Dragon
Snow Moon Dragon

Dragon Isles
Liza
Cherry
Rena
Sasha

ABOUT SHELLEY

USA Today bestselling author Shelley Munro lives in Auckland, the City of Sails, with her husband and a cheeky Jack Russell/mystery breed dog.

Typical New Zealanders, Shelley and her husband left home for their big OE soon after they married (translation of New Zealand speak - big overseas experience). A twelve-month-long adventure lengthened to six years of roaming the world. Enduring memories include being almost sat on by a mountain gorilla in Rwanda, lazing on white sandy beaches in India, whale watching in Alaska, searching for leprechauns in Ireland, and dealing with ghosts in an English pub.

While travel is still a big attraction, these days Shelley is most likely found in front of her computer following another love - that of writing stories of contemporary and paranormal romance and adventure. Other interests include watching rugby (strictly for research purposes), cycling, playing croquet and the ukelele, and curling up with an enjoyable book.

Visit Shelley at her Website

https://shelleymunro.com

Join Shelley's Newsletter

https://shelleymunro.com/newsletter